ABOUT THE AUTHOR

Ten years or so ago, Roxanne Bouchard decided it was time she found her sea legs. So she learned to sail, first on the St Lawrence River, before taking to the open waters off the Gaspé Peninsula. The local fishermen soon invited her aboard to reel in their lobster nets, and Roxanne saw for herself that the sunrise over Bonaventure never lies. Her fifth novel (her first to be translated into English), *We Were the Salt of the Sea*, was published in 2018 to resounding critical acclaim. *The Coral Bride*, which was a number-one bestseller in Canada, was shortlisted for the CWA Translation Dagger and won the Crime Writers of Canada Crime Book of the Year Award. *Whisper of the Seals* is her third book to be translated into English. Roxanne lives in Quebec. Follow her on Twitter @RBouchard72 and on her website: roxannebouchard.com.

ABOUT THE TRANSLATOR

David Warriner grew up in deepest Yorkshire, has lived in France and Quebec, and now calls British Columbia home. He translated Johanna Gustawsson's *Blood Song* for Orenda Books, and his translation of Roxanne Bouchard's *We Were the Salt of the Sea* was runner-up for the 2019 Scott Moncrieff Prize for French-English translation. Follow David on Twitter @givemeawave and on his website: wtranslation.ca.

Whisper of the Seals

ROXANNE BOUCHARD

Translated by David Warriner

**ORENDA
BOOKS**

Orenda Books
16 Carson Road
West Dulwich
London SE21 8HU
www.orendabooks.co.uk

First published in the United Kingdom by Orenda Books 2022
Originally published in French as *Le murmure des hakapiks* by Éditions
Libre Expression 2021
Copyright © Éditions Libre Expression 2021
English translation © David Warriner 2022

Quotation on page 137, from *Aimez-moi* by Yves Boisvert,
Éditions XYZ, 2007. English translation by David Warriner.

A catalogue record for this book is available from the British Library.

ISBN 978-1-914585-24-1
eISBN 978-1-914585-25-8

Typeset in Garamond by www.typesetter.org.uk
Printed and bound by CPI Group (UK) Ltd, Croydon CR0 4YY

Seal icons created by Freepik – Flaticon

*We would like to thank the Société de développement des entreprises culturelles
(SODEC) for its financial support*

For sales and distribution, please contact info@orendabooks.co.uk

For Audrey Pelletier, whose heart is as open as the ocean.

« Je suis l'océan

Qui veut toucher ton pied »

'I am the ocean

Trying to touch your toes'

—*Tu m'aimes-tu?*, Richard Desjardins.

English translation by David Warriner.

The crew

The blade sliced the flesh into thin strips, then little pieces. Meat cuts easily when it's half frozen. Tony McMurray used the knife to scrape it into a stainless-steel bowl. The seal loin left a carmine-red, nigh-on black, trail of blood on the kitchen countertop. He wiped at it, but the liquid ran away from the dishcloth, found its way to the edge of the counter. A drip fell, making a star-shaped splash on the tip of his shoe.

With an involuntary roll of his left shoulder, a tic deep-seated in his body since his teenage years, McMurray wrung out the dishcloth and wiped down the work surface. A stain would remain, a sanguine stream, the relic of an incident sealed into the hardwood, one the homeowners could only erase by sanding down the whole counter, letting the sawdust blow away in the sea breeze.

The chef's eyes were drawn to a sudden brightness. The headlights of a truck sweeping the fringe of grey spruce, a pickup making painful progress into the sunset. From where he stood in the Vigneaults' house, he caught a glimpse of the logo on the door in the dying evening light. The vehicle came to a halt in the neighbours' driveway.

'Well, fuck me ragged!' he cursed out loud.

In a flash, he switched off the hallway light, dimmed the one in the kitchen. Lucien had said, when he dropped him off on the Belle-Anse road, that this place had been left empty for the winter.

He rubbed his thick, hairy hands under the tap and, drying

his fingers, went over to the front window, which had a better view of the house next door. He squinted into the nascent darkness. He was sure it was the Fisheries and Oceans Canada logo he'd seen, but the pickup was parked on the other side of the house. The angle of the driveway meant that all he could see was the back door, the woodshed and part of the living room, when the lights were on.

'You've got to be kidding me.'

He went back to the task at hand, laughing into his beard as he finished preparing his tartare.

'Just wait till Lulu gets wind of this.'

Lucien Carpentier had been forced to sell his lobster-fishing licence some years ago, after his run-ins with the fisheries officers. Tony McMurray remembered that well. He had been working with the guy when it all hit the fan.

Opening drawers at random, rummaging through the pantry, he found a few jars of spices and herbs the owners must have grown, harvested, dried and packaged with care the previous autumn. Picking the ones he wanted, he tossed a handful into a bowl and set about making the vinaigrette.

That afternoon, his former skipper had picked him up from the ferry and handed him a frozen pizza. McMurray had taken it without saying a word, but when Lulu had dropped him off at the Vigneaults' place, he had shoved the box straight in the bin. Because there were limits to the sacrifices to which Tony McMurray would consent. He had agreed to come up from Mexico for a couple of weeks during the worst of the winter. He didn't mind biding his time until Carpentier's return, alone in a vacant house while the couple who owned it were away on holiday. But there was no way he was putting that kind of crap in his mouth. Wherever he went, he made sure he ate well. So as soon as he was inside, he had gone to see what he could find in the freezer and found a filet mignon of seal meat. Now that was a meal. Potatoes he had found in the cold room, as well as some asparagus and carrots canned by the owners that summer. He had opened the jars and helped himself like he owned the place.

Rummaging through other people's things could be a recipe for trouble. Tony McMurray knew that and would even admit to a fair few dalliances that didn't reflect well on him. But these didn't outweigh his merits. No, there were two qualities the Newfoundlander prided himself on. One: he was a good cook. Food was so sacred to him, it had landed him some decent jobs. That was how he got to spend the winter in Cancún, working as a chef in a hotel for tourists. Two: he had a long memory. When he owed someone, he owed them. And he paid them back. If someone helped him, he remembered it, and he was willing to drop anything to pay his dues. That was the very reason he'd come up to the Islands, to do Lulu a favour.

With an eye as curious as it was inquisitive, he peered out at the house next door. No one in the living room. The guy must be making a bite to eat too, he figured. Since his own troubles with the police, McMurray had hated anyone who wore a uniform and carried a book of tickets – patrol cops, fisheries officers and all; but he reasoned with himself: Lulu had said he'd only be here a matter of hours. Nothing to get himself worked up about, really.

He stirred the meat and vinaigrette together and let it sit.

Lucien Carpentier had said it would be a lucrative expedition. He had asked McMurray to put together a menu for ten days or so and said he'd take care of the food shopping. The time would fly by. By the time Valentine's Day rolled around, he'd be back with his pals, enjoying some cheap Mexican skirt.

He took the potatoes he'd sliced into chips out of the water they were soaking in, dried them off and put them in a bowl, then oiled and spiced them, gave them a stir and spread them out on a baking sheet in the oven. Then he went back to the front window.

The living-room light came on next door. For a second, McMurray was transfixed.

'Well, fuck me ragged. It's a woman.'

He went to grab the telescope he'd figured the Vigneaults must use to look out to sea, then he set it down in the hallway and focused the lens. Lucien had told him how Normand Petitpas had been given a fine – no longer ago than yesterday, out around Pointe-aux-Loups – because his hakapik was a centimetre too long. The sealer had taken it the wrong way and gone on a rant: the animal-rights activists were already making their lives hard enough, so the fisheries folk should just keep themselves to themselves. But most of all, and to add insult to injury for Petitpas, the officer who slapped him with the fine was a woman. A young twenty-something, still wet around the ears, she was.

The next-door neighbour was prancing around. The floor must be cold on the feet.

'Ooh, she's a frigid one too!'

McMurray thought that was funny. He could see her more clearly, now that she was lighting the wood stove. As if she were right there in the next room.

These heartless little woman officers who threw their weight around, they deserved to be put back in their place. And McMurray, he knew how to give a lesson to a bitch who was asking for it.

He closed one eye to get a better view of her. She stood up, put a parka on and went over to the patio door at the rear of the house. *That's nice of her*, McMurray thought, *she's staying right in my line of sight.* She was taking a while. She had to pull on her boots, he figured. And then she stepped out onto the porch. A gust of wind made her take a step back. She tugged her hood up over her head, stray locks whirling wildly in all directions. She went over to the woodshed and loaded her arms with firewood. She had picked up more than she could carry, he could see that much. She faltered as she climbed the porch steps, dropped a few logs, ducked inside, closed the door behind her, probably with her foot. McMurray wondered if she was going to lock it.

It would be easy to sneak over there. He wouldn't even need to go via the road. The ground was frozen, the snow blown away by the wind, all he'd have to do was walk across the dune, between the bowed heads of the sea wheat-grass, to reach the neighbour's patio door.

She put the firewood down by the stove, took off her coat. If she had been keeping an eye on the seal hunt all day, she must be cold. She would have a shower, maybe sit down to eat in her dressing gown. Unless she had plans to go out.

He went back into the kitchen, flipped the chips over on the baking sheet and put them back in the oven.

He liked it when a girl put up a fight. Those Mexican chicks, they came cheap, but they were too much of a pushover. No, a woman had to scream a little. It wasn't as satisfying if she didn't.

He returned to the hallway, dug around in the closet until he found a grey balaclava. He had some condoms in his bag. The more he thought about it, the more excited he got. No one knew he was in the area, and as soon as this hunting expedition with Lulu was done, he'd be headed right back to Mexico. The girl would think it was Petitpas doling out her punishment for that ticket. Tony McMurray liked the idea of dragging a local's name through the mud. He would get his revenge on the fishermen out at Grande-Entrée, for that run-in they had a while back. But that was only if she reported it. They didn't always report it, he knew that from experience.

His phone rang. It was Carpentier. McMurray answered, peering into the eyepiece of the telescope again.

'Have you eaten?'

'Not yet, why?'

A light came on in a small window upstairs. The girl was in the bathroom. If she came down in her dressing gown, then she didn't have any plans. She would be easy to take by surprise. And by force.

'I'll come by soon to pick you up and take you out to the boat. I've done some asking around and the skipper's there already, so you can sleep on board tonight. We should be setting off tomorrow lunchtime.'

The shower was almost in line with the window. McMurray could see a hand closing the shower curtain. She was so close, he reached down and gave himself a rub through his clothes. He was starting to get hard. The oven timer beeped. He stood up, went through to the kitchen, took the chips out of the oven. His left shoulder rolled back mechanically.

'Give me an hour. I haven't eaten yet. And I'm ravenous.'

While McMurray devoured his seal tartare, Simone Lord shivered in the shower.

She had spent the afternoon on a quad bike, patrolling the beach at Pointe-aux-Loups. The grey seal hunters were in a hurry to pile up their prizes before the storm. Already, by the day's end, they could sense the wind turning to the northwest. She thoroughly scrubbed her hands with soap, red as they were from the greasy lingerings of blood, then tilted her head back in the warm stream, lathered her hair with shampoo, touched a finger to a vertebra that teased beneath her skin, or so it seemed.

At the end of an investigation on which she had collaborated with Sûreté du Québec detectives the previous autumn, as she was poring over her report at the Gaspé police station, the fisheries officer had felt a gentle stroke, almost a caress, on her neck. She had been startled, turned her head away. Detective Sergeant Moralès, her superior officer on the case, had withdrawn his hand in shame, as if he had surprised even himself by making the inappropriate gesture.

'There's … you've got a … er … a vertebra showing, there.'

She had blushed like a teenager, prudishly pulled up her collar, before realising he had been quite overcome, too. He had apologised and made for the door. But instead of crossing the threshold, he had stood in the doorway.

'When are you leaving for the Islands?'

'In a few days' time.'

'And when will you be back?'

'At the end of March.'

'Shall I … er … give you a call when you get back?'

She had whispered a shaky yes, and he had left the room, but not without bumping his shoulder against the door frame.

She heard something, pricked an ear. Her phone was ringing. She had left it downstairs, on the counter in the kitchen. She turned the water off, towelled herself dry, patted at her hair. She hesitated. Her young colleague, officer Stéphanie Poirier, had invited her to come for a drink with the new recruits at the bar, Le Central. Simone checked the time. She could get dressed, make a quick supper and go and meet them. But, nah, she didn't feel like it. They were the kind of youngsters who egged each other on to write tickets left, right and centre; she was past that age. Especially tonight. She donned a dressing gown and slippers and went downstairs.

The warm aroma of the *pot-en-pot* pie in the oven was beginning to fill the kitchen. Simone wasn't gifted in the cooking department; ready meals were more her thing, and those from the local Côte à Côte butcher's she found comforting in her solitude. She picked up her phone and went over to the dining-room window.

The light from the moon was softened by the off-white silk lampshade of the clouds.

To the west, the cliffs bisected the terrain. A week earlier, a slab of red sandstone had collapsed into the sea. Not a big one, barely one metre by two, but Simone had been outside when it slid. She had heard the ground crack, seen the slab fracture and, with a dull groan, fall in one swift movement into the Gulf of Saint Lawrence. The ice had shattered under the weight of the earth. Stacks of water had spurted skyward, fallen on the land, then flowed seaward once more. Like a watermark, great fingers of frost remained imprinted in the edge of the escarpment, as if a sea monster had clawed its way up the cliff to the house.

To the north, a path led to the dunes, where the beachgrass, bending under the late January frost, whispered amidst the haunting howl of the northwesterly wind.

The other sides of the home were protected by thickets of black spruce; in places they were nothing more than snarling grey trunks bristling with broken branches, their spikes sharp as daggers. They had grown leaning eastward. Buffeted relentlessly by the brutal blasts of the wind, their full heads of hardy needles were nodding in the heaviest gusts like those of youngsters in a mosh pit, rocking out to a halting heavy-metal crescendo.

Her Fisheries and Oceans Canada supervisor, Jean-Guy Thériault, had left her a voice message. As Officer Lord was about to listen to it, her phone rang again. Érik Lefebvre's name appeared on the screen. She answered the call.

'Hey, Simone! How's it going?'

The voice of her friend in Gaspé was brimming with enthusiasm.

'All right.'

'Is that all? It's been two weeks since we last talked and that's all you have to say: "all right"?'

'The forecast says the northwester's going to keep on freshening. The sealers are all going home. My supervisor's told me the January grey-seal outings are wrapping up. And since the harp seal season's not starting for another month or so, once the pack ice is solid and the pups are weaned, he thinks we'll have a bit of respite.'

She opened the oven door. The *pot-en-pot* was nearly ready. After a silence, Lefebvre piped up again.

'Wow! I never thought that one day we'd have such a close, confiding relationship.'

Perhaps she wasn't that gifted when it came to intimacy either.

'What about you? Have you made any headway with your packing?'

Standing by three huge suitcases that were wide open and crammed with stuff, Érik Lefebvre found himself confronted by one of the greatest mysteries of his life: how to differentiate the necessary from the superfluous. In other words, how should he separate the wheat from the chaff? It was a question he had been struggling with for the past three weeks.

'I can't wrap my head around it. At first, I followed the trip organisers' advice. I dug out a regular suitcase and a small backpack, but then…'

'Did you go and get those two big suitcases from my storage unit?'

Lefebvre had to admit the truth. 'To be honest, I've lost my handle on it.'

Simone Lord smiled and poured herself a glass of wine. 'Take out everything that isn't essential for a ski trip.'

'It's not as easy as that. What's essential for one person isn't the same as for another. Take shirts, for example. You need a certain minimum to choose from for the occasion. If the situation's right, I'll happily wear the one with the pink palm trees.'

Simone Lord went through to the living room, put another log on the fire and moved towards the patio door. Earlier, across in the Vigneault house, she had thought she'd seen a light being switched off.

'Well, do you really need to travel that light?'

'It's best. We're flying to Montreal, and the organisers have chartered a cruise ship from there that'll be our hotel. We're two to a cabin.'

'Oh, really? I thought you were staying in the Gaspé. Skiing around the peninsula.'

'No. We're going to be skiing along the way too, in Quebec City, Sainte-Anne-des-Monts, Carleton, Paspébiac…'

The clouds were compacting, shrinking the visual space sharply. Darkness was swallowing the sea and the spruce, forcing the gaze to retreat. The wind had swept the path she had carefully cleared at the beginning of the week, sculpting waves of powder between the bottom of the steps and the woodshed.

'Lucky you. It'll be spectacular to ski your way along the river and up in the Appalachians.'

'We got an email today. They've had some last-minute cancellations, so there's still room on board. You should come along, Simone.'

Earlier, she had gone out to fetch some wood. Her arms too full, she had dropped a few logs on the porch. She would be needing those in the morning. Might as well bring them in now.

'I can't, I'm working.'

'Take some time off.'

She stepped into her boots and pulled the handle; the glass door slid open on its track in silence.

'I'll take some holiday time in the spring when I'm back in Gaspé.'

The wind was wild, whipping at her dressing gown, sending shivers between her thighs. Simone bent down and quickly retrieved the wood, bracing the phone awkwardly against her ear with her shoulder.

'I knew you'd say that.'

Back inside, she slid the door shut with her foot, making sure it was closed all the way, otherwise it tended to whistle in a northwester. No, she didn't lock it. No one did that in the Magdalen Islands.

'Has our friendship reached the level where you can read my mind, Érik Lefebvre?'

'You're not hard to read. You've got overachiever syndrome.'

'Overachiever syndrome?'

When her supervisor had driven her here at the beginning of November, Simone had been surprised to find the door unlocked. Jean-Guy Thériault had laughed: 'If a thief came and pinched something, where would he take it? Two streets away, and they'd catch him three days later.' He had added that the last time they'd had a sex offender on the Islands, the fishermen in Grande-Entrée had made him walk the plank.

'Loads of you women suffer from it.'

'I thought you were a police officer, not a psychoanalyst.'

The absence of petty thieves had quickly been confirmed by the fact that the owners of the house had gone away for the cold season and rented out their home complete with everything it contained of their personal lives: recipe books, records, happy snaps of them together, on holiday, at family parties.

'A good police officer has to know his way around the human soul. Especially a woman's. Plus, I've read a lot of pop psychology magazines. It helps.'

'Well, do explain this to me, doctor.'

Lefebvre cleared his throat.

'As young schoolkids, when the bell rang at four o'clock, we boys used to barrel outside to go and play soccer, pinch penny sweets from the store or hang out on the beach. But not you lot. You lot, you overachievers, you'd hurry straight home to scourge yourselves by cramming for the test the next day. You always had some sort of homework to do, some pressing deadline to meet...'

Simone went over to the wood stove while Érik went wild with his theory.

'You weren't hard to spot. You were the only ones who raised your hands to come up to the blackboard.'

Framed in driftwood and screened by glass, the photographs of the all-embracing family saga that lined the walls of this home reminded Simone Lord that she was an outsider, standing out of the frame, not in anyone's arms, smiling.

'You never learned to tell a lie. You were always guilty or ashamed of something no one was even blaming you for. So you made a habit of being obedient.'

Encumbered by the phone, Simone was struggling to find a way to free herself gracefully of the logs.

'You overachievers, you've made the world your burden, so instead of having fun, you spend your life shouldering responsibilities.'

Screw it, she thought, letting the wood tumble out of her arms. Lefebvre carried on as if he hadn't heard a sound.

'Then when you're grown adults, it gets worse. You're not just top of the class, you're the schoolmarm as well, so you set the bar too high, then you punish yourselves afterwards.'

Taking a quick step back to avoid dropping a log on her toe, she bumped into a photo frame, sending it crashing to the floor.

'You, Officer Lord, are the type to have your very own firing squad; and you'd stand in front of it and shout "open fire!"'

She saw the glass shielding a photo of a couple kayaking had shattered. Simone left her boots by the fire and went to fetch a broom and dustpan to sweep up the shards.

'You'd have been better off putting all that aside and coming out to play with the rest of us.'

Tiny fragments peppered the woman's face. Simone didn't know how she could fix the mess she'd made. Lefebvre spluttered, as if hesitating, then went on with his revelation.

'And you know what, you overachievers, you're no good at loving.'

Simone threw away the glass shards, put the broken frame on the shelf beside the hi-fi. It occurred to her that she could put some music on, once in a while. Lots of people did that. They would turn on the radio or TV to give themselves the illusion of company. But she, Officer Lord, would navigate evenings in a heavy silence inhabited only by the crackling of logs and flames in the fire and the relentless gusting of the wind.

'You're so desperate to get good marks that you refuse to let yourselves lose your footing, relinquish control, let yourselves go, allow yourself to wander with your head in the clouds, dream, or allow a man to distract you, entertain you, sweep you off your feet.'

Her eyes were drawn once more to the shattered glass in the frame, the gashes in the photograph.

'Listen, Simone … you might remember I had, let's say, a moment of grace with your sister when she came to visit the Gaspé, four or five years ago?'

'Yes.'

The oven timer beeped. Dinner was ready. Simone went into the kitchen, took out the pie and sat down at the table.

'Well, she and I had a bit of a talk … about the choices you'd made, about your family—'

This time, she interrupted her friend.

'What are you trying to tell me, Érik?'

She had left her slippers in the living room, but didn't feel like going back to get them. She rubbed her feet together to warm them up and took a sip of wine while Lefebvre went for broke.

'Right, well, have you heard from Moralès at all?'

She gagged on her wine.

'Simone, are you all right?'

Bending double in a wild coughing fit, she put the phone down on the table, then she stood up straight, poured herself a glass of water and tried to catch her breath and hold back the suffocating tears. Simone felt a sudden cold draught between her calves. She pulled herself together, drew herself tall, her senses on alert. There was a noise out there, on the porch. She took a sip of water and picked up the phone again. The floor beneath her feet was still a block of ice, so cold it felt like it was burning.

'Someone's coming. Talk to you soon.'

While Officer Lord left her phone on the table and went to the door, Lefebvre, satisfied with Simone's reaction, added a baseball glove and half a dozen balls to his third suitcase.

🦭

Standing in the wheelhouse of the *Jean-Mathieu*, as the hull swayed beneath his feet, Skipper Bernard Chevrier looked at his brother-in-law, and the boat's owner, Denis Éloquin, who was rocking his weight back and forth, hands planted in his pockets. Denis wasn't the nervous type, but this was the first time he was hiring out his trawler.

'It's Nancy, eh?'

Éloquin made no reply, just turned his head towards the deserted wharf of Cap-aux-Meules. Chevrier understood. The lamplight out there was flickering. The wind was turning northwest.

Nancy was angry at her husband for letting the Painchauds charter his crab trawler, but what else could Denis have done? The Painchaud son, Marco, he was who he was, but he was still Denis' nephew. The kid whose mother buggered off from the Islands and set him adrift at not even twelve years old.

Denis could understand his little sister walking out on a drunk of a partner who came home to the wrong house every night, and had to be fetched every morning and brought back to the right living room. But he could never accept her abandoning her child. When she left, it was Denis Éloquin who kept an eye on the kid and paid for his schooling, even when he went to study in Quebec City.

Last year, when he'd found out what Marco was doing in the old walled city, Éloquin had missed three days of fishing while he went to flush his nephew out of the lowest parts of the Lower Town. He had pulled up alongside the kid in his car, like his customers did, strong-armed him into the backseat and taken him home to his father. Bernard Chevrier knew all this. It was Denis, too, who had put his hand in his pocket when the time came, in order to land the kid a job on a lobster trawler, drill some sense into him and sprinkle some salt of the Islands in his heart. All summer long, he had paid Marco's wages himself, on the sly, so the skipper would keep him on board.

That was the way he was, Denis Éloquin: he wouldn't sleep easy until he'd brought his nephew back onto the straight and narrow. And Nancy knew her husband: she hadn't married him for his money, but for his wide-open arms.

Some time ago, Marco Painchaud, together with his father, had come to see his uncle about chartering the *Jean-Mathieu*. His father had said he'd pay. Denis Éloquin had agreed, once more, to bail out his nephew, but standing here in the wheelhouse of the twenty-metre-long midshore trawler, he was still worried. If something were to break, the time it would take for the repairs might mean missing the harp-seal harvest. Maybe even the entire summer fishing season. Bernard Chevrier knew that, but neither he nor Denis dared to voice the possibility. That was what Nancy was worried about. As an accountant, she fussed about the money; as Denis' wife, she fretted about her husband spending a season in dry dock. The two brothers-in-law had spent enough years navigating the waters together for Bernard Chevrier to understand the stakes. He and Éloquin were cut from the same cloth. They loved the sea and everything about it. And land was nothing but a compromise.

The forecast said a big northeaster would arrive in a few days' time, and a storm would swallow the horizon by the weekend. In an attempt to be reassuring, Chevrier decided to take a sympathetic tack.

'If the northeaster picks up, we won't go to Pictou Island.'

Denis Éloquin stared intently at the wharf. He had insisted that Marco Painchaud hire his brother-in-law because Bernard was one of the only skippers he really trusted.

'It's not up to me to tell you where to go.'

'I'm going to head out Nova Scotia way. If we don't make a killing on Margaree Island, maybe I'll motor on to Henry Island.'

'Not sure there are still any seals around those parts. Weaning's been done for a while now, so the colonies must have moved on. If you don't take the guys to Pictou, chances are you'll come back light. Marco's old man didn't give me much, but he's still paid for a proper charter.'

Bernard Chevrier didn't need his brother-in-law to draw him a picture. No crew wanted to come ashore empty-handed, and Painchaud and his mates were no exception. And Bernard himself didn't want Denis' nephew to be humiliated either.

The trouble was, to get to Pictou, in Nova Scotia, they had not only to skirt around Prince Edward Island, but also venture deep into the Northumberland Strait. And when they got there, if the northeaster started to blow, then the *Jean-Mathieu* would have to make one hell of a quick getaway, or else the ice would grip them in its vise, and even though the hull was made of steel, anything might break. That northeaster was supposed to pick up for sure, and blow hard. It was for that very reason that all the seasoned sealers were on their way back to shore.

But Marco Painchaud was adamant about going out now on this expedition of his. With the bad weather, they wouldn't have the animal activists on their backs, he had said. That was an argument Éloquin could understand; he detested activists as much as he hated white sharks. It had to be said too that now was the only time Painchaud could hire his trawler. In a few weeks' time, everyone would be getting ready to head out for the harp-seal harvest. Even to get a crew together, it couldn't have been easy.

'Do you know if Marco's brought Réjean on board?'

'Réjean Vigneault? No. Him and his wife, they've gone off skiing in the Gaspé. But he did say he'd hired a guy from Pointe-aux-Loups. And two from Grande-Entrée, I think.'

'So it's just the five of you?'

'Maybe an observer from Gaspé too.'

'Aye.'

'I'll keep my phone on, even at the hospital. Don't hesitate to call me.'

Bernard agreed. If Denis Éloquin's daughter wasn't about to give birth to her first child, he'd be taking the helm himself for sure, but there were some family situations that seemed like a strait you had no choice but to navigate, in spite of the foul weather some days and the waves hitting you head on. And Nancy'd had to insist her husband stay home: it wasn't every day a man became a grandfather.

A pickup truck came down the wharf and pulled up alongside the *Jean-Mathieu*. Denis Éloquin emerged from his thoughts and turned to his brother-in-law.

'I'll leave it up to you to manage your crew. Don't forget: protect their lives first, then the boat.'

'I'll be careful.'

'And above all, remember that after the Man Upstairs, you're the only master on board.'

Denis gave Bernard a look of such intensity it left him feeling a bit shaken, as if he had just heard news of an impending disaster. Outside, the pickup's passenger was grabbing his bags. As the brothers-in-law exchanged a last handshake, they heard the slam of a truck door.

'Worst case, I bring your boat back empty, Denis.'

'Worst case, you leave the boat. But you come back, Bernard.'

Skipper Chevrier had barely a second to nod his head before the owner was gone. Just as he disembarked by the bow, the newcomer came aboard at the stern.

It was that time of the tide when the gunwale sits at the same height as the wharf. Without a backward glance, Denis Éloquin hopped into his car and disappeared into the night. From the wheelhouse, Bernard Chevrier spied the newcomer as he edged his way around the rowboat moored to the starboard-side bulwark and the all-terrain vehicle chained to the deck, then stepped inside. He could hear him calling from the vestibule.

'Anyone there?'

The skipper leaned towards the stairs.

'Yep.'

'Is Painchaud here?'

'Not yet.'

Saying nothing more, the newcomer took his things down to the sleeping quarters. Chevrier turned on the TV screen, slid a recording of a hunting show into the DVD player. It was his wife who recorded those for him, when he was out at sea. The new guy came back up.

'You the skipper, then?'

'Yep. Bernard Chevrier. Who are you, then?'

The guy extended a hand. Tattoos licked at his wrist.

'Michaël Lapierre, Pointe-aux-Loups.'

Chevrier frowned. So many Lapierres around these parts, there were, the name alone didn't tell him much.

'Never heard of you.'

The other guy smiled, remembering how here in the estuary, you had to say what line you were from for the Islanders to place you.

'Eudore's Normand's Michaël.'

'Eudore's Normand's Michaël? Are you serious?'

'Yep.'

Chevrier extended a gracious palm, and Lapierre shook it with vigour.

'Sorry, I didn't recognise you. Wasn't sure what to make of you.'

'No sweat.'

'How's your dad?'

'Same as always, but his knees are getting worse.'

'It's been a while … How old were you when you left the Islands? Sixteen?'

'You've got a good memory.'

'And when did you get back?'

'Couple of weeks ago. With Marco Painchaud. He's the one who got me to come aboard.'

'You're a family of hunters, then…'

'Since forever.'

Bernard Chevrier was relieved. Painchaud had sworn to his uncle he'd find an experienced crew and perhaps he was true to his word. Michaël Lapierre looked at the time.

'Why's no one else here? What are they playing at?'

'Not in any big rush, are they? We won't be off until tomorrow.'

The other guy nodded.

'I'm going to check the rifles.'

Lapierre went down to deck level. Chevrier followed. They went through the vestibule, where the parkas, jackets, waterproofs and warm toques were hanging, and also the hakapiks, long wooden shafts with a head like a hammer on one side and a hook on the other, designed especially for seal hunting. The boots were strung up there too. Between the vestibule and the galley was a narrow corridor crossing the trawler from port to starboard, ending at the top of another set of stairs that ran beneath the first, down to the hold and the engines. Along the corridor, Éloquin had built in a fitted cabinet to hang the rifles on the wall.

One by one, Michaël Lapierre unhooked and inspected them. Chevrier looked on in approval.

'Of course, your dad did say you were in the police.'

His companion shot him a sideways glance. 'Is that what he told you?'

'Yes. Him and your uncles.'

Pointing to his tattoos, Michaël Lapierre laughed out loud. 'Do I look like a pig?'

'You could be the kind of cop who infiltrates biker gangs. That would make sense.'

The newcomer shook his head. 'Nope. I work in a bar.'

'Aye. But I hope you know how to shoot.'

Lapierre gave him a wink.

'Don't worry, I'll manage.'

ᴥ

A balaclava-clad Tony McMurray crept on to the back porch of the house next door to the Vigneaults'. He silently slid the patio door open, six inches or so, then paused, on his guard. Was that a noise he had heard?

The woman was in her dressing gown, as he had predicted. From his observation post, he could see her, barefoot, making her way over to the front door. He couldn't really see what was happening, but figured she must have opened it. A male voice spoke to her. For a second, he thought about giving up, then it occurred to him that the man was just a visitor, otherwise he would have come in without knocking. With a bit of luck, the guy wouldn't stay long. Huddled in the shadows, McMurray figured he could wait a few minutes. He still had time.

The woman returned to the kitchen, followed by a big, hefty guy wearing a jacket with a Fisheries and Oceans Canada logo. McMurray pricked an ear. Silence. Maybe they were kissing. No. The stairs creaked; the woman officer must have gone to get dressed. So the guy wasn't her lover. The sound of voices returned. The man apologised; he had an order to relay.

The tone was formal but warm. The woman said she didn't understand something. McMurray was cold, but he wasn't discouraged. She would end up understanding, and the guy would end up leaving. Except they'd have to hurry up about it, because he had a boat to catch.

Suddenly, a ringing sound pierced the air. Tony McMurray scrambled down from the porch and dashed behind the woodshed. He pulled his phone out of his pocket. Lucien Carpentier was calling. He tried to answer, but the screen died. The cold had got the better of the battery. He craned his neck, trying to see what was happening inside the house. No one seemed to have heard the phone. In any case, neither of the two officers had approached the patio door.

He crept back to his post, saw the woman turn the light on in the hallway. She was walking her visitor to the door.

'What time do I have to board?'

'At noon. Stop by the office first, I've got a tagging kit for you, then I'll give you a ride.'

'And what's the name of the boat?'

'The *Jean-Mathieu*.'

The man was about to take his leave.

Then all of a sudden, the aggressive, repeated honk of a horn sounded over at the Vigneault place. As the two Fisheries and Oceans Canada officers peered curiously out the window overlooking the Belle-Anse road, a furious Tony McMurray pulled off his balaclava and retreated through the dunes, curses flying in his wake, to grab his bag and join an increasingly impatient Lucien Carpentier sitting in his truck. But as he settled into the passenger seat, he turned to the seaman from Grande-Entrée with a smile on his lips.

'What's the name of our boat again, this week?'

'The *Jean-Mathieu*, why?'

McMurray's left shoulder rolled backwards of its own accord.

'No reason.'

Or rather, because a good lesson could also be given out at sea.

⌀

When Simone Lord rolled up to the *Jean-Mathieu* on the wharf shortly after noon, skipper Bernard Chevrier had a sense of foreboding about the expedition. A satisfied Tony McMurray opened a porthole to spit into the water, but the thick gob of drool met with a gust of wind and splattered against the black hull instead, where it slowly dribbled downwards, then stopped and froze. Marco Painchaud nibbled the edge of his left thumbnail, sniffing frantically, and Michaël Lapierre shook a disapproving head. Only Carpentier, the poacher, didn't react at all, because he hadn't seen her; he was setting up his bunk.

She picked up her bags, slammed the back door of the truck shut, then strode with a firm and determined step towards the vessel. She had a pack on her back and another bag, bearing the Fisheries and Oceans Canada logo, slung across her shoulder. Already the northwesterly wind was gusting at up to fifty kilometres an hour, and she was struggling to stand up straight.

Michaël Lapierre's face turned to stone.

'Weren't we supposed to have a guy?'

Marco Painchaud kept nibbling at the edge of his thumb. 'Yeah, but I haven't heard a thing from him since lunchtime yesterday.'

'What do you mean, you haven't heard from him?'

Tony McMurray approached the rear wheelhouse window so he could look out over the deck. 'I know her. She's the one who slapped us with a fine eight years ago. I was with Cassivi, from Rivière-au-Renard. We were ten miles outside our zone. She came down on him like a ton of bricks.'

Simone Lord put one of her bags down on a pathway muddied by sand and de-icing salt. The boat heaved fiercely, yanking at its mooring lines then slamming back into the wall of tyres strung along the wharf to cushion the impact.

'Call your mate at Fisheries and Oceans back,' Lapierre told Painchaud, putting his foot down, 'and tell him we're not having her on board.'

McMurray's left shoulder rolled back in its socket; his grey balaclava sat perched on top of his head, hitched back a bit. 'You can forget that. They do what they want, that lot.'

But Lapierre was undeterred. 'Call that guy of yours, Painchaud.'

With every ricochet of the hull against the rubber buffer, long blades of spume shot into the cold air and shattered as they fell. Fleeting streams of the stuff flowed across the bluish white of the trawler's deck. The seawater ran like a swarm of scarpering pests, down the slope of the deck, pouring out of the spouts at the stern, leaving in its wake a sticky skin of saline frost, a carpet over the hold hatches sitting flush with the surface.

Simone Lord clambered aboard, edged her way around the dinghy and the quad bike, opened the door to the vestibule, tossed her backpack inside, at the foot of the stairwell, and returned to the wharf to fetch what remained of her luggage.

Marco Painchaud put his phone back in his pocket. 'He's not picking up.' He had made an effort, that was enough.

In the cockpit, the four men stood still, spying on the officer on the deck a floor below as she battled with the boat's movement.

'She'll cost us the afternoon.'

Marco Painchaud cursed. Bernard Chevrier turned away. It was his fault if they were lumbered with an observer. He had chosen to go to sea while the bad weather was sending everyone else back to the dock. It was obvious the maritime authorities thought that was suspicious. Instead of getting the coast guard's icebreaker to follow the *Jean-Mathieu* in these harsh conditions, Fisheries and Oceans Canada must have decided to stick an officer right under their feet. Had to be expected.

'Aye.'

The skipper resumed his scrutiny of the chart, cross-referencing with the handwritten notes he had taken while listening to the weather report. Since he had sold his own boat some twelve years ago, any urgency to get going had floated away from him. He had taken this job because his brother-in-law, Denis Éloquin, felt like he was in a jam, and his sister Nancy had insisted. If it had been up to just him, he would have opted, like all the other Islanders, to take a couple of weeks off before things started ramping up for the harp seals. To boot, there was a storm forecast for the weekend, and if you asked him, no seal pelt was worth risking his own skin for. That said, he wasn't the type to stay shored up when he had the chance to go to sea. He was born to be on the water, and that was where he'd die. Still, the foul weather was really rocking the boat. It was yanking at its moorings like a lunatic in shackles. That kind of tipping and turning wasn't good for the trawler or for the crew's morale. The fisheries officer had better not keep them from setting off for too long.

Lucien Carpentier was just unpacking the last of his things when Simone Lord came into the cabin. Her backpack drew his eye. Some women sure travelled light. Which was a rare thing. He knew something about that, did Carpentier, because his wife always filled three and a half suitcases whenever they went away. The other half was for him and his stuff: a few pairs of clean boxers and not too well-worn socks, three or four shirts and a spare pair of trousers. Sometimes he stretched to swim shorts, but not often. He'd been fishing since he was twenty years old and he'd pulled so much disgusting stuff out of the sea any temptation to take a dip was a thing of the past. Resort pools he was even more wary of, especially those with a wet bar, where holidaymakers would park their butt cheeks on the stools under the water and sit drinking all day long. No way was Lucien Carpentier forking out for a luxury hotel to dip his toes in a bunch of drunk guys' piss.

Not that the destination made any difference. Whether it was for a four-day city break or a week at an all-inclusive resort in the sun, Ida never travelled light. He had even heard her telling the neighbours' wives, as if it was something to be proud of, how often they'd been dinged for excess baggage at the airport. Not to mention, she'd added with a naughty wink, she only took her finest things away with her. Once, on the tarmac in Varadero, the zip on a tall blonde's bag had broken, and the unfortunate contents had spilled out. Everyone had seen that the woman, embarrassed by her mistake or by the exposure of her intimate belongings, was carrying a practically empty suitcase. While Lucien's eyes had tangled themselves up in the finer fancies of a woman's underwear, Ida had learned a more practical and categorical lesson from the incident: 'When you travel on a shoestring, you'd better make sure you've got a good, strong zip.' Lucien had been lost for words. Once again, his wife had shown she could find meaning in even the most everyday of events. Also, when they got home that year, he had thought it sensible that Ida invest in a new set of suitcases, and agreed that it would not be completely unreasonable for her to refresh her wardrobe regularly. The last thing she wanted was to look like 'a pleb of the sea'.

Fortunately, the kids had stopped tagging along on holiday with their parents the year before, which had lightened the load on the shock absorbers of their rusty car as well as the family packhorse's arms. The packhorse still had a worrying financial load to bear, though.

Their eldest had gone to university that autumn. And not to just any old institution, no: to the University of Montreal, thank you very much, to study veterinary medicine, no less. Lucien was on the hook for all of it: his son's tuition, his apartment, his clothes and his books. Not to mention the nights out that kept eating into his line of credit. But Lucien didn't say a word, because the Islanders had their pride to wear in the city. They would never be the first to leave the party or the last to buy a round of drinks.

Still, such vanities had ended up quietly boring a hole in the mortgage. When Lucien had his own boat, money was never a problem, especially as he'd had it all figured out: he would sell three quarters of every catch offshore, to Asian traders. That used to fill pockets the tax man never got to see. But five years ago, Fisheries and Oceans Canada had come down on him like a ton of bricks. They had confiscated his equipment, his lobster trawler and his pickup truck, and slapped him with fines he could never pay. He had teetered on the brink of bankruptcy. Carpentier the poacher had had to offload his fishing licence and get a job as a deckhand.

His income had taken a tricky dip for a time, but he hadn't dared to broach the subject with Ida, who kept buying her glad rags like there was no tomorrow, even though her fashion sense tended to be a touch flashy for the Islands. Three weeks previously, when Lucien had attempted to express a doubt about the need for so many frills and fancies, his sweet lady love had cast her glare of wrath at him and proclaimed in no uncertain terms: 'Just because you're a deckhand now, doesn't mean I have to dress like one.'

He had bitten his tongue, ashamed, both of his unwise comment and the difficulty he found himself in. He had not yet told her about his maxed-out credit cards, nor had he mentioned the second mortgage. Principally because his other half had seized the moment to reveal that she'd donned her party-organiser hat and was planning festivities that ranged from the romantic to the frisky ahead of their twenty-fifth wedding anniversary next month. She had reserved the whole bar and restaurant at Les Pas Perdus, hired a group to play music, ordered a seafood buffet and was about to send out the invitations. She was umm-ing and ah-ing about the bar though. Should she put a limit on how many free drinks people could have?

Sitting at the kitchen island, their teenage daughter had rolled her eyes. Since Léa-Jade had started at the local college, she had grown critical of her parents' lifestyle. An enthusiastic Ida had marched right on without waiting for her husband to reply.

'And I've booked us a little getaway in the Dominican Republic too. I went for the bridal suite with a jacuzzi to recreate the same atmosphere as our honeymoon.'

Léa-Jade had snapped. 'The Dominican Republic? There are slaves there, you know.'

Ida had given their daughter a condescending look. 'That's precisely why we're going to a hotel, to escape our own slavery. If they're fed up working, they should just do what we're doing.'

In that regard, Lucien had conceded his wife was right, but Léa-Jade wouldn't drop it.

'Why don't you go somewhere else? Cuba, for example. It's a communist country that—'

Ida had put her foot down. 'Because Cuba is Cuba, and the Dominican Republic is something else. And anyway, there are no slaves at the hotel. It's a five-star resort.'

Lucien couldn't argue with that. Exasperated, their adolescent daughter had sighed loudly, looked at her father and sneered: 'And I suppose you're paying for all that, are you?'

He had not reacted, because it was a stupid question and the answer went without saying. Léa-Jade had stormed out of the room and slammed the door behind her.

Fortunately, though, their youngest was a bit of a bohemian eco-warrior, a vegetarian and a charity-shop bargain hunter, because otherwise, Lucien had to admit, he was so strapped for cash, he wasn't sure he could stretch to a couple of pairs of new fishing gloves for himself next summer.

To put it simply, all that explained why Carpentier, when he heard Marco Painchaud was plotting a grey-seal expedition during the week of a storm, had gone to prop up the bar at Le Central in Cap-aux-Meules. Lucien Carpentier had done enough poaching to know that if a guy made a call like that, it was going to be a lucrative outing.

At the pub, he had spotted Marco Painchaud knocking back

the beers with a stranger. He hadn't wasted any time, and had gone over to broach the subject before the young guy had one too many.

'Just to let you know, I'm free next week, for the sealing…'

Already a sheet or two to the wind, Marco Painchaud had mocked him. 'Tell me, why would I hire a poacher?'

Then Painchaud had erupted in a crazy laugh, to which Carpentier had taken an immediate dislike, clenching his fists. Sure, he was broke, but he had his pride; no one would make a fool of him. He was a man of few words – small talk was more Ida's department – but knew when to stand up for himself and wasn't afraid to give a big talker a knuckle sandwich.

'You say you're free, but are you really motivated? Because we're looking for guys who've got what it takes, eh, Lapierre?'

The mention of the word 'poacher' had piqued Michaël Lapierre's interest enough for him to start sizing up Carpentier, and not just his lanky frame.

'We're looking for men we can trust…'

'I've been sealing for twenty years at least.'

'…who'll do whatever it takes to come back with a full load in the hold.'

Lucien had thought he'd understood what that meant.

'I'm the best man for the job.'

'Are you sure?'

'Don't you worry.'

Michaël Lapierre had traded a wink with Marco Painchaud, then hired the former skipper on the spot.

'You can get your gear together.'

Painchaud had given him a slap on the shoulder. 'You won't regret it, poacher man!'

Carpentier had chewed his cheeks, like someone who didn't

know what end of a shit-covered stick to pick up, but Lapierre had cut his attempt to express himself short by asking him if he knew another hunter, not necessarily an Islander, who'd be up for the trip as well.

'A guy as reliable as you.'

That was when the poacher had told him about Tony McMurray, a guy from Newfoundland who would go wherever the work was. McMurray owed Carpentier a big favour, so he'd be on board and, it went without saying, he'd keep his mouth shut.

The previous day, Lucien had taken care of his right-hand man, getting him set up on board, and this morning, while, back home, Léa-Jade chuntered on again about human rights in countries invaded by tourism, while his son dragged himself out of bed after a heavy night of drinking on the paternal credit card, and while his wife was getting ready for a little session at the tanning salon, the poacher parked his truck on the Cap-aux-Meules wharf and carried his bags, his rifle, his hakapik and his knives aboard the *Jean-Mathieu*.

He said hello to the woman who'd just walked in and pointed to the top bunk, on the starboard side.

'That's the only one left.' Then he gestured to the port side of the cabin. 'I'm on the top bunk, too.'

She gave a nod of her chin, as if to say that was all right by her, and tossed her backpack up there in one long movement of her body, twisting from the hips.

'You don't travel too heavy, do you?'

Simone Lord didn't reply. She'd had a hard time settling the night before, and was in no mood. That morning at the office Jean-Guy Thériault had told her what he knew about each of the men. She couldn't fathom why the boss in Gaspé was sending her – *her* – aboard that boat. It had left nothing but a bitter taste in her mouth.

'Below you, there's McMurray. He snores like a diesel generator.'

She had run into Lucien Carpentier once or twice at Le Central. She had recognised him when she walked in. She had heard he was the kind of guy who forgot it was his turn to buy a round and pinched the waitresses' tips when they weren't looking. As the trawler bucked and tugged at its mooring lines, Simone climbed up the two bunks below hers and over the wooden edge to sit on her mattress. A handrail on the ceiling might have done double duty as a curtain rod, if there'd been a curtain to hang.

'I hope you're a sound sleeper.'

She had a sleeping bag, but not a very heavy-duty one; it was the kind they sell in a sports store. Carpentier would never go anywhere with bedding like that, because fashion was all very well, but it didn't look warm.

'And down on the bottom bunk, there's Lapierre.'

On the ceiling was a burned-out bulb no one had replaced. That way, the light wasn't as harsh when there was a shift change in the night.

'He's from Pointe-aux-Loups, but he's been living in the city for a long time. He looks more like a grunge rocker than a sailor, but when you're flat broke, everyone's a seal hunter.'

Simone hated those kinds of petty, hypocritical remarks.

'So that's why you're here then, is it? Short of a buck or two, are you?'

Her voice, and the wry, harsh tone of it, surprised him.

'Me? I don't have any money problems.'

'Oh, no? I thought I heard you'd had to sell your livelihood for a song.'

He recoiled a step, as if her words were a snakebite.

'I was fed up of being skipper. It's a big responsibility, a boat is.'

'And word is, that wife of yours has an expensive taste for trinkets…'

The lanky seaman pointed clumsily at Simone's sleeping bag and the rest of her stuff. 'You've got an eye for nice things too…'

'I'd better not catch you nosing around in my bags, you filthy poacher.'

That was when it sank in for Lucien Carpentier that the latest arrival wasn't a biology researcher or an intern from the university in Rimouski, but a Fisheries and Oceans Canada officer. He hadn't paid any attention to the logo on her bag, but all of a sudden, it was like acid thrown in his eyes.

He could feel his ears burning, he knew he was going red with shame.

Ida had always said that women had no place on a boat of men. She herself never came aboard. Lucien Carpentier had tolerated one or two, on occasion, because he'd had to, but now they were lumbered with another one, and a fisheries officer, to boot. Marco Painchaud had never said a word about that.

Five years, that was how long the poacher had been ruminating about the comeuppance he'd give to one of that lot, someday. With the fines and the seizures, there was a heavy buildup of resentment in his voice box. His jaw quivered. *Fuck off, bitch!* That was what he wanted to say, but the words churned around his mouth like a semi-soft cheese, and he ended up just swallowing them.

Simone glared at him. Anger and a sense of injustice caught like a poison apple in her throat. 'Have you got a problem?'

Ida would have known what to say back to her. Carpentier, he just clenched his fists. He had never laid a finger on a woman, but when an airhead like her came aboard, trying to be clever, she'd better not complain if she ran into trouble.

In spite of himself, he heard himself saying *no*, and took a few backward steps.

'I'll leave you to settle in.'

He grumbled his way out of the cabin. Bitches like that, they deserved nothing but a good whack on the back of the head with a hakapik.

The end of eternal bands

There are some, rare, mornings, when a man takes off a ring and it's thirty-two years of his life that he puts down on the polished wood surface of the kitchen table.

Four months earlier, Joaquin Moralès had reached into Gaspé Bay and pulled out the body of a fisherwoman in her wedding dress who had spent three days in the water. Her frock had been tainted, her eyes fallen prey to sea fleas, her face maimed by crabs and autumn-spawning fish. He had crouched down beside the woman and called her by her name, as if she could not only answer his questions about the investigation, but also speak to his woeful wondering about love. When he had closed the case file, he had understood that it was the end of his own marriage he had seen in the gruesome effigy of the young bride's body. Once he was back home in Caplan, he had gone to knock on Chiasson the notary's door.

The wise legal man had expressed some reservations about the necessity of divorce.

'Thirty-two years of married life don't come to an easy end. Think this through. I've seen plenty of people cry in that armchair.'

A box of tissues on the corner of the desk and a wastebasket on the floor lent a semblance of truth to these words. But Joaquin knew from experience that the dead were beyond resuscitating. He had driven out here, to the Gaspé Peninsula, at the beginning of the summer, his car loaded to the roof with the kinds of objects that tell the story of a couple's life fulfilled, and he had patiently waited for his wife to come and join him here. But she had tarried. Distance had made old misunderstandings resurface, things neither of them had worked through, and with the weight of the years, the scales of resentment had suddenly tipped the wrong way. Sulking had sullied the sheets of their marital bed, so the notary had resigned himself, and retrieved the form used to file for divorce. Joaquin and Sarah had signed the end of their love story separately and in silence. They had penned its prologue together long ago, in front of an altar.

The previous day, Joaquin had collected the documents that confirmed the end of his life as a married man. Chiasson the notary had shaken his greying head, supported as it was by three dignified and well-meaning chins, and impressed upon his client the triviality of all those official stamps, the true burden of which was now his, and his alone, to bear.

'You'll see, signing those papers isn't the hardest thing.'

Feeling the weight of that fateful foresight, Moralès had taken the envelope and carried it home. He had not slept well.

Fortunately, today he was going away on a skiing trip. As if he were making a getaway. His luggage was waiting at the door. When he came downstairs in the morning, he liked to be ready.

'You're travelling light.'

His eldest son was at the kitchen counter, getting himself a bowl of cereal.

'It's not supposed to be a fashion parade.'

They had been living together since Sébastien had rolled up at his door a few months earlier, the worse for drink. Like a man who'd lost it all. Now he had a job at the microbrewery in L'Anse-à-Beaufils and was talking about moving to Percé at the end of the following week. They got on well, but Moralès senior was still keen to see the last of his son's dirty socks in the house. He was past the age of kids living at home.

'What time's your flight?'

'Half past twelve.'

Joaquin went over to the patio door and looked out at the bay. It was so cold, everything was immobile. The ice had encroached on his little patch of beach a while back, and the tide, seemingly on the ebb, was elevating the bluish slabs and their spiky peaks. The sky was transparent.

'Are those your divorce papers?'

Seated at the table, his son half opened the envelope Joaquin had abandoned there. It had too much weight to it for him to feel able to put it anywhere else. Where were you supposed to file a document like that? What sort of folder is made to hold a certificate of divorce? He had been replaying the notary's words in his mind. Between which year's tax return and which month's bank statement were you supposed to slip thirty-odd years of love, laughter, intimacy and dreams that were meant to be shared?

'Are you going to keep wearing your ring?'

With a lump in his throat, Joaquin refused to think about that.

'I'll take it off when it's all over.'

With his mouth full, Sébastien scraped the bottom of his cereal bowl.

'I hate to break it to you, Dad, but it *is* all over now.'

Joaquin was about to react, but realised with regret that his son was right. It was all over. What would it say about him if he kept wearing that band of gold? He bowed his head, grasped the ring between his right thumb, index and middle fingers and observed his gesture with a growing ache in his stomach.

Whenever he might have doffed his wedding ring in the past, for work or a workout, it was only ever a temporary thing, of no consequence. Now, as Joaquin slipped the ring off his finger, he was painfully aware that he was bidding farewell to Sarah and the whole story they had shared together, since the moment they met in Mexico, since he emigrated and set about laying down roots in another soil, another climate, another culture, all while their boys were being born, while he was becoming a police officer, then a detective, and while their life together was growing stronger, or so he'd thought.

He turned his back on the frozen sea, and on the table he placed the band of gold, the words of love whispered in two tongues over their children's cribs, the ripples of laughter that would swell through Sarah when he grumbled about the winters, her earthy hands in April, the wind in her skirts in June and the sultry scent of her silky skin between the sweaty sheets of their embrace.

He took a step backwards.

Sébastien, suddenly ill at ease, felt obliged to add something.

'Back in the autumn, you told me there were some days you had to take it all, and others, it was better to let it all go.'

The silence caught in Joaquin's throat like a ball of papier-mâché. He couldn't find the words to express how that ring had deep roots, that by taking it off he had ripped everything up. He was devastated. He walked out of the kitchen, over to the front door.

Sébastien said something, but his father didn't hear it. Inside him, nothing was left but an empty echo. He put his coat on. Sébastien got up to come and say something, but Joaquin was already out of the door. He didn't want his son to witness his turmoil. He carried his bags to the car and put them in the back.

He had no desire to stand in front of a young man whose future and potential stretched in abundance before him, now that he himself was straddling the chasm of his life. Sébastien gave him a sad sort of wave from the veranda as Joaquin sat behind the wheel and drove away. Where was he even going? He had moved out to the Gaspé Peninsula to make his wife happy. Now he was divorced, which way would he turn?

Disoriented, he drove with an eye on the Baie-des-Chaleurs and parked outside Renaud's bistro as if on autopilot. He stepped over the threshold without thinking, the way someone calls for help.

'Ah, well let me tell you, if it isn't the inspector himself who's come for a shot of espresso, but make it a long one!'

It was still early, but pillars more solid than a winter shore were already propping up the bar, keeping a watch as wearied as it was caffeinated. Men of his age, or older, expecting only from the spring what it was sure to offer: a breath of warm air, a few fleeting tourists and a bit of fresh lobster.

A shallow wave of salutations rolled like a three-word canon sung by an off-key choir. Renaud Boissonneau, the barkeeper, was holding his left hand high in the air, wrapped in a big white bandage. Before Joaquin even thought to ask the question, the answer was fired from his right.

'The cook's had his knives sharpened.'

Vital Bujold the fisherman, his eyes a darkness in the doldrums, was leafing through the sheets of a national daily. Victor, his deckhand, completed the news flash.

'It's l-l-like that every year at the end of J-J-January.'

He swivelled on his stool to look out of the window at the sea, which stretched beyond the rocks like a motionless field of ice.

The curate got up and went behind the bar to make the coffee. The bistro was on the ground floor of the old rectory. He still had an apartment upstairs, but made himself quite at home in the kitchen there, especially during the off season.

Renaud followed his every step.

'Let me tell you, he's going to need a sugar bowl…'

The man of the cloth cautiously placed the cup in front of Joaquin, who reached for it with his left hand, as if on autopilot.

'You're not wearing your wedding ring anymore?'

In a near-synchronised movement, they all leaned in for a look at Joaquin's naked finger.

'Jesus, Mary and Joseph, it's such a shame. Let me tell you, what are we going to do?'

'Christ in a chalice! Calm down, Renaud, you're not the one who's got divorced; you're not even married.'

'Oh, but it does get me all in a flip, that kind of thing.'

In a movement of melodrama, the barkeeper wiped his nose with his bandage. Joaquin took a sip of coffee to shroud his sorrow.

'Y-y-you must be feeling the emptiness.'

Moralès nodded.

'I kn-kn-know what that's like.'

'You lot, in the police, don't you get to see a shrink or something?'

Joaquin replied to Vital Bujold. 'If you've witnessed a trauma, you get the privilege of seeing the psychoanalyst in town once a month. If not, then…'

'Then what?'

'Same as everyone else. They send you to Doctor Samson.'

A wave of low whistles rippled around the bar. Originally from Quebec City, Doctor Samson was a life coach who had an office in Saint-Siméon. The thing was, she had a diploma in sexology and had been struck off the register of her professional association after she had confused psychological research and manual therapy on half a dozen occasions. Few serious men in those parts had any desire for their fellow citizens to see their car parked outside Doctor Samson's. Her office was in the basement of her house, right on the main road.

Vital shook his head. 'Forget it.'

'Why? I've been to see her before, and let me tell you just one thing, her technique is—'

The curate cut him off. 'In truth, Renaud, this isn't the right time for a confession.'

'W-w-when I had my accident, I b-b-bought a book.'

'A book?'

Boissonneau was on the brink of a heart attack.

'You think I should read something?'

Vital was at the end of his rope. 'Not you, Renaud. Victor's saying that for Moralès.'

The curate pursed his lips. 'In truth, there's only one text to help a man gone astray, and that's the Bible.'

Boissonneau couldn't argue with that.

'And let me tell you, your holiness, there's one only tourist brochure for me, and that's the missel you read from at mass!'

Proud of his little repartee, the barkeeper slapped a palm on the bar, but ended up hopping in pain because he'd used his bad hand.

'Christ in a chalice, Renaud, just go home if you're that much of a cripple. We've had it up to here with you getting on our nerves.'

Victor took advantage of the diversion to lean closer to Moralès. 'G-g-good booksellers are l-l-like psychologists.'

'There's one who runs the bookshop not far from the wharf in New Richmond.' Vital ventured the information like it was an insider secret and gave the curate a glare to keep his mouth shut.

The curate turned his back as a stroppy Boissonneau went about having the last word.

'Let me tell you just one thing though, they might have a bookshop, but they don't serve coffee!'

Even the silence fell flat, and the men went back to their missel, their newspaper, their looking out to sea. Now he was off the hook from the chit-chat, Joaquin sipped his coffee slowly. Back in the autumn, Sébastien had given him grief for cutting himself off so completely from his Latin American roots. Perhaps that was the way he should turn in order to ground himself again, to fill the void. He got up and paid, said his goodbyes all round and headed for New Richmond.

He hadn't read a book in a long time. Not since he was a student, when he would scan the words of the prescribed Spanish authors with an uninterested eye, between jaunts to the beach with friends, where Luisa Guzmán ruffled her colourful skirts and stirred hopeless dreams of what they concealed from him and his peers – much to her parents' delight, she was seeing a man ten years her senior, a well-built lawyer from a well-to-do family. As it happened, that older hunk had ended up marrying her and having some charming children. It just went to show that life was only fair for pretty women and sons of the rich. He had stuck his nose between the covers of publications about his future career as a detective too. But did that really count in anyone's mind as 'reading'? Moralès couldn't help but wonder as he pushed open the door to the little bookshop in New Richmond, which stood facing the sea.

The tinkling of the bell sounded around the whole shop, and a self-conscious Joaquin ducked to his right to avoid meeting the owner's inquisitive gaze too quickly. He found himself in the children's books section, organised by reading age, in the midst of toys and jigsaw puzzles. He made his way to the end of the aisle, feigning an interest in some how-to guides about plumbing and electrics before surreptitiously sneaking in the direction of a whole stack of books about yoga, spirituality and meditation.

'Are you looking for some book in particular?'

Joaquin was startled and turned towards the counter. An attractive bookseller with very short black hair and a radiant smile was looking his way. She gave him the nod of a confidante. She was probably too young to understand.

'Is it for a special occasion?' she persisted.

If Victor and Vital had advised him to come here, he'd have to spit it out.

'I've just got divorced.'

The bookseller nodded her head. 'Long time, was it?'

He cleared his throat. 'Thirty years.'

'Feels like a bottomless pit?'

'Yes.'

She thought for a moment, then made a decision. She came out from behind the counter and headed for the far end of the shop, where the poetry collections were.

Joaquin scurried after her. 'Do you have any books by Mexican writers?'

She pointed to the translated fiction section. 'This isn't a very big bookshop. We carry a few Latin American authors.'

Moralès recognised a name, Gabriel García Márquez, on the spine of a book. 'That one.'

'He's not Mexican.'

Joaquin picked up the book and peered at the blurb on the back cover. 'He's Colombian, but he wrote this novel in Mexico.'

The bookseller looked Moralès up and down. 'Are you sure about that?'

'Yes.'

'All right, but don't tell anyone I was the one who recommended it to you.'

She grabbed another one on her way back to the till.

'I'll sell it to you along with this one. It's for you, but you'd better lend it to Érik.'

Joaquin frowned. 'Pardon me?'

'You've got a police badge and a tan that hasn't faded. Let me deduce that you're the Detective Moralès who works with Constable Lefebvre. He should like this collection.'

She tapped the prices into the till. 'I'll take ten percent off for you and here's a loyalty card.'

As the bookseller slipped a bookmark into each of the titles, a flabbergasted Joaquin Moralès handed her his credit card.

Michaël Lapierre and Bernard Chevrier were the only ones to greet her when she entered the wheelhouse. Surrounding the skipper were two screens showing the deck and the engine room; the radar, VHF unit, depth gauge and other instruments were switched on too. A small television, mounted to the ceiling, was playing a show about hunting. The sound was down low; no one was really listening. The generator was running to preserve the heat in the living quarters and the food in the fridges. Officer Lord introduced herself and announced the inspection procedure.

'Let's start with your permits, the paperwork for the boat and the firearms registry documents.'

Marco Painchaud nibbled the edge of his left thumb nervously. 'Do I look like I've got any fucking papers on me? Do I?'

Tony McMurray, lounging more than sitting on the grey leather bench that stretched the length of the wheelhouse down the port side, was chomping on something – sunflower seeds, chewing tobacco, or maybe his own drool. Simone strode over to Painchaud, who was wriggling like an electric eel in holy water. Jean-Guy Thériault had said he'd had a run-in with the guy last summer, over Grande-Entrée way. Her boss had not minced his words, telling Simone he was the worst lowlife of a cokehead he'd ever met. A real parasite, with a greasy face and eyes that were up to no good.

'Marco Painchaud, I presume? Denis Éloquin's nephew, aren't you? I understand the charter is in your name.'

'Yeah. This is my boat.'

Officer Lord smirked at him. He was all brag and boast, but he schlepped his secret around like a puppet with string for brains. Everyone knew he didn't have two cents to rub together and it was his old man who had chartered the *Jean-Mathieu*, getting himself into debt to encourage his boy to take some responsibility. Not to mention that his uncle had probably done him a deal because he was family. Simone decided to hold him to his word.

'Well, since you're the boss, you're going to give me the grand tour.'

'No. You can forget your papers and your sightseeing. How

come you're here? It was supposed to be Maxime – my mate Maxime Laurin, from Gaspé.'

Bernard Chevrier was sizing up the young lad, telling himself that in their house, his dad must be crossing his fingers and hoping this hateful son of his didn't get up to too many hijinks, or else he wouldn't see a cent of the money he'd fronted for the charter.

If there was one reason Painchaud senior had agreed to put some trust in his spawn, it was because he'd had his own roller-coaster ride of a life. He had lost his house during a night of poker, as well as his wife – the next morning, when he stumbled home after sleeping on a neighbour's sofa. On his own with his young son, he had moved into a friend's basement and kept wagering his wages, swearing he'd give up gambling and drinking when the cards let him pay his debts. Since, on the odd occasion, some benevolent deity does open half an eye and look favourably on an unlucky player, one day Painchaud had filled his pockets. Keeping his word, he had then abstained from his excesses, bought a cabin, done it up, and started saving.

Growing up, his son Marco had, naturally, inherited a similar taste for trouble. Setting his sights on wherever, he had gone off to the mainland for a few years, claiming he was going to college, then university. Until his uncle Denis fetched him and brought him back to his dad's front door. He was skinny, scruffy and reeked of all the wrong things to get mixed up in, but his old man had still welcomed him by killing the proverbial fatted calf. No later than the very next morning, Éloquin had found him a job on a lobster trawler. Painchaud senior had kitted his son out with some fishing waterproofs and dropped him off at the wharf.

It had turned out to be a decent lobster season and, surprisingly, Marco had pulled his socks up and worked hard. But then, when autumn came, he had followed the flocks of Canada geese and taken off for the mainland again. He had returned only twenty days earlier, still down and out and stinky, with Michaël Lapierre riding shotgun beside him and a plan to harvest seals hatching in their bags. Was his dad up for an opportunity?

While Painchaud senior hadn't set foot near a card game in years, the gambling streak still ran deep, and he had decided, just this once, to bet on his offspring. And so he had gone, with Marco in tow, to persuade Denis Éloquin to let him charter his boat in the worst week of weather, making sure the fridge was as full as the fuel tanks, hoping his boy would bring home a good haul.

The boat's owner had insisted on Chevrier being on board and promised he'd sniff out a spot in the Maritime provinces that was as well stocked with marine mammals as a pasture in the American West could be with big, beefy cattle. Then the men had gone to get their permits. What could possibly go wrong?

Officer Lord sighed. It was going to be a long week.

'If you don't have your papers, you're not casting off from the wharf, Marco Painchaud.'

'I'll cast off if I say so.'

'Since you're not in a rush, we're going to take our time. I might as well make the most of it to inspect your weapons and measure your hakapiks.'

Bernard Chevrier got up and fished out his wallet. He wasn't keen to go against what Denis Éloquin's nephew said, but the young lad was pushing it. Giving the fisheries officer grief wouldn't do any good. He tossed his skipper's licence and sealer's permit on the counter that ran the length of the front window.

Tony McMurray followed suit. The more they messed around, the longer it would be before he got back to Mexico. Anyway, he already knew how he was going to punish her, he had his ways. He threw a crumpled piece of paper on the counter then grabbed his crotch and gave it a good tug.

'There's my hunter's permit. And this here's my gun. Want to inspect that now or later?'

Michaël Lapierre gave a nod of his chin and rummaged through the pockets of his jeans.

'I might borrow that, McMurray, if mine's out of action…'

Lapierre placed his own papers beside the others and looked down at the hand between the legs of the Newfoundlander in the grey balaclava.

'The thing is, though, I'm used to handling bigger calibres.'

Marco Painchaud erupted in a laugh like the back and forth of a timber saw biting into an oak plank. Simone Lord glared at him.

'I didn't know you had epilepsy, Painchaud. Are you having a fit?'

The laugh stopped dead in his mouth, and his lips glued themselves to his gums in a grimace.

'I'm not epilepsic.'

Thin and borderline bony, with a sunken chest and dangling arms, Painchaud was a picture of wonky teeth, persistent acne and long, greasy hair that was matted to his scalp as if he'd been wearing a cap all day.

'If something's funny, it's funny, and I can laugh if I like. Is that clear?'

His jaw never stopped moving, caught in anarchic shakes, as if he'd had a line of coke cut with more than it probably should have been.

'And it's my boat, so you're either on board – with everything – or I'll send you off for a swim right now.'

Michaël gave him a harder slap on the shoulder than he had to. 'Hey, Eight-Inch, it was only a joke.'

That was what his long-time friends called him, since the day they dared him to sniff a line of coke eight inches long in a high-school toilet cubicle.

'Yeah, yeah, I know.'

Since then, he had never quite been 'all there'. That might well have been the case long before the incident too, but no one had ever really stopped to think about it. He gave the corner of his nail a quick nibble and said his last piece.

'Hey, I know how to crack a joke too, you know.' He turned to Simone. 'Is that clear?'

Officer Lord addressed him as if she were speaking to a child.

'All right, then. Now you're going to put your serious face on and show me your papers. All of them.'

Eight-Inch pulled out his wallet, while Lapierre waved at Carpentier the poacher, who was out on deck, mumbling to himself with clenched fists, to come join them.

ઝૈ

Moralès walked out of the airport and tossed his bag and his gear in the back of a taxi just in time to hit the rush-hour traffic with a driver whose ear was glued to a talk show the whole way to Old Montreal. He paid the fare and carried his bags, skis, poles and all, into the pub. Langlois, a portly sexagenarian with thick glasses, came over to greet him with open arms.

'Hey, Moralès! Haven't seen you in a while.'

It was the first time he'd been back in the city in nearly a year.

Langlois stashed the luggage in a tiny staff room before walking his customer to the bar. Joaquin cast an eye around the room.

'Looking for Doiron, are you?'

'Yes. And Lauzon.'

'Not here yet.'

Joaquin sat on a stool.

'Can I get you a tequila?'

'No. I'll have a beer.'

Langlois poured him a pint of amber ale and in spite of the crowd, stuck around to get the gossip.

'Doiron told me you were on a temporary loan to a team out in the Gaspé…'

Joaquin smiled in spite of himself. Langlois was a typical bar owner, the type who'd dangle a half-truth to lure his customers into opening up.

'If you say so.'

'Must be good to be back?'

'Right.'

Buoyed by the banter, Langlois leaned across the bar. 'I've got a sailboat in Contrecoeur. I've spent a few summers sailing down around the Lower Saint Lawrence. Things aren't as hectic down there. There's more action in the city.'

'It's different.'

Down there, an accident sends shock waves through a whole community. In Montreal, it takes more than a gruesome murder to shake the streets.

The barman went on. 'I don't eavesdrop, but I hear your colleagues talk. And I've often wondered why you do the job you do.'

Intrigued, Moralès waited to see where this was going. 'To serve and protect,' he would invariably reply when asked this question. The truth was more complex and rooted in his own personal past and place of birth, a country choked by the challenges of drug trafficking and corruption in the legal system. Of course, when he immigrated to Quebec, he could have changed career paths, but what would he have done?

Langlois nodded pensively. 'Because the adrenaline gives you the powerful sense that you're more alive than everyone else.'

'Perhaps.'

Joaquin took a swig of beer and immediately regretted his choice; he should have ordered a tequila, a rum, even a mojito. Alcohol that would have left a taste of getting away from it all on his tongue, that would have spread its heat in his mouth, reminded him of summers to savour and brought on a quick buzz.

'In any case, it's not an easy job.'

'Neither is running a bar.'

'You don't suffer so much.'

Joaquin fell silent. These days, his torments had nothing to do with his work, but he wasn't in the habit of sharing confidences in the space between the beer pumps.

Langlois straightened up. 'But, hey, suffering's all part of being alive.' Without another word to his customer, he slipped away into the hubbub and the music.

Moralès checked his watch. His friends were late. That was a bad sign.

He couldn't help but flick an eye to his fingers, to the naked ring finger.

At the end of the street was the river, and on the other side, Longueuil. That was where he'd raised his children. And where his ex-wife had bought a condo. A place of her own. He could have called Sarah, suggested they go for a drink, or have dinner together at that Italian restaurant they used to like so much.

He gulped. He would have rather the ski trip start from somewhere else, Quebec City, or Rimouski. Being here was a brutal reminder of everything his life had been for thirty years. Now he was a tourist visiting his past.

Since he moved out to the Gaspé Peninsula, there had been one tidal wave after another, barrelling in from the depths, bringing fragments of himself surging up his throat. Mexico, his every love, his boys' childhood, his first few years on patrol with the Sûreté du Québec: the shards of his story were washing up in a jumble of softened colours on the shore, and Joaquin didn't have the strength to throw them all back in the sea. He turned the sea-glass lenses of memory over and over in his hands, not knowing whether to take them home, expose them to the light of the sun or abandon them to the next tide. He made do. With the artefacts and the indecision. With this baggage of his, at nearly fifty-three years old, he had to learn all over again how to … to what?

To not wear a wedding ring anymore?

To no longer be a detective in this city that was not easily shocked?

To be a tourist collecting scattered glass treasures from the beach of his life?

The plan, for now, was to go skiing. It was Lefebvre, a friend from the Gaspé detachment, who had twisted his arm to come on this package trip. It was the kind of holiday Moralès hated, but the kind a man in the midst of a divorce agrees to in order to fill the void. And to divert his mind from the suffering.

He felt his phone vibrate. He retrieved it from his pocket and read Lauzon's text: *No can do right now.*

Shit! He hurried to reply, while she had a moment: *Think you'll make it later tonight?*

Nadine Lauzon was supposed to be coming on the ski trip too. The first stop for the skiers was right here, the next morning, alongside the wharves in Montreal. Then the ship, moored in the Old Port at the moment, would be setting sail for Quebec City at the end of the day.

The reply came quickly: *Hope so.*

Moralès winced. If Nadine couldn't get away, that meant something serious had happened that urgently required the forensic psychologist's attention. He wondered what it could be. Maybe a gang-related crime. With an involuntary movement, he pushed his beer away from him. Unless it was a hostage-taking. His phone rang. Number withheld. It must be Doiron. He stiffened, on alert, answered the call. The voice on the phone didn't bother with a greeting, just got straight to the point; it was a force of habit, had been for years.

'Serious assault on a teenager.'

Langlois, accustomed to a police officer's reactions, brought his customer the bill for the drink, even though the beer wasn't finished. Detective Moralès put the money on the bar. He felt the sudden surge of adrenaline in his body.

'A teen? How old?'

'Seventeen.'

His heart rate accelerated.

'Small-time dealer?'

'Probably.'

'Messed up bad?'

'Looks like it's headed for homicide.'

If the kid was in that bad a way, they had to act now. Reflexively, Moralès pulled a pen and notepad out of his pocket. His hands were clammy. But it wasn't an address that Doiron had to share with him.

'Sorry, I won't be able to make it for that drink.'

Joaquin opened his mouth, closed it again, lost for words. He could hear the music again now, the voices in the bar. He could feel the heat in his body and sense the state of hypervigilance slowly dissipating.

His friend misinterpreted his silence. 'I'm sorry. You know how it is. We've all got to be on standby now.'

Joaquin put the pen and notepad back in his pocket. 'It's all right.'

'I'll make arrangements so Nadine can come aboard tomorrow.'

'Thanks.'

'Listen, Moralès…' He paused for a moment, and Joaquin gathered the boss must be stepping away from the other detectives on his team. He cleared his throat, then carried on. 'I've been putting the go-slow on the paperwork for your official transfer to the Gaspé. I'm telling you this, just on the off chance…' Doiron didn't say any more. He had been promoted to the rank of lieutenant not long after Moralès's move, and Moralès understood what that unfinished sentence implied.

When Sarah had fallen out of touch, Joaquin had asked his former colleague to see what was happening in Longueuil. It was thanks to Doiron that Moralès had learned his wife had bought a condo – and it had sunk in that she would never come out to the seaside to join him. If Doiron was yet to finalise the transfer for Moralès, it was because he knew the detective's marriage was coming to an end and he wanted to leave the door open for him to return to his old team in Montreal.

Moralès turned to the frosted-up window and saw passersby, nose down in their coats, battling the icy late-January wind on the slippery flagstones of this city that used to be his. He looked down again at his naked left hand, beside which the glass of beer sat barely half empty. He had spent more of his life married than single and now, a new civil status would be written after his name: Joaquin Moralès, divorced.

⚓

Bernard Chevrier started the engines.

The day was drawing to a close as Officer Lord stepped out on deck to lend a hand with the unberthing of the *Jean-Mathieu*. Marco Painchaud had spent nearly an hour looking for his permit before remembering he'd left it at his dad's, who was out at work at the salt mine in Havre-aux-Maisons. He'd had to ask a neighbour to do him a favour and bring the piece of paper down to the wharf. Bernard Chevrier, comfortably seated in his captain's chair, had spent the afternoon watching hunting shows.

Making the most of a moment to herself, Simone had gone down to the cabin and discreetly sent a text to Érik Lefebvre to explain her imminent departure. She might be hard to get hold of for the next week and didn't want him to worry. She hadn't complained about the wayward crew, no. It wasn't the first time that men had kicked up a stink about taking a woman on board. She had even had to field that sort of thing from some of her colleagues in the coast guard a while back, and she had always emerged unscathed. If she had wanted to be well accepted at work, she would have chosen another career. She would have become a nurse or, like her sister, opened a yoga studio. But she had chosen the sea.

Tony McMurray was fiddling with the mooring lines.

'There's still time to jump ship, lady.'

'Don't let me be the one to stop you, McMurray.'

Calling fishermen by their last name wasn't ideal, because they tended to think hers sounded a bit high and mighty. Érik Lefebvre would say she was trying to be top of the class, teacher and headmistress all at once. Perhaps he was right.

A long time ago, Officer Lord had begun to take certain measures to distance herself from not only men in general, but also, and especially, the crews she joined at sea. Lots of seamen found their lewd tongues when they left the wharf behind, as if the open water were giving them permission. Calling the fishermen by their first name might lead them to believe that Simone was seeking some sort of proximity. Proximity was something she eschewed, to avoid the potential for ambiguity in a situation, and because slapping a fine on someone you were friendly with could be seen as an act of treason. Insults were quick to fly around on the deck of a boat, she knew that already.

The Newfoundlander with the balaclava perched on the top of his head glared at her with a darkness in his eye.

'Eight years ago, you slapped my skipper with one hell of a ticket.'

Simone Lord stared right back at him, but couldn't remember where or when she had seen the man before.

'I'd be surprised if I did, because this is the first time I've come on board to watch a seal hunt.'

She made a point of stressing the 'watch' to make it clear what her role was on board and mark the distance that separated them.

'Cassivi, in Rivière-au-Renard. We were out fishing.'

Carpentier the poacher jumped down onto the wharf from the bow. Tony McMurray did the same at the stern. The wind was solid, steady and right where it was meant to be, and had been for hours. The boat was still tugging at its lines, but not as aggressively as before, as if it knew they'd be on their way soon.

The men pulled up the fenders and coiled the ropes before tossing them onto the deck. The one at the stern landed like a dead snake at Simone's feet.

'He was just a poor guy who'd not had his trawler for long.'

'I imagine that if he was poaching, he could afford to pay a fine.'

McMurray stopped for a second and gave her a menacing stare. 'The guy was nowhere near rich, but he kept me on board the whole rest of the season and not once did he talk about cutting my pay. Generosity, that means a lot to me.'

Carpentier freed the foredeck of the *Jean-Mathieu* and jumped aboard at the bow. McMurray, still on the wharf, stooped over the mooring bollard, unhooked the breast line and tugged it towards him.

'Now you mark my words, Cassivi asked nothing of me, but I reckon I owe him something all the same. And when I owe someone, I pay them back.'

The hull at the stern pressed up against the tyres as the bow swung towards the way out of the port. With one end of a line in his hand, McMurray jumped back aboard.

'That's loyalty, and that's something you officers don't understand.'

He gave the heavy rope a hard shake, and it hit Simone's boots. She didn't budge an inch.

'That's why, sometimes, you need to be taught a lesson or two.'

He coiled the line as the boat slowly moved away from the dock.

'Maybe you should have gone ashore.'

Rope in arm, he passed close by Simone.

'Because, you know what, I still owe that guy something.'

His left shoulder rolled back in its socket as he went on his way. He lifted the coil onto a hook and followed Carpentier into the vestibule.

As they left the shelter of the marina, the skipper gunned the engines. Behind the trawler, a hefty wash made a rolling wake. It was sharpened to a blade by a frothing sea turned bloody by a crimson sun that was slowly drawing the scarlet curtains of the day. Simone, momentarily thrown off balance by the acceleration, staggered back into the wall by the door and braced herself against the mooring line coiled by McMurray. The land dissolved and vanished before her eyes. All that remained, atop the raging waves, were flat clouds, their carmine bellies stacked heavy amidst layers of grey in a harsh, foreboding sky.

The Hawaiian music was lapping at the portholes of the ship. And Érik Lefebvre was dancing with his arms in the air in the middle of a group, who were mostly women with garlands of multicoloured faux flowers around their necks. In a classy yellow shirt dotted with earthy-toned chimpanzees, Érik was undeniably a picture of elegance, rocking a neatly trimmed moustache, a most becoming pair of brown trousers and his signature cowboy boots.

When he noticed Moralès, he made a show of excusing himself and bounded over to greet him enthusiastically. He pointed to a couple on the dance floor, who turned and waved at them.

'That's Réjean and Réjeanne Vigneault, my friends from the

Magdalen Islands. They've got a slaughterhouse and butcher's shop in Cap-aux-Meules, and—'

Joaquin cut him off. 'I will come and join you, Érik, but first I have to put my stuff in the cabin.' Having found the reception desk unstaffed, the newcomer was still encumbered with his coat, boots and the luggage he had just tucked away in a corner.

Lefebvre frowned. 'Weren't you supposed to be having a happy-hour reunion with your old police friends?'

'Yes, but they stood me up. They had an emergency.'

'An emergency? Do they need you, then?'

Moralès shook his head, no, but Lefebvre liked to guess.

'They asked you to come, didn't they?'

Joaquin tried to steer the conversation onto a different course. 'Where's the cabin?'

'Listen, Joaquin, don't worry about the week away. If you'd rather jump into an investigation with your old homicide team, just go for it.'

'Where's our cabin?' Moralès insisted.

Lefebvre didn't reply. He shouldered Moralès's ski gear and led the way down the corridor.

'Everyone's skis are down in the hold, but we'll stick yours under your bunk for tonight. The boat is amazing. It's got bars, a cafeteria, a cinema, a gym, you name it.'

At last, he opened a door and held it open for Joaquin, who tripped over the suitcases his roommate had left in the doorway, just managed to break his fall, felt for the switch, turned on the light and regained his balance.

The room was minuscule. Two narrow bunks were arranged either side of a small table, with a porthole in the wall above it. Stuff was spread out in such a consistently disorderly way it was hard to tell which bed Lefebvre had claimed. Joaquin smiled.

His colleague was more than messy, he knew that from having worked with him at the station in Gaspé, and he'd have to live with it for the next few days.

'I texted you to let you know we were having a bite to eat in the cafeteria. Is your phone turned off?'

'No.' Moralès pulled it out of his coat pocket. 'The battery's flat.'

'It must have frozen. It happens. I've got a charging cable right here.'

As Érik plunged an able hand into a jumble of a suitcase and pulled out the right cord on his first try, Joaquin cleared a bed and tossed his backpack on it. Lefebvre plugged his roommate's phone in.

'Doiron's asking you to come.'

'Are you reading my messages?'

Érik put the device on a shelf. Clearly it was still turned off. 'I just made that up.'

Moralès felt like an idiot. He'd been had, like a rookie. He hadn't even been texting with Doiron.

His friend looked him in the eye. 'What's happened?'

For months, Moralès had believed he had moved house because his wife wanted to, but earlier, in the pub, he'd had to admit that he had left Montreal of his own accord. He had been feeling old – old and ridiculous – around the recruits who were slowly pushing him into obsolescence, with their new technology and oh-so modern ways of understanding a crime scene.

Lefebvre was insistent. 'I can do the Tour de Gaspé without you, you know.'

To resist that sort of sidelining, some seasoned detectives went out of their way to find fault with the youngsters, to remind them they still had a lot to learn. He, Moralès, had preferred to hang up his hat.

'I told you, I'm not going.'

'Not even just for the night?'

Working on Doiron's current team, he would find himself the target of the rookie's ironic stares, and he had no doubt the competition among them would overshadow the real issues in the case. No, that was no longer his place.

'Not even just for the night.'

Lefebvre was puzzled. 'Is your colleague Lauzon coming to join us?'

'I think so. But not before tomorrow.'

'I suppose she'll bring a copy of the case file with her.'

Moralès dreaded the thought. In any case, he was assigned to the Bonaventure detachment now. There was no point encouraging another pang of nostalgia. He had his frustrations with Lieutenant Marlène Forest, and had vented about them, but he knew that behind her sarcastic-boss facade, she held him in high esteem and boasted all over the Gaspé Peninsula that she had a 'real' homicide detective on her service. Out there, he felt less old, still useful and not completely ridiculous.

'Stop it, Érik. I'm on holiday.'

Lefebvre mulled it over and agreed with himself. 'I bet she will. In the meantime, do you have a shirt you can wear tonight?'

'Not really.'

'Right, well, did I tell you eighty percent of the people on this trip are women and that we're all going cross-country skiing?'

'Yes.'

'Can you imagine how many women are going to need warming up this week? How many are going to be needing a massage?'

'Listen, Érik…'

'Just wait till I tell them you're a police detective; you'll go down a storm! Did you bring your handcuffs?'

Lefebvre glanced at his colleague's left hand, then opened the cabin door. 'Ah, you've taken your wedding ring off. Fantastic!'

'I've just got divorced, I don't know if I'm…'

Moralès had to concede, Lefebvre's whirlwind of energy in some way relieved him of the weight he'd been carrying. Out in the corridor, his friend turned to him.

'You'll have to remind me to give you an update about our lovely Simone, when we've got a minute…'

Leaving his sentence trailing behind him like bait on a hook, Érik led the way to the dining room with a spring in his step.

The ice singer

After supper, half the crew disappeared to the sleeping quarters. Tony McMurray left some grub for the night shift and decided to bunk down until dawn. Lucien Carpentier, who'd spent the evening stewing and seething, and Painchaud, who'd gone out like a light, were dozing ahead of the midnight watch they were taking together.

Simone Lord made herself comfortable in the wheelhouse, on a little stool to the skipper's left, looking out of the window. She placed a document portfolio on the counter. Bernard Chevrier was wary: the northwesterly wind had severed the ice from the shore; great hard chunks were looming out in the darkness. The boat was making very slow headway.

'So, you married, then? Got any kids?'

Simone looked across at him, intrigued, then understood that the skipper was talking to Michaël Lapierre, who had sprawled out on the leather bench that ran the length of the portside wall and had picked up one of the hunting and fishing magazines from the cubbyhole beneath him. Lapierre tilted his head to one side, stretched his neck a bit, rubbed his shoulder, tugged at the collar of his shirt. In so doing, he revealed the tattoos clawing at his neck.

'I've got a girlfriend.' He said it with no great conviction.

'It ain't always easy.'

'No. How about you?'

'Thirty-seven years of marriage in May. And love. Don't go thinking any different: you can be old and in love.'

Chevrier pulled a thick leather wallet out of his pocket and opened it with one hand. He fished out a photo and held it out for Michaël Lapierre to have a look. The young guy sprang to his feet, as if this were his tattoo artist showing him a new design, grabbed the snapshot and leaned closer to Simone so she could see at the same time.

'Look at all of you, in your glad rags!'

'Aye.'

Standing in front of a tinselled tree at Christmas in a new shirt and narrow tie, Bernard Chevrier was the picture of a happy man. He had his left arm around his wife, who was wearing a black dress, white necklace and a sparkling smile. He was holding a young woman's hand.

'My daughter Amélie. She's expecting, due in May. Behind her, that's the dad-to-be. And next to him is my eldest, Marc-André, and his boyfriend.'

'Your son's gay?'

Chevrier gave him a stern look. 'Aye. And?' He reached out to retrieve the photo.

Michaël handed it back to him. 'You're right. I just find it surprising that—'

'That what?'

Through the big picture window, in the light of the trawler's powerful headlights, Simone could see the sea and the long, heavy waves they were slamming into almost head on. She wasn't sure if it was a blessing or a curse. As they crested the peaks, she and the skipper were keeping an eye on the lurking ice that threatened to slide up and over the deck.

'Yeah, that's a fine family you've got there, Bernard Chevrier. I admire that.'

To Simone's left, a corner of the window that lay in shadow

revealed a reflection of Lapierre, who had returned to sit on the bench. 'What about you, then, Officer Lord?'

This startled her.

'I suppose you have a name as well as a rank, do you?'

'Simone.' She all but whispered it, affected by the sudden intimacy of the moment.

'Where are you from, Simone?'

'My family was from Laval, but I've lived in the Gaspé about thirty years. In Douglastown.'

'Have you got any photos in your purse?'

'No.'

She said it so quietly, the men deduced more than heard her reply. In spite of the growling of the engines and the groaning of the waves, the wheelhouse was abruptly awash with fragility.

The previous autumn, Simone had retrieved the body of a woman in her wedding dress from the water. In her diving suit, the officer had descended to see the dead woman suspended beneath the surface and looked into what the sea fleas had left of her eyes. The sight had devastated her. In that woman, she had seen her own reflection. In the thick of the investigation, she'd had to make herself scarce and seek refuge in her own space. Stunned, she had spent a long time in the shower not only to cleanse her skin but also, and especially, to erase the haunting image that had imprinted itself on her pupils. In vain. Since then, saltwater had tended to be quick to fill her eyes.

Chevrier could see that without turning around. 'Aye. But you're young, still.'

To veil her discomfort, she reached into her portfolio for a pen and a sheet of paper.

That day, Simone had felt bound to admit that, by absent-mindedness or indifference, Eros had neglected to send a true love knocking at her door. No one had ever swept her off her feet, given her the kind of feeling that could move mountains, as people say, that could spark a desire to exchange eternal bands of gold.

'So you came out to the Islands on your own, then?'

'Yes.'

One evening, some time after they had found the bride's body, Detective Sergeant Moralès had invited her to dinner and, without realising it, incised her heart the way a blunt blade scores a jagged line into the lid of a tin can. Standing before him, Officer Lord had seen how, as the years had gone by, she had clothed herself in cumbersome armour – the heavy layers of frosty sarcasm and a cold demeanour – quite in spite of herself. And how she had ended up condemning herself to the spinster-hood that some men laughed about; and facing it now, as her fifties came into sight, she felt like crumbling.

'Autumn's tough, in the Islands.'

Simone had been left with the impression that she and Moralès had experienced something powerful that night. They had eaten and said barely nothing, shrouded in the unsettling silk of a silence that seemed complicit.

'In the summer, there's all the tourists, retirees and Islander kids who flock here from the city. You've got to plan weeks in advance to reserve your spot on the CTMA ferry. But after Thanksgiving, there's a big gust of wind that blows everyone right back to the mainland. The shops and the restaurants close their shutters. Then the boredom sets in. When did you get here?'

Simone was sketching something on the paper with the tip of her pen. 'Beginning of November.' She'd been transferred for the cold season.

'That's the worst time. November's the month when the storms are raging. It's like this string of islands sinks into the sea. And then you know you're in for the winter and you're not getting out. The roads are going to close for blizzards and the ferry's going to stop coming because the ice sets in, and all the flights are going to be delayed by the wind. Where are you staying?'

'Jean-Guy Thériault's found me a house in Belle-Anse.'

Officer Lord's supervisor had taken her under his wing so kindly, as soon as she had stepped off the ferry, that she'd cast her doubts aside and decided to learn from him. With wit and wisdom, the loyal family man had shown her not only the ropes of seal hunting – from the art of their ancestors to the rules of the present – but also, over the course of their long, silent watches on the beaches, how to live with the endless howling of the wind.

'The Vigneaults' place? Can't be, they've only just gone on holiday.'

Still poring over her paper, Simone was tracing curved lines that intertwined.

'No, Michel Arseneault's place.'

Chevrier gave an admiring whistle. 'Aye. You're not slumming it then, are you?'

The wind in the Magdalen Islands stops at nothing. It sweeps dunes, traverses lagoons and wraps itself around people to get the gossip, then it blows the bluff and bluster out to sea. Simone had allowed herself to be buffeted by the gusts, to let go of the dark traces of her most turbulent of torments. And so she had settled, standing at the patio door of the magnificent home in Belle-Anse, marvelling at the sun rising, casting the sea in a delicate yellow light, and setting just at the cliff's edge, between the dining room and the lounge, cloaked in its fabulous scarlet finery.

'Still, you must get a bit bored sometimes.'

'Is that a question?'

'No. I know my Islands. Me, I've got my wife and my kids. But on my own I'd find the season hard. When you step outside, that cold, dry wind from the north has a real nip to it. So you hole up in a house that's shaking in the squalls, and you wait for autumn to blow itself out.'

The day before, when Jean-Guy Thériault had broken the news that the boss in Gaspé had decided to assign her to monitoring this seal hunt, Simone had felt like she was going from exile to confinement. Her supervisor had offered to take her place, but she had refused. She had gone aboard the *Jean-Mathieu* with clenched teeth, but with a sense of duty and a heavy heart. Like an overachiever.

'Winter's a wonder in the Islands. You can't argue with that. The whiteness as far as the eye can see, the northeaster that bends the sea wheat on the dunes, sends the spray flying over the barren lands and slices the cliffs like a carving knife. But it's so intense, it hurts to look at it.'

Lulled by the skipper's voice, Michaël and Simone lost track of the hours passing in the night.

'What have you been writing, then?'

Simone flinched. The arabesques she had been drawing had capsized ever so slightly with the rolling of the trawler. Chevrier kept one peeper on her as he steered the ship.

'I've been doing this for years, and you're the first person, skipper Chevrier, who's noticed there's text in there.'

Albeit abashed by what he took to be a compliment, he turned his head to read the sentence. 'Aye. I'm a bit of a poet too.'

He opened his mouth as if to say the words she'd written out loud, then closed it again and motioned to Lapierre, who was still lounging on the leather bench, leafing through the back issue of an old hunting-and-fishing magazine. He would not pronounce the phrase he had read with the guys in earshot.

Chevrier thought for a moment. Perched on that little stool, which was too low for her, the woman was dutifully folding her paper, agonising over it. She looked like she was in the naughty corner, being punished for something. Maybe that was it.

'How about you, skipper, how long have you been seal hunting?'

Time to divert attention away from herself.

'Since I was eight years old.'

'That's young.'

'Aye. And I'd have started before then if I could've. Our house was that close to the sea, you could hear the seals singing, so we knew when the season was close. My old man had a copper telescope, like a pirate's spyglass it was, but long as your arm. Every winter, before the hunt, he used to unscrew it and blacken the lens with a candle so there'd not be so many reflections. And then he'd spot where the colonies were. But he wouldn't let me tag along. He said it was too dangerous.'

'You went all the same, though.'

'Yep. One afternoon, I figured I'd skip school. I came home, I picked up one of the hakapiks and off I went onto the ice. It's treacherous, walking on the ice. They must have told you that in your training. You have to know which way to go. I followed the footprints the guys had left a few days earlier, but then at one point I strayed from the trodden path to get to a seal. Ten steps later I stuck my foot in a patch of nilas and in I went — water up to here.' He tapped a hand to his waist.

'What do you mean by nilas?'

'A granular kind of snow that's pretending to be solid ice. Didn't they tell you that in your training?'

'They mostly taught us the rules for the slaughter.'

'Well you'd better be a fast learner if you don't want to go under.'

She would remember that.

'I jabbed the hook of the hakapik into a chunk of hard ice, hauled myself out of the hole and went home. Was I ever feeling down on my luck? When my old man got wind of it, he said, I told you not to go out there on your own. Saturday, you're coming with us.'

He was steering a smooth, skilful course, letting the long, rolling waves carry the *Jean-Mathieu*.

'We set out at dawn. My dad stuck a sealer's badge on my hat and a permit in my pocket. He found a club for me, 'cause there was no way he'd let me borrow his, and he sharpened me a knife and stuck it in a little wooden holster on my belt. Leather holsters, they freeze stiff.'

'Weren't you afraid?'

'I've always been less afraid to run on the sea ice than I am to take the metro in Montreal.' Simone paused her folding to lend an attentive ear.

'Back then, sealing crews were families. So we had two of my uncles and three of my cousins, older than me, with us. My dad said walk in our footprints, never anywhere else. After what I'd been through a few days earlier, I wasn't inclined to disobey. All of a sudden, we spotted a group of seals. Harp seals, they were. My dad waved me over. There, you give that little one a whack, he said. We're not allowed to lay a finger on the pups anymore, not for more than thirty years. But back then, there was a big market for the white fur. And for the meat. Tender as lamb, it was.'

Ahead of the *Jean-Mathieu*'s prow, the sea was steadily filling with chunks of drifting ice, forcing their vessel to slow its progress on its way to Margaree Island to what seemed sometimes like a complete standstill. Chevrier wasn't taking any risks. He wasn't the type to play captain of the *Titanic*.

'So anyway, I picked up my hakapik and I made my approach.'

A sudden glassiness came over the old sea dog's eyes.

'Because of the cold wind, seals always have a tear in their eye. And a little one's still a baby…'

He trailed into silence, and cleared his throat meekly before he went on.

'It's hard to kill. From far away, with a rifle, the adrenaline, the sight and the sound of the shot, it's not the same. But when you've got the creature at the end of your club … you don't want it to suffer. Your first experience makes you conscious of your actions, then and every time after that. You're not taking a life for nothing. You're putting food on the table and earning a wage. They say the Inuit thank every animal for giving sustenance to their families.' He nodded slowly. 'You've got to be grateful.'

He went quiet. The sound of the hull tearing through the water, the echoing of the engines in the steel shell and the faint hum of a moose-hunting documentary from the television filled the air in the wheelhouse once more. The other screens still showed the engine room in the glow of the night light, and the deck steeped in shadows. Simone wondered if Chevrier had seen McMurray circling around her aggressively while they were getting ready to leave the wharf, if he'd seen her lose her balance when he opened up the engines.

She picked up her paper again and kept on folding.

'So, are you a fan of the seal hunt, then?' Lapierre was the one asking her the question.

'No, but I'll admit I'm a hypocrite. I don't like seeing animals slaughtered, but I like meat. Pork, beef, chicken, even a bit of grey seal. So I can live with it.'

'By keeping the hunters in check.'

She turned his way for a second. He hadn't moved, still had his nose in the magazine.

'Fishing, hunting, I figure if I want to eat lobster, fish and seal, I'd better make sure there's not much poaching going on, so there's plenty left to last me.'

'Look at you with your schoolmarm's morals.'

Michaël Lapierre turned to Simone and gave her a mischievous, disarming smile. She returned to her meticulous folding. After a silence, she heard her own voice emerging and was surprised to find herself telling a story in her turn, sharing a memory she thought she'd forgotten that was suddenly resurfacing in the nautical night.

'When I was young, my mum had a pair of sealskin boots. My sister and I, we used to drool over them – wished we could wear them. We had no idea where the fur came from. We had no idea it was sealskin. We just thought those boots were beautiful. At seven and ten years old, long before our feet were big enough, we used to have fun strutting up and down the hallway in them, even though they were dragged on the floor. When we were older, we used to take turns wearing them to go out, like trophies on our feet.'

'Sounds like a rite of passage for girls growing up.'

Simone laughed. 'Boys want to become men by going on the seal hunt. We became women by stepping out in sealskin boots.' She leaned back in her seat, cradling the folded paper in her hands.

'Seals, seals, where are all the seals?'

Eight-Inch Painchaud made a coked-up entrance into the wheelhouse with a face full of tics, followed by a still-groggy but already exasperated Carpentier. The midnight shift was here.

'There's lots of little ice floes starting to pop up…' Chevrier was clearly hesitant to leave the helm to them.

'Yeah, and? Who says I can't steer a ship in the ice?'

'Go get your head down, skipper,' said Lapierre. 'I'll stay up for a bit and come wake you if things get sketchy.'

Chevrier stood down. Lapierre was right. He couldn't take every shift at the helm, anyway. 'I'll take the wheel when it's necessary.'

Everyone turned to Carpentier. They tended to forget, or preferred not to remember, that the poacher had earned his skipper's licence and had owned a boat for years.

'Who says I can't steer this ship on my own if I want to?'

Chevrier got up and stretched. No one was listening to Painchaud.

'There's the automatic pilot anyway. Just got to avoid the big bits of ice out there. Night, then.'

He gave Simone a nod and went downstairs. She was reluctant to retire to her bunk. She wasn't sleepy.

Painchaud sat down in the captain's chair and immediately switched off the automatic pilot. 'Yeah, baby!'

Carpentier was horrified. He went and stood right behind Painchaud to make sure he was staying on course, and barely two minutes later he had to intervene.

'Turn the automatic pilot back on, Painchaud, we're going all over the place!'

Eight-Inch ignored him and gunned the throttle, then slowed right down for no reason, spun the wheel every which way, like a crazy kid with a new video game console. Carpentier raised his arms, clearly to grab Painchaud by the shoulders and strong-arm him away from the helm, but Lapierre motioned for him to cool it. The poacher restrained his rage, chewing on his words as if they were solid chunks of lard:

'Marco, put the automatic pilot on before I throw up.'

Painchaud hesitated.

'Put the pilot on!'

The stroppy young cokehead stood down and Carpentier took over at the helm.

'Anyway, I hate doing that. Is that clear? I hate it.'

Tiring of these pointless power plays, Simone decided to go to bed. On her way downstairs, she caught the look in Lapierre's eye, so calm and sure of himself. How was it that Painchaud would do what he said? The cokehead plonked himself down on the stool Simone had vacated and nibbled the edge of a nail.

'There!'

His nasal cry was a slap in the air that gave everyone a start. Marco was pointing out the window to starboard.

'There's a seal. There's a seal!'

Then he leaned over to the captain's chair with that snide smile of his. 'Had you there, Carpentier, didn't I?'

Simone descended the narrow stairs.

Down at deck level, the galley kitchen between the wheel-house and the hold took the brunt of the sounds and bounced them around. The roar of the heating system rattled to life, accelerated its rhythm, exhaled its hot air with the purring of a giant monster, then groaned to a halt. It was hard to tell these metallic cries apart from the creaking and cracking of the trawler in the dark waters, and the screeching of the hull as it swished through the drifting ice.

Simone entered the cabin cautiously. She was in the top bunk on the starboard side, with two bunks below her. On the port side, Chevrier was drumming his fingers on his pillow. She was relieved to hear McMurray's snoring amidst the rumbling of the engines. She approached without a sound. The man's breathing was still regular. She placed a foot on the wooden edge of the bottom bunk, stretched tall and started up the rungs of the ladder, found a foothold on the edge of the middle bunk and built some momentum to hoist herself over the edge of her mattress, but at that very moment she felt McMurray's fat palm clamp around her ankle.

'Come to have some fun, have you, big girl?'

He yanked at her leg. Simone dropped the origami she was holding and took a firm grasp of the handrail on the ceiling. With her free foot she gave McMurray a swift, solid, effective kick in the elbow. It landed so hard, it forced the joint back on itself. The guy stifled a groan of pain and let go. Her heart pounding, Officer Lord threw herself onto her mattress. Lapierre came in right that second. The light in the galley was on, so he must have seen what had happened. But neither he nor Chevrier breathed a word.

Simone stayed like that for a long while, barely moving in the gloom. In the cabin, the snorings took hold at last, rolling into one another and adding to the other noises. Sliding a stealthy hand between the wooden edge of her bunk and the mattress, she retrieved the origami bird she had dropped in the scuffle. In the night, with shaking fingers, she gently unfolded its wings and placed it beside her pillow, against the cold wall of the hull.

ൄ

Joaquin jammed the tips of his boots into the ski bindings. The cold was biting on the riverside, where a track had been set for the occasion. Érik, sporting the very latest in skiing apparel, pulled his neck warmer up to cover his mouth, the elegance that was his thin moustache and his nose. He seemed to be on top form, unlike his colleague, who had drunk too much, danced too much and gone to bed too late the night before.

Moralès had gone back down to the cabin after they'd had an aperitif, still unsure which way he wanted the evening to go. But he'd had to admit that it was absurd to be checking his text messages behind Lefebvre's back, to be feeling the weight of Lauzon's and Doiron's silence, to be overwhelmed by guilt at the sight of the lights over in Longueuil. Phone in hand, he opened the contact file for Simone Lord. How many times in the last few months had he done this? Érik had promised he'd let him know how she was doing. Joaquin had been meaning to send her a message, but what would he say? He had ended up telling himself it wasn't the right time. A man didn't engage in communication with a woman like her when the empty indentation on his ring finger was still clear to see. In any case, he and Simone had agreed to meet up on her return from the Islands, in March. What would he look like if he wrote to her now? A half-witted teenager, or some soppy hanger-on. Before he could admit to himself that it took more courage for him to approach a fisheries officer than it did to chase a lawbreaker, Joaquin had gone back up to the dining room.

He and Lefebvre had dined in the company of Réjean and Réjeanne Vigneault, a husband and wife from the Magdalen Islands with a duo of names you couldn't make up. A couple in love and fun to be around, they were on the Tour de Gaspé trip not only to ski, but also because they were sponsoring a seal-steak dinner, they said. Their good humour and tight connection were a constant reminder of Joaquin's solitude, and he'd had to work hard not to wallow in his regrets.

Fortunately, their conversation was cut short by the arrival of Chris Hadfield, who was on board to give a talk. The famous Canadian astronaut had spoken about his extraordinary experiences in space. The weightlessness. Listening to him, Joaquin had told himself that was what he needed: to feel light. He had remembered how Sébastien, his eldest son, had sought that sensation of weightlessness in drink, dancing and sport, when he had gone through the doldrums of his own break-up.

Coming to the conclusion that he might be able to shake off his apathy by doing the same, Joaquin had ordered a round of tequilas for himself, Érik and the couple from the Islands.

After the talk, the four of them had carried on to the bar and hit the dance floor, keeping the night lubricated with regular rounds of bad tequila. Moralès had embraced the music and had twirled around with women who had no names or faces, and he had drunk. Because he had to move on. Break the promises of the past, put them down on a tabletop with peeling varnish, accept that the dust would settle on top of them, and embark on a new adventure. He had whimsied with weightless abandon until the DJ killed the music shortly before two in the morning, and then he had retired to the cabin and to sleep, still with Lefebvre by his side, promising it would be an incredible week.

That morning, the alarm had erupted in hysterics around half past five. Lefebvre was already singing in the shower at the top of his lungs. Reflexively, and in spite of himself, Joaquin had checked his phone: still nothing.

At breakfast, he had failed to spot Nadine. Now, with his skis in the tracks, as the mayor of Montreal was delivering an official speech to get the Tour de Gaspé under way, he looked around at the crowd of skiers, bundled up in their thermal layers, bouncing up and down to stay warm while they waited for the starting whistle to blow. He couldn't see her.

'Have you seen that pretty woman with the long blonde hair giving you the eye?'

'No.'

'Right there.'

Sure enough, a woman with a spectacular head of hair topped with a big, blue-grey woolly hat was looking his way with a sparkle in her eye.

'Right, well, you danced with her last night, you know.'

Ill at ease, Joaquin turned away and saw the Vigneaults giving each other a little kiss before pulling their neck warmers up to their noses.

Suddenly, Joaquin wasn't so sure *la fiesta* was as good a fit for him as it was for his son. The whole ski trip – the festive atmosphere, the healthy breakfast, the course laid out ready for their skis, the hundred and fifty people on board, the accordionist, the group warm-ups, the smile of a strange woman – in the blinding morning light it all seemed like a hopeless bandage on a gaping wound. It wasn't even noon and already he was feeling the urge to flee.

'You said you'd heard from Officer Lord?'

Érik nodded, but his head was in the clouds. 'Yeah, yeah. I really should fill you in.'

At last, the group could set off.

'You'll never guess what she's up to.' Lefebvre stepped ably into the track reserved for the most seasoned skiers. Moralès followed, hoping he would be able to keep up, after a night that had scrambled his thoughts and softened his muscles.

'Right, well, she only asked after you, didn't she? Like she always does.'

'Oh, really?'

'I'll tell you more later.'

Lefebvre strode on ahead, quick to lead the way along the river, over which a thick plume of mist was rising. He did a little happy dance inside. He was really quite pleased with himself. Joaquin had taken the bait.

The previous autumn, they had all worked together on a case in Gaspé. And the fiery outbursts between Simone Lord the fisheries officer and Joaquin Moralès the detective had been nigh on incessant. Although he'd never call himself an expert in matters of the heart, Érik Lefebvre was enough of an agony uncle to know that passionate arguments like this were often a sign of a simmering erotic desire. He had therefore expected the two of them to unleash their frustrated libidos in the room the Sûreté du Québec had reserved for Moralès for the duration of the investigation. Always one to stick his nose in, Lefebvre had quizzed his friend Corine, who ran the auberge. But she had given him a formal report: the sheets on the detective's bed had remained scrupulously unrumpled.

Lefebvre had deduced that the conjugal equation was missing a variable, for which he had neglected to account. The said equation had been solved no later than a week ago, over dinner with his friend, when Joaquin had mentioned his ongoing divorce proceedings. That, Érik Lefebvre had concluded, was just what the handsome Mexican detective was lacking in his attempts to get a little warmth flowing in the fisheries officer's veins. Why hadn't he told she-who'd-be-the-first to benefit what he was thinking? Did ardent lovers who maintain the icy silence of winter not risk an eternal frost setting in around potential love? As Valentine's Day approached, Lefebvre had decided to draw a proactive arrow from Cupid's quiver and took the liberty of phoning Simone, the night before her departure, to see if he was on the mark. The way she had sputtered on hearing Moralès's name inclined him to suspect that he was.

He'd better not get too carried away though. Maybe it's just a little nibble, his old man would have said when out fishing. Before you reel in the line, you've got to make sure the fish has bitten down hard on the hook. All the same, the matchmaker knew he could titillate Simone with a text when he got back to the boat, to make sure both catches ended up in the same landing net.

Feeling perked up, Lefebvre pushed the pace without realising it. Following him, Moralès was in a sweat, as if by holding the cadence he would somehow become weightless. Behind them, the Vigneault couple were taking the brisk day in their stride.

The river, to their left, was blanketed in broken ice, its surface blasted by the wind with a fine powder of hard, bitter snow. The brittle blue light was a sign of the harsh, intense cold that lay ahead.

Simone was alone in the cabin when she woke. She had slept restlessly, in fits and starts, and ended up drifting into slumber after sunrise. She took advantage of the peace and quiet to slip into the bathroom for a quick wash. Like the rest of the crew, she was mindful not to waste water and would only shower when she had to. In a hurry to get to the wheelhouse, she inhaled her breakfast in the company of Tony McMurray and a still-grumpy Lucien Carpentier, who were chatting about a mutual acquaintance. Marco Painchaud didn't look up from the game he was playing on his phone.

Chevrier the skipper said good morning to her. 'We won't be at Margaree Island before tomorrow.'

Michaël Lapierre gave her his usual friendly, amused smile. Binoculars in hand, he was looking out to the horizon. The two men carried on a conversation they'd started before she walked in.

'True, I could have retired years ago,' Chevrier said. But the excitement keeps bringing me back; that, and the memories.'

Officer Lord took a seat on the leather bench. All there was to do was wait. She sipped slowly from the travel mug she had filled with coffee. The wind and the current were whipping the waves into stiff peaks that slammed into the hull, and surprise chunks of ice were surfacing in the folds of the sea.

'When we were young, we used to hack our way through the shore crust with an axe. Then we'd walk for a good three to five kilometres on the ice. We'd leap over the trickles of water like it was nothing. We didn't tell our mother everything, but she knew it was dangerous.'

There was a sudden thickness to Chevrier's voice. And a softness to his eyes. Now they were all slipping back into the lazy, tranquil nostalgia of their last watch.

'One time, the northerly died down without us expecting it to. We always went out in a north wind, because it keeps the slabs close to the shore. But then, the ice played a nasty trick on us and we started drifting. My dad and me, we spent the night on an ice floe no bigger than this ship. We wrapped ourselves in seal pelts, didn't matter that we stank to hell. We kept walking in circles and curled up tight together to keep warm. Boy, were we ever glad when the helicopter found us the next morning. My mum thought we were done for, that we'd never come back.'

He was breathing in the broad draughts of a happy man.

'We saw it all, when we were young.'

Michaël Lapierre put the binoculars down and braced his hips against the stair railing. 'You still love it, too.'

'I love everything about the seal hunt. I love the ice: it's like the sea – calm as anything, but if it makes up its mind it can take you in two minutes flat. I love the meat. When we were young, my mum used to cook little roasts of grey seal, with potatoes, carrots and onions. I even love the seals themselves. I had a neighbour once who asked me to go over and put her goat out of its misery. You'll never believe it, the creature had hurt a foot and it was rife with gangrene. She was a martyr to that hoof, so don't try and tell me that woman loved her goat – and if she did, I was glad she didn't love me like that. And she had a sick old dog that had hip dysplasia too. Me, I'm against leaving animals to suffer. When you've got a chance to put them out of their misery, you should make it a moral duty.'

Simone was watching Lapierre. He was wearing the same T-shirt as the day before, over which he had put on what looked like a sleeveless leather vest and a warm coat. She wondered what it said on the back of the vest. What he had tattooed on his chest.

'So when you do eventually retire, what are you going to do?'

'I'm a hunter, Michaël, I'm not going to start planting spuds in my garden.'

Lapierre laughed, and went on interrogating Chevrier. Simone recalled that he hadn't been back in the Magdalen Islands for long.

'Still, there must be some things you get sick of. The grease on the boat, the smell…' He seemed to be genuinely enjoying chatting with someone from his home patch, an Islander who must be the age of his father.

'Aye.'

The skipper was searching his mind, though. And found something.

'What really riled me for years, was feeling betrayed. When the animal-rights groups noticed they could make millions off our backs, with their fundraising, they came out to film us. It's true, the blood on the ice does make for some impressive photos. There's no denying, it's spectacular. But when I saw the picture they painted of us and it sank in that the world – even folk from around here – thought we were murderers, that made me furious. I was angry for years. But did that help me? No. One time, there was an activist who landed his helicopter on the Islands, supposedly because he'd run out of fuel, and then he went off somewhere by boat. Obviously we went and smashed up his helicopter. After that, he came back with a TV crew and filmed a documentary that made us all out to be monsters and bloodthirsty killers. It was all rigged that way, you understand? And us lot, we weren't smart enough to see that it was provocation. We were too worked up. We were bitter and we were outraged.'

Chevrier marked a brief silence before he went on.

'But then I got to a point where I could actually see myself flying into a rage. And I didn't like what I saw. From one day to the next, I stopped. I was over it. I'll be honest, I still feel betrayed and resentful. But I won't let the activists wear me down, and I won't act on a grudge.'

Without warning, Eight-Inch Painchaud and his nasal twang joined the conversation as he came bounding up the stairs.

'We're gonna rake it in with this trip. You just wait and see, we're gonna rake it in.'

'Aye.'

Lapierre gave his friend a look. 'Chevrier's not in it for the money, Marco.'

Eight-Inch shook his head to the point of putting a crick in his neck. 'Why are you even here then, eh?'

'Because your uncle hired me to skipper you through the ice and bring his boat back to Cap-aux-Meules.'

Lapierre pursed his lips, as if he'd been dreading that answer.

Eight-Inch abruptly jabbed a finger to the west. 'Looks like we've got company.'

Bernard Chevrier picked up his binoculars. At the same time, the VHF transceiver boomed with the deep voice of authority:

'*Jean-Mathieu*, *Jean-Mathieu*, *Jean-Mathieu*, this is the Canadian Coast Guard vessel *Guardian*, *Guardian*, *Guardian*. Acknowledge. Over.'

The skipper reached for the handset.

'Hey there, Canadian Coast Guard vessel *Guardian*. This is *Jean-Mathieu*. I hate to say, go ahead.'

His tone was weary. Chevrier had better things to do than immobilise a boat already making slow headway, but he sensed that was coming. He released the button on the handset.

'All right, *Jean-Mathieu*, I will go ahead. Please idle your engines. We're going to pay you a little courtesy visit. Over.'

Lapierre snatched the transmitter out of the skipper's hand. 'No need to bother. We've just left port, we've got nothing in the hold. We've even got an officer aboard and she'll tell you everything's all right.'

'A woman officer, you say, *Jean-Mathieu*? Who is she? Over.'

Lapierre frowned. The skipper, guessing he hadn't grasped the sense of the question, took back the handset as Tony McMurray made an appearance in the wheelhouse, as if he were coming to answer the VHF call.

'A watcher from Fisheries and Oceans. We've got an observer on board. Over.'

The reply came quick as a flash: 'We're on our way. We haven't seen a woman at sea in a long time. It'll be a pleasure to meet her. Idle your engines, *Jean-Mathieu*. Out.'

Chevrier grumbled his way through the manoeuvre.

Lapierre turned to Simone. 'Why are your friends coming to pay us a visit?'

'They're not my friends. I'm a fisheries officer. Not a coast guard.' That was all she said.

But McMurray wasn't satisfied with that answer. He scurried over to the leather bench and sat down facing Simone.

'Seems it was one of your colleagues who was supposed to come aboard. Then at the last minute you show up, batting your eyelashes. And already, you're rubbing us up the wrong way. My pal Carpentier here, it makes him sick to see a woman worming her way aboard a trawler. But what's riling me is, instead of keeping boats like that out of our way, you're reeling them in. Tell us why you're doing that, then, why don't you?'

Simone held his gaze, then looked down at his knees as if to say he was sitting too close.

'I've no idea why leeches keep latching on to me.'

'You cheeky bitch. Haven't you had enough of—'

The skipper's voice cut him off. 'Bloody hell, McMurray!'

The Newfoundlander stared at Chevrier, who was giving him the evil eye.

'I've just put two and two together. I know who you are,

now.' But the skipper hesitated. He figured it wasn't the right time to reveal all.

Uncomfortable, McMurray got up and walked away from Officer Lord and over to the window that looked out on deck to watch the boarding manoeuvre. Only Simone stayed where she was, keeping her head down. Even though the hunter was out of her hair, at least for now, she had recognised the voice on the VHF speaker and knew she was in for a rough time of it.

The coast-guard vessel came to a stop and lowered a Zodiac loaded with four men into the sea.

There was one coast-guard crew Officer Lord detested. She had worked with them for fifteen years before she was hired a decade ago by Fisheries and Oceans Canada.

The Zodiac threaded its way cautiously through the patchy ice.

The familiar voice belonged to a former colleague, Filiol. McMurray was right. It was probably because Lapierre had said there was an officer on board – a female one – that this lot had decided to come for a look-see. There weren't many women working in the field. Steve Filiol was the worst chauvinist Simone had ever encountered. He'd go hundreds of kilometres out of his way to hassle a woman he worked with.

The motor launch docked alongside the *Jean-Mathieu* by the port gunwale.

Filiol had always been ugly as sin and envious as hell of his immediate superior, who was barely three years his senior but handsome as a Hollywood movie star. What gave Filiol a thrill was challenging his boss, Pascal Ouellet, to have his way with every fresh piece of skirt, and putting money on it. Ouellet was happy as a clam to be the alpha male strutting around. Because the challenge was all about preying on women in house, within the coast guard's ranks. All women were targets in his sights; it didn't matter if they were secretaries, new recruits or couriers. If the big guy who cleared the snow out front were ever to show up to work one day in a skirt, he'd better not turn his back, Simone had even gone so far as thinking.

Two men hopped aboard.

Officer Lord, when she started out in the department at twenty-two years old, had herself fallen for the tall, fair-haired charmer with green eyes. Going out with the head of her team was like hanging a rack of antlers over the headboard of her bed. Until the night when she'd gone back to the office to grab a jacket she'd left behind and caught her buck mounting an intern.

Carpentier the poacher, always someone who liked to stay in the background, scheming, opened the door to the vestibule for the two coast guards.

But for Ouellet there was more to the bet than just having his way with the women in question. He also had to prove he'd done the deed.

Simone could hear their heavy boots in the stairwell. Ouellet was the first to show his face and bypassed the others to address her directly.

'Officer Lord, is everything all right?'

Simone turned away without replying. Lapierre frowned again. Chevrier kept his mouth shut, but was watching. Filiol wasn't far behind his boss, and gave a long, sarcastic whistle of admiration that came out like a screech.

'Wow, look at you, boys. You brought the singer on board.'

In order to win his bets, Ouellet would get his conquests to moan loudly during their exploits, claiming it turned him on. He would secretly record them and play the tapes back to Filiol and his bunch of pervy little punters, who'd get a hard-on and pay up.

Filiol, rotten as a rabid rat, gave Ouellet a nudge of his elbow. 'You should tell them why we call her that...'

When she had found out that Ouellet had recorded them against her knowledge and that the whole team had heard their every intimacy, Simone had held her head high, making up her mind to become one of the best officers in the coast guard. She worked later than everyone else on investigations, dived deeper than them at sea, intervened on vessels better than them, without force, but with assertiveness; she stepped in front of them when she had to, interrupted them, went out of her way to make a fool of them. This had not earned her a good reputation and she couldn't say she liked her own attitude, but this fighting instinct had saved her from drowning on the inside.

'Well fuck me ragged. Of course we want to know,' said Tony McMurray with a sleazy snigger.

After fifteen years and all the training, she had ended up joining Fisheries and Oceans Canada, where she was despised by the fishermen as much as she was her colleagues. She was used to the haters.

Michaël Lapierre shook his head. 'We're not interested.'

Eight-Inch, who didn't seem to have been following the conversation, now barged his way in: 'Yeah. I'm the boss around here, all right, and we're not interested, is that clear?'

Bernard Chevrier hoped this wouldn't turn sour. 'What do you want?'

Pascal Ouellet drifted slowly away from Simone and, while Filiol licked his lips, addressed the owner's nephew.

'All right, since you're the boss, I'm going to ask you to

accompany my colleague here, who'll be inspecting your safety equipment.'

Eight-Inch shook his head sharply, but stayed where he was. The skipper gave him a nudge on the shoulder.

'Aye. Show him the survival gear, Marco. You know where it is.'

The youngster pulled himself together enough to walk Filiol over to the rack where they kept the flotation devices.

'How many of you are there on board?'

'Six.'

'Including the singer?' asked Filiol.

McMurray leaned his behind against the counter that ran the length of the wheelhouse window and gave Simone a predatory stare.

'Including Officer Lord.' Chevrier set the coast guard straight.

Steve Filiol, who was leaning forward to inspect the survival suits, drew himself tall and turned to look at the man who'd answered him.

'She used to work with the coast guard, this lovely lady of yours. We had plenty of fun with her.'

McMurray liked the sound of that. 'Oh, really?'

'Yeah. Eh, Pascal?'

His superior made no comment, but didn't tell him to shut up either. Again, it was Chevrier who spoke up. 'Are you here for her or for our safety?'

'The two go hand in hand. Now I'm not sexist, but everyone was glad to see the back of her. Had to have eyes in the back of our heads all the time, didn't we? Would you trust a lovely lady like that to save your skins? Not me. I'd never trust a woman to haul me back on board.'

Pascal Ouellet intervened. 'Stop it, Steve. You've never hauled a guy aboard with your bare hands. We've got cradles and hoists for that.'

Steve Filiol looked Officer Lord up and down. All this time, she'd been staring obstinately out to sea.

'I just don't trust these feminists who insist on being part of a crew. What is it with you – wanting to muscle in on a man's job, eh?'

Seeing she wasn't rising to it, he turned to Lapierre. 'They're everywhere, these days. Watch your backs, 'cause she'll get a kick out of giving you all a ticket.'

Michaël Lapierre gave him a sly smile. 'Don't get laid much, do you?'

Steve Filiol flushed as red as an overcooked lobster. He shoved away the gear he'd been inspecting and barked at Painchaud: 'Your suits are all right. Got any flares?'

The youngster nodded wildly and led Filiol into the stairwell. As he ventured down the stairs, the coast-guard officer launched into an off-key rendition of a chorus from the opera *Carmen*.

'*Toreador, en garde! Toreador! Toooreador!*'

The others heard Painchaud cackle crazily, then an awkward silence set in.

Ouellet motioned to Simone. 'Officer Lord, can I have a word in private?'

She hesitated, then followed him into the stairwell. She grabbed a coat from the little vestibule and they went out on deck. The frigid air felt like teeth nipping at her face and neck.

'Are you sure you're not out of your depth, Simone?'

'You're not my boss anymore, Sergeant Ouellet.'

'You can come aboard with us, if you like.'

She didn't reply, because there would be too much to say. She settled for glaring at him as if she'd just spat in his face. He pursed his lips and lowered his eyes, but still came back for another try.

'They're not a big crew for a hunt like that. There should be at least eight of them, and you know it. The forecast says the temperature's going to plummet, and there's a storm coming any day now. I can't fathom why your boss sent you out here. You'll likely get stuck in the pack ice and if the…'

Lapierre was coming their way, and Simone wondered whether he'd been listening in the shadow of the gantry where they'd hidden from the wind, as well as from prying eyes, while they had been talking.

'We won't get stuck,' said Lapierre.

Caught off guard, Ouellet didn't know who to address next. 'Well, we're headed back for shelter, and we've got an icebreaker twice as sturdy as this.'

Lapierre took a step closer. 'Your friend's finished his inspection. Another douchebag joke or two and he'll be on his way out here.'

Pascal Ouellet gave Simone a look, was about to open his mouth, but Lapierre stopped him short.

'You're not trying to take off with our singer, are you? Where else are we supposed to turn for a bit of fun if we don't find any seals?'

ᘛ

Simone didn't watch the coast guard's icebreaker sail away.

She went back into the wheelhouse to seek refuge in the horizon, keeping a keen eye on the tough headway the *Jean-Mathieu* was making towards Margaree Island. The end of the afternoon was nigh. It stretched out slowly, from Bernard

Chevrier's short shift into Lucien Carpentier's longer leg; Chevrier had now gone to catch forty winks so he'd be fresh for the coming night at the helm.

McMurray was busy in the kitchen; Painchaud was lounging on the leather bench, playing a game on his phone. All of a sudden, Carpentier the poacher started cursing.

Painchaud looked up. 'What's going on?'

'Didn't you hear the weather?'

The radio had been on for a while, but everyone, it seemed, had been deep in their own thoughts.

'No. I wasn't listening. What's the problem?'

Carpentier, immersed in the map and the meteorological data, didn't answer. Simone came over to the screen.

Painchaud was losing patience. 'Is there someone who's gonna tell me what the problem is?'

'The wind's pushing the ice towards the coast of Margaree Island.'

Eight-Inch nibbled at the edge of his finger. 'Yeah, so what?'

Officer Lord spoke to him the way she would to a child. 'Margaree Island, that's near Nova Scotia, north of Inverness.'

'Yeah, and?'

'Grey seals stay on land, Marco. If the wind keeps blowing, it might form a barrier of ice along the coast of Nova Scotia. And if the ice pack surrounds the whole island, the colony will be hard to reach.'

'I knew that. Is that clear?' Painchaud slouched back down on the bench to sulk. 'Is that clear enough?'

Carpentier, who had no desire to continue the discussion with the officer, mumbled an end to the subject. 'Chevrier's about to get up. He's the skipper, so he'll deal with it.' In the meantime, he would keep the boat on course.

Realising it was about time she had a bite to eat, Simone turned to the stairwell and found herself face to face with Tony McMurray. She hadn't heard him coming upstairs.

'So you like to sing then, do you?'

Surprised to see him so close, Simone buried her hands in the pockets of her coat and swallowed what was rising in her throat. McMurray ran a thick, lolling tongue over his lips, scratched his head through the grey balaclava he almost never removed from the top of his head, and took a step in her direction.

'The first time I saw you, I said to myself, now she, she needs to be taught a lesson.'

He came another two steps closer to the officer, forcing her back towards the wooden counter that ran the length of the forward lookout. Simone inhaled deeply, backing away from his advance, looking for an escape route. He unbuckled his belt.

A wide-eyed Painchaud was glued to the scene; he looked like he was watching a wrestling match, his right knee jiggling up and down nervously, his head going from one to the other, his body ready to jump for joy if his favourite KO-ed his opponent.

'And then today I find out that you're a singer as well…'

McMurray was fat, like those oxen farmers once used to pull carts – fat with the strength of a working animal, with a fat neck protruding from his navy-blue windbreaker, thighs like tree trunks and chiselled hands that could kill a seal with a punch to the middle of the forehead.

'I do like it when a woman gets vocal.'

McMurray prowled closer still. Then his stocky body pushed her, abruptly, crushing her and shoving her back against the counter.

Carpentier the poacher cast an eye in their direction,

approved with a satisfied nod of his chin, rolled a brief chuckle in his throat, kept on steering the ship. His wife had always said, a woman who went aboard a trawler, she was a hussy. He wouldn't touch that, not with a bargepole, but McMurray was confident. He knew what he had to do, and he was doing it.

McMurray forced a knee between the officer's legs, pressed it into her crotch, let his hands wander to her waist.

In one swift movement, Simone pulled a flick knife out of her pocket, snapped it open and pressed the tip of the blade to her assailant's carotid. Breathing heavily in his face, she spoke in a low voice, as if the words were surging from the loamy depths of her throat.

'You're fishing outside your zone, McMurray.'

He laughed, aroused by the challenge. He liked it when they put up a fight. 'Knives like that are illegal in Canada.'

Painchaud couldn't keep a lid on it. 'Yeah, they're illegal, they are.'

Simone kept her cool. 'You can't report me if I slit your throat, you fat pig.'

'Fuck, you're making me hard.'

'Get a hard-on, and it's not your throat I'll be cutting.'

Painchaud applauded the riposte. Sitting on the edge of the grey leather bench, lapping up the show. 'Look who's getting poached now, eh, Carpentier?'

At that moment, Chevrier appeared at the top of the stairs. 'The girl's with me.'

Painchaud turned to the newcomer as if he were a third wrestler entering the ring: who did this guy think he was? Lucien Carpentier stood fast at the helm, staring out to sea as if he'd not seen a thing.

Tony McMurray didn't turn around. 'Since when?'

'Since I said so. I'm the skipper. I'm the one who finds the seals, so I'm the one who gets to make the mermaid sing.'

Painchaud approved of that. 'Yeah, that's right. And since this is my boat, I'm the one who decides. Is that clear? Is that clear enough?'

The hunter's excitement had shrivelled, anyway. The magic of the moment was shattered. He recoiled three steps, touched a finger to his throat to wipe away a trickle of blood. Dismissing Simone with a disdainful chin, he spoke to Chevrier. 'Well, you're the specialist when it comes to the sea ice.'

'Aye. Go finish making supper, will you. I'll be wanting to eat before my shift.'

McMurray buckled his belt and glared at Simone. 'We've got all week together. Plenty of time for me to poach her. And make her sing.' And he disappeared down the stairs.

Painchaud applauded the exit. 'It's gonna be a helluva great week!'

Chevrier made a move for the radio, turned up the volume, reached for a pen. He hated having an officer along for the ride, and the fact that she was a woman made it worse.

Simone glanced at Marco, who was already immersed once again in the game on his phone. She sensed that Lucien, a man of few words and two faces, would have been happy to see her pushed around. Her supervisor Jean-Guy Thériault had warned her: 'Carpentier hates fisheries officers. Has done since the day he was caught poaching red-handed and it cost him his livelihood.'

She pressed the tip of her knife into the wooden countertop, pushed the blade back into its handle. She thrust her shaking hands deep in her pockets, brought her breathing discreetly under control. If the situation had degenerated, neither of those two, she realised, would have intervened. Neither to stand up for her, nor to stop her from slitting McMurray's throat.

ॐ

Nadine arrived at a run as the skiers came out in force on deck to wave a mittened farewell to the big city, as the undocking orders were being shouted out, and the Tour de Gaspé ship was about to raise the ramp and set sail.

Joaquin hadn't dared text her because there was no point rushing her. He knew Nadine would clutch at every second and put every moment she possibly could into the case; she might even delay boarding until the next port of call, in Quebec City, if she had to.

Leaning against the guardrail, the police officers out on deck saw her coming. It looked like she had a lot of bags to carry, so Moralès went down to meet her. Érik Lefebvre buried his phone in his pocket and wasn't far behind. He craned his neck so far, he might have put a crick in it, eyes immense with amazement.

'Is that her?'

Joaquin said yes, it was. One kind of tension released within him, while another stiffened. He was both relieved to see that his friend had made it, and nervous because she'd clearly brought a copy of the case file with her – she was carrying the messenger bag she'd been using as a briefcase for years. His Gaspé colleague shoved him to one side and strode forth alone to introduce himself to the newcomer.

'Érik Lefebvre. If you hadn't made it in time, I'd have got them to hold the ship for you.'

Nadine offered a hand, but Lefebvre reached right past it: he was in a hurry to relieve her of her gear.

She frowned. 'Are you the captain?'

Érik feasted his eyes on her, completely gaga. 'No. I'm in love.' He handed her luggage to Moralès.

'Is this your colleague from Gaspé?' Nadine asked.

Lefebvre grabbed hold of her ski bag and didn't give Joaquin a chance to reply.

'Yes, I'm the colleague. And it seems you're the Sûreté du Québec's top forensic psychologist. Right, well, I've been looking forward to you getting here. Honestly, I could use a good psychoanalysis session. Freudian, if possible.'

The gangway was raised.

'Is this a ski trip or a blind date?'

'I've always dreamed of a love boat. Haven't you?'

Abashed, Nadine adjusted her hat in such an involuntary show of charm, Érik took it for a small victory, a first point scored.

'Right now, I'm dreaming of taking a shower.'

'I'll put your gear in the hold and be right back with the soap.'

She burst out laughing while Lefebvre, rather pleased with himself, disappeared into the crowd as the Tour de Gaspé ship set sail with a whistle to the joyful cheers of the cross-country skiers.

Joaquin walked with Nadine to the reception desk. She looked exhausted. Her hair was stuck to her forehead, her makeup made rings around her eyes and had run into the purplish bags left from the previous night, and her pale lips were dry from hours shut away in meeting rooms with no fresh air. Still, Joaquin thought, Érik was right to be charmed by her delicate features, the bright twinkle in her eye and that cracker of a smile.

At the desk, the receptionist was expecting her. 'The organisers have put you in a different cabin, Ms Lauzon. You'll find a meal waiting for you on the table. Welcome aboard.'

Nadine thanked her, took the key and led the way down the corridor, ahead of Joaquin, his arms full of her luggage.

'Doiron put in a call to the ski-trip people for me; I've got a cabin all to myself. I've got some work to do. If you feel like joining me…'

'Erik would be too jealous.'

She stopped at a door and opened it. Joaquin followed her into the cabin, put the big backpack on the floor while Nadine relieved him of the messenger bag and tossed it onto one of the beds, which would now serve as a makeshift desk.

'Doiron told me you didn't want to get mixed up in the case, Joaquin, but—'

'How long has it been since you had any sleep?'

She shrugged her shoulders, pulled the plastic wrap off a tray of raw vegetables and nibbles they'd put out for her. She took two bites of carrot and wiped a hand across her forehead. She'd raced to make it aboard in time.

Moralès could feel the ship moving slowly, smoothly away from the wharf. Through the porthole, he could see the south side of the river and the city of Longueuil, emerging on the shore then fading away in the reddish rays of the setting sun. Nadine tugged off her boots and tossed her coat on the floor. She sniffed her armpits.

'I really need a shower.'

Embarrassed, Joaquin turned away. 'I'll leave you to it.'

He opened the door. 'I'll be in the bar with Érik, if you feel like letting your hair down a bit.'

As Moralès stepped out into the corridor, Nadine's voice piped up behind him. She weighed her words carefully.

'The mother of a seventeen-year-old youth called 911 the day before yesterday. She'd just been at a family gathering, with her two daughters. When they got home, she found the house turned upside down. Her son had been beaten up. He was unconscious. We lifted the prints of the sicko who did it. They were everywhere. The guy lost it completely in there, and clearly didn't take any precautions. He's a lowly foot soldier with the Hells. Buster's his name. We're on the lookout for him.'

Fingers on the door handle, the detective said nothing. He was absorbing the information smack dab in the middle of his back, between his shoulder blades, right where he would often feel a stiffness set in.

'The kid's in a coma. He's not going to make it.'

Moralès looked to the floor, the drab, narrow corridor stretching to his left. He could hear the joyful cries and happy voices echoing out on deck. He took a deep, broad breath, then closed the door behind him.

⠪

Simone had decided to shadow Bernard Chevrier on his shifts. This one was due to end around one in the morning.

For more than three hours, they hadn't said a word to one another. The skipper was lost in his thoughts. He had spoken to Denis Éloquin earlier. The northeaster was filling in, a phantom sweeping down from the pole, headed right for them. It was going to blow hard. His brother-in-law hadn't reminded him not to venture into the Northumberland Strait, he'd just said: 'Be careful.' But Chevrier was old enough to interpret the subtext. 'Aye, we'll hit the islands then come back, even if the hold's empty,' he'd said. Then he'd asked how things were going with the baby. 'He'll be born in the thick of the storm,' Éloquin had replied. It was Nancy who'd predicted it. 'She says you be careful, too.' Chevrier had dodged his brother-in-law's questions about the crew. The nephew with a nose full of coke, McMurray and the attempted rape, Carpentier the poacher just being there, none of that would reassure a boat owner. What good would it do to worry Denis? This wasn't Bernard's first seal hunt. He would sort things out.

Michaël Lapierre was also tagging along on this night watch, but he had dozed off on the leather bench, dropping a magazine by his side.

Nervous, shaken by the day's events, unable to draw or fold a bird from paper, Simone was sitting on the little stool by the front window, still as could be in spite of the pitching and rolling. Staring out across the dark depths of the sea as the surface erupted in sharp peaks of foam and ice in the cold night.

The trawler was already labouring up the crests and down into the troughs of the wind-driven waves before they passed the tip of Prince Edward Island, at around supper time, and the current in the Northumberland Strait started to slap at the starboard flank, making the trawler heave from side to side.

Marco Painchaud had joked that these conditions were what separated real men from weaklings, but he kept his mouth shut when his friend Michaël Lapierre very calmly got up to recycle his meal in the toilet.

The course of the conversation, in any case, had been diverted by the ringing of Carpentier's phone when the boat passed close enough to the town of Souris to pick up a signal. The crew were quick to pull out their devices, listen to and read their messages with a glee not unlike that of children opening their Christmas presents. Simone avoided checking hers in front of McMurray and the others.

Not long before midnight, Lucien Carpentier went out on deck with a wooden sledge hammer to break up the ice that was weighing the ship down. Since then, the crew had been sleeping.

Discreetly, her hands shaking slightly, Simone Lord reached for her phone in her inside coat pocket to see what was new.

Chevrier the skipper glanced in her direction. She stopped what she was doing. Was he going to ask her sarcastically if she'd heard from her boss or check if she'd had any news from the coast guard and tease her for being a 'singer'? No. He just made sure Lapierre was out for the count, and then went right back to steering the ship.

Simone sighed, then turned to her phone. She made sure the ringer was off, opened her inbox. She scrolled through the office memos, skimmed over the missives from her sister, read the message from her friend, which drew a brief smile of relief, though she still had a lump in her throat. Érik had told her how the start of the ski trip was going: *The cabin's not very big, but I don't regret bringing those two suitcases of yours. Moralès says my baggage doesn't bother him. He's divorced now, did you know? He asked me how you were doing.*

Simone swallowed her smile, switched the phone off, returned it to her pocket.

Joaquin was divorced.

Everything had started off on the wrong foot with him. She had been short with him at the police station in Gaspé, and they had got on each other's nerves. Then, there was that evening when she had stopped by the auberge where he was staying to share some information. She had walked in on him making supper. Without meeting her eye, he had started telling her about his youth, about Mexico, the tacos his grandmother would make for him, the sacred stool where she would sit, the legacy she had left him by teaching him the gentlest of gestures. Simone had been leaning back against a kitchen cupboard, on her feet and ill at ease, intimidated, as she listened to him.

Unsettled by the memory, she tilted her head to one side. On the edge of the counter, just there, she could see the mark in the wood left by the tip of her knife when McMurray had finally let her be.

She closed her eyes. The boat was shaking her every which way. She steadied herself against the counter.

That night, Joaquin had spoken of his grandmother with the mildest of accents, his voice carrying those delicate inflections that belong only to nostalgia. At one point, he had approached her. Simone had stood still as could be. She had held her breath, thinking he was going to kiss her.

Some seconds in life seemed like they'd remain ingrained, in her memory and in her body. The second when that guy lost control of his vehicle, the second when that neighbour broke her neck falling down the stairs, the second when she walked into that office and saw her lover cheating on her with the intern, the second when she pressed the tip of her knife to the carotid of a man who wanted to rape her. Seconds that created cracks in certainties.

Joaquin Moralès had extended a hand, reaching for a rolling pin behind her. He had been so close, she had breathed his scent, sensed him entering her intimacy. She had choked, like a teenager, on her glass of wine. And he had invited her to dine with him.

Behind her, Lapierre moved. He was awake. 'You've got a vertebra protruding at the nape of your neck…'

She drew her head up straight.

'Sorry. I wasn't saying that to give you grief.'

She sprang to her feet in a flash.

'Are you all right?' Lapierre asked.

Chevrier motioned at him. 'Leave her be, she just wants a bit of peace and quiet.'

Simone turned, tore down the stairs, through the vestibule, dashed out onto the deck. The bow crested a wave. Officer Lord grabbed hold of the guardrail and threw up overboard in great spurts.

Winter carnival

'Your friend, Nadine, is she single?'

'Yes.'

At the wharf in Quebec City, the ship was disembarking a sunrise shivering of skiers keen to get going on the last urban leg of their trip. Today, they would be skirting the old walled city, skiing out around the Plains of Abraham and back along the waterfront Samuel-De-Champlain promenade. The skiers were dapper and dashing, in spite of the biting cold. Their muscled bodies would warm up quickly on the course that awaited them, some twenty kilometres long. After dark, the ship would set sail again for Sainte-Anne-des-Monts. From there, they would enjoy the rest of their week in the grand, sweeping scenery of the Gaspé Peninsula.

'And she's not a lesbian?'

'Not that I'm aware.'

It was a relief for Joaquin to no longer have Montreal or Longueuil in his field of vision. Over dessert the previous evening, the skiers had been treated to a sneak peek of today's course as well as a talk by an ice-cap explorer. The good spirits of the group must have been contagious, because when he retired to the cabin, Joaquin had been surprised to find he had strayed a little from his stresses, taken a step into holiday territory, engaged with the launch into orbit, as the astronaut would say. But he had sensed it was a fragile thing.

'Right, well, I'm not taking her away from you, am I?'

Now Lefebvre only had eyes for Nadine. He had managed to

keep her sitting with them for nearly two hours before she retired to her own cabin.

'No.'

The weather conditions were unusually harsh, more merciless than in recent late Januaries. It was clearly a concern for the trip organisers, who were cheering the disembarking skiers with the nervous energy of those who motivate others in order to convince themselves that everything will be all right. They had announced that they would be bringing the start time forwards, since they were concerned the river might freeze and the ship might otherwise not be able to reach its next port of call. Everyone was promising to pick up the pace, giving one another a companionable wink.

Érik smoothed his thin moustache and smiled at Nadine, who was tinkering with her gear as she approached. She seemed like she hadn't had much sleep and, over breakfast, in spite of Lefebvre and his devastating charm, she had remained lost in her thoughts. She stepped into her skis and joined Moralès, who was jogging on the spot to stay warm, waiting for his turn to cross the start line. While he had grown used to this season – thanks mostly to Sarah, who would often take him and the kids out to enjoy winter sports – the Mexican in him had never really learned to love the dark days and the bitter cold.

'I'm wondering why Buster lost it so completely he ended up beating the crap out of a small-time dealer who was only seventeen. A kid.' She looked into the detective's eyes. 'He went there alone, as well. Why? It's as if he panicked. What made him panic?'

Moralès stopped breathing for a second. He didn't ask her any questions, but he didn't turn away either. The line of skiers was moving at last. What was he doing there, wallowing in the wake of his divorce and pretending to have fun on a group holiday? Did he spend all his time making bad decisions?

Nadine adjusted her neck warmer and glasses. 'Our guys are going to the kid's school today to try and track down his partner.' Often, small-time dealers were like bikers in a gang: they rolled as a duo. 'We're hoping he's still alive.'

One push and Nadine was off, followed by Lefebvre, into the cheerful throng of skiers. Moralès fell into stride behind them. He was cold and wanted to gain some speed, but the group was still slow to get going and there was nowhere for him to pass at this point on the course. To his left, Réjeanne and Réjean gave him friendly smiles, which he returned with difficulty. All of a sudden, he felt like he was short of breath, for no physical reason. The horizon seemed to fade from sight and he hung his head. The surface beneath his skis was hard, and the snow was screeching bitterly.

🦭

Lucien Carpentier slapped the table with the flat of his hand.

'Didn't your mother ever teach you any table manners?'

Simone gave a start, lifted her nose from her coffee. She was surprised to hear the poacher's outburst. He struck her as being more the type to stew in silence. Not like Eight-Inch; he was always on the attack.

'What's your fucking problem, this morning?'

'You're slurping your yogurt. It's one thing to slurp your bloody coffee, but when you slurp your yogurt it's like you're gurgling snot in your throat and it grosses me out.'

Painchaud got up with his yogurt pot in hand and hovered brattishly over Carpentier, who stabbed a raging fork into his omelette.

'You're nothing but an employee, OK? This is my boat and I'll slurp whatever I want, whenever I want to. Is that clear?' Painchaud leaned over Carpentier, pretended to lick his ear, then erupted with his nasty laugh, which sounded like a saw rasping back and forth. 'Is that clear enough?'

The poacher was on his feet in a flash. He grabbed the collar of Marco Painchaud's plaid jacket with both hands, backed him up against the fridge, lifted him off the floor. *I'm going to smash your shitty coked-up face until it's so small it'll fit inside your yogurt pot, you cheeky little fucker.* That's what Carpentier wanted to say, but the words slipped and slid around his mouth like a greasy sausage. It was always the same: when he lost his rag, he couldn't find his voice. Just his clenched fists. And he was really getting sick of Eight-Inch now.

Simone stiffened in her seat. The table was covered in bread crumbs and omelette remnants. The poacher had overturned his plate when he got up, sending the other guy's yogurt skittering onto the floor to rest by the stove, leaving behind it a trail of bleeding raspberries caught in their viscous liquid. Painchaud, at the end of the galley, was kicking his heels against the fridge door like a crazed puppet.

'Lulu, are you trying to teach my man Eight-Inch how to dance a jig?'

Michaël Lapierre's slow, sombre voice sent a trickle of cold sweat down the poacher's back. Coming from Lapierre's mouth, those words were a threat. Carpentier released his catch reluctantly. Painchaud's feet were back on the floor, but he stayed there, between the fridge where his hair had left a greasy mark and the lanky poacher, who stood a good foot taller than him. He made long slurping sounds before erupting in another fit of his nasty laughter.

McMurray came out of the bathroom. He glanced in their direction, scratched his head through his balaclava and then put everyone in their place with the authority of a bossy cook no one would talk back to: 'If you lot want to eat at lunchtime, then clear out of here.'

Painchaud sniggered. 'Lulu Carpentier was just about to clean up the mess he made, is that clear? Is that clear enough?'

While the men continued their stand-off, attempting to stare each other down, Simone got up, put her dishes in the sink and left the room. If they were squabbling among themselves, at least they were leaving her in peace.

She went up to the wheelhouse.

Chevrier didn't say a word. He had heard the scuffle, seen Lapierre go down the stairs and gathered that he had calmed Carpentier down. He wasn't sure he quite grasped where Michaël Lapierre fit into the group. Granted, he was Eudore's Normand's boy, but his authority was too striking, even when it came to Painchaud, who was so keen on playing at being boss since it was his old man who'd chartered the boat. The others were afraid of him, almost, even though none of them were exactly altar boys. Take Lucien Carpentier and his pal who'd come up from Mexico, for instance. You wouldn't put your family's life in the hands of guys like that. Obviously, Chevrier wasn't on board to oversee who got hired, but this was the first time he'd been lumbered with a crew like this one.

'Officer Lord?' He motioned for her to approach. 'It's your first hunt.'

It wasn't a question. Chevrier was making a statement. He was gauging her, the woman.

It irritated her to be treated like a rookie. 'I've monitored harvests on land.'

'Aye. That's not the same, though.'

'No, it's not the same.'

Marco Painchaud bounded up the stairs, wound tight as a spring. 'Margaree Island in sight!'

The men all came up to the wheelhouse for a look at the coast. Painchaud and Carpentier were glued to their binoculars, sweeping the shore, while Lapierre sat back and watched the action with a mug of coffee that had probably gone cold. The air was glacial, in spite of the heating that was on almost all the time. The crew were all wearing warm clothes, even indoors.

'There!' Lucien Carpentier pointed to the west. Simone reached for her binoculars.

A couple of nautical miles away, there were some seals resting on a short stretch of shoreline at the foot of a cliff. Not many. Seven or eight. There might be more, but the ice piled up near the shore made it hard to see.

Painchaud, Carpentier and Lapierre went below. McMurray joined them. They pulled on their outdoor layers, grabbed their rifles and went outside. Chevrier stayed in the cockpit, steering a course towards the seals. The ice was thick. Despite the cold, the hunters were warmed by adrenaline. Clambering up on the prow, they were talking among themselves in hushed voices. Around half a nautical mile from the shore, Chevrier motioned to them to say they couldn't go any further, and put the engines in neutral. They would have to go ashore in the dinghy.

'Listen here, girl.'

Simone gave him a wry smile. 'Girl?'

Chevrier didn't care what she thought. 'If we run into another boat, you go aboard and you get out of here.'

'I'm not—'

He looked her straight in the eye and that was enough to

mute her. 'It's not a suggestion. When Denis Éloquin trusted me to skipper the *Jean-Mathieu*, he told me to bring everyone back safe and sound. And I don't want anything to happen to you. So the next time you get a chance to jump ship, you jump ship. You forget about this mission of yours, you get your stuff, your little paper bird, and you go right back to that house in Belle-Anse.'

'I'll do what I—'

'That's an order, from your skipper.'

The hunters brought their weapons to their shoulders, set sights on their targets. They fired. Simone saw the heads of three seals snap skywards, as if in surprise, then fall dead to the ice. Immediately, she heard another shot and a fourth seal followed. She looked out on deck to see who had fired in such quick succession.

It was Lapierre.

More detonations rang out, one after the other. Chevrier was watching the action with interest.

'He's got a hell of a good aim for a guy who reckons he's only hunted with a hakapik before.'

Simone didn't react. She stood there, observing.

'I'm pretty sure it's Carpentier who missed his shot. McMurray might have a balaclava over his face, but that's not stopping him from shooting straight.'

Simone made a move to venture outside.

'Until you get a chance to jump ship, you be sure to walk in the sealers' tracks. Don't stray to the wayside. Take a hakapik with you on your way out. If the ice gives way beneath you, you jab the hakapik at a right angle to your body so you don't sink. Then you use the hook to haul yourself out of the water. You claw it into the ice and you—'

'I get the picture.' She turned, mildly insulted and ready to hurl a scathing comment in his face, but Chevrier was so serious she bit her tongue. He held her gaze like a parent trying desperately to explain to his child the depth of the danger she would be wading into if she went for a swim alone at night, in the big lake where the leeches were lurking. She nodded so as not to antagonise him, and went on her way.

Bernard Chevrier had come close to drowning the first time he went on a seal hunt, so that had to be what was worrying him. It was normal: Simone was a woman, she was younger than him, she wasn't from the Islands. McMurray's showboating must be putting him on edge too, but it wasn't the first time a man had tried to intimidate Simone on board a ship. Last night she had spent some time thinking about her first few experiences at sea. She'd dealt with some rough crews – who had swiped her blanket, who had locked her outside on deck at supper time in the pouring rain, or who had taken her bunk for a urinal. Simone Lord had never sobbed and sniffled. She was one of those officers who carried their career like a challenge, so she held her head high and got the job done. It wasn't this crew that was going to make her back down and retreat. In any case, the hunting and skinning of the seals was going to keep the men so busy, they'd all but forget about her.

She pulled on her warm clothes, looked at the long wooden shafts with hooks on the end, reached for one, weighed it in her hand. Chevrier had said, the other night, that it was hard to kill with one. Unlike a rifle shot and the noise of its detonation, the action of the hakapik was subtle. The weapon would arc through the air with a whisper and the metal mass of it would murmur the mightiest of blows. A whisper, a murmur, and the seal was dead, in the calm and the cold of the sea ice.

Simone went out on deck. The wind felt like a slap in the face.

Carpentier the poacher was working one of the two winches, lowering the gangway towards the water while McMurray used the second to lower the dinghy. Simone hopped aboard the dinghy with the four men. In their anticipation of the first kill, they barely noticed she was there.

Carpentier steered the craft through the arteries of water between the ice. A hundred metres or so from the seals, unable to go any further, he drove the bow of the dinghy up onto a flat slab of ice. 'I'll wait here for you.'

McMurray looked up to the sky as he clambered overboard. 'For fuck's sake! What the hell is that thing doing?'

To the west, a helicopter emerged, seemingly from out of nowhere. It was headed for Margaree Island at a surprising speed, where it dropped off four people before taking off again.

'Fucking activists!'

Carpentier spat on the ice. 'That red logo. It's the girl from your neck of the woods, McMurray. Do you have any idea how much she raked in in donations last year, with her photos of the seal harvest? A hundred and thirty million. There's no way she's going to stay out of our way?'

'For fuck's sake.'

'Just wait till the storm starts blowing, that fucking helicopter of theirs will drop like a stone.'

Marco Painchaud got out of the dinghy and joined McMurray on the ice, but Michaël Lapierre stayed aboard and signalled for Carpentier to disembark instead. 'Change of plan: I'm the one who's staying put. I hate having my photo taken.'

As the poacher complied, Lapierre added, for the fisheries officer's benefit: 'You, make sure you walk in his footprints.'

He wasn't expecting an answer. It was an order, one that was sure to be obeyed. Simone had no desire to stray very far, anyway. The ice was a patchwork of slanting piles connected by gullies they would have to jump over. These trickled into little pools that were filled with a compact, granular, deceptive snow. She followed the crew, using the hook of her hakapik to keep her footing on the slippery surfaces.

The four newcomers, in their bright-red snowsuits, were also struggling to make headway towards the dead seals. Three of them were weighed down with gear: a video camera, some still cameras and a microphone at the end of a pole. The woman at the head of the group was forging ahead with the arrogant air of someone conquering the territory. Simone recognised her. She was the most fractious of the activists she had encountered on her patrols.

Plenty of Islanders had told Simone how some years ago, a similar group had daubed the seal pups with red paint, supposedly to protect them from the hunters. But the smell of the paint had driven the mothers away, and thousands of baby seals had starved to death, out there on the ice. The men would go on about that in their hoarse voices. Simone had often heard sealers yell at the activists to watch out because a bullet could ricochet off the ice.

Painchaud set foot on the shore and stopped. He let Carpentier, who looked like he was chewing on a chunk of rancid bread, go ahead and waited for the fisheries officer, addressing her with a seriousness to his voice she had not yet heard. 'You take care of that lot, all right?'

'There's nothing I can do.'

'I don't want to see them take a step in our direction. Is that clear?'

Simone knew what he was getting at. To capture their

aggressive expressions and make them out to be bloodthirsty killers, the activists would be looking to raise the hunters' tempers. It wasn't hard to rile them – she had seen that in her duties as an officer – not just because the hunters were fed up with being portrayed as murderers, but also because the campaigns urging foreign countries to boycott the trade in seal meat and pelts were losing them a significant chunk of their annual income, which was low enough already.

'That's not my role.'

'What is your fucking role, then?'

'I'm here to oversee the culling, to make sure they don't say you're making the seals suffer. That's the most I can do.'

'We're not making them suffer. They're dead.'

'I'll make sure they don't get in the way of your work.'

Painchaud smiled through his filthy teeth. 'Now we understand one other. You keep them well clear.' He went on his way.

Suddenly, the woman leading the activists disappeared. It looked like she had slipped on a mound of ice.

Simone saw Painchaud's shoulders shaking with laughter. Then he mumbled something, clearly not happy. Moving closer, the officer saw what had happened. The activist's fall had been heavy, and her boots had smashed into the seal pup's face, ramming it into its mother. The baby was bleeding heavily from its snout and looked to be in a bad way.

The film crew were right on it. The cameraman moved into position to film the bleeding seal pup, which the woman had now taken into her arms and was stroking with a look of desperation on her face. Behind her, the mama seal, whose eyes were streaming from the cold, was writhing in anger. The camera was likely capturing the dead seals in the background too, and the hunters advancing towards them.

Simone veered away from the men and cautiously approached the woman. Then she pulled out her notebook and stood deliberately in the camera frame. The leader of the group simply moved aside. She wasn't happy to have a fisheries officer getting in her way, but laid the charm on thick for the camera.

'Today, we've saved more than sixty babies, little harp-seal pups, from the claws of these bloodthirsty murderers…'

The woman was speaking at the top of her voice, not just to cover the howling of the wind in the microphone, but also to get the hunters' backs up. The fiercer they looked, the more lucrative the film shoot would be. Carpentier had sunk his face into the collar of his parka, Painchaud was in the grip of some nervous movements that threatened to send him sprawling between two slabs of ice at any moment.

McMurray was the only one to speak up. 'They're grey seals, not harp seals. Whelping's not for another three weeks for them.'

The woman noticed the Fisheries and Oceans Canada logo on Simone's coat. She pointed a finger at it and carried on with her spiel.

'As you can see, even the authorities are in on this massacre of millions of innocent lives.'

Officer Lord reached for a marker pen. It was time for an intervention. 'There are six men here who witnessed you hitting and causing a potentially fatal injury to this seal pup. Culling them at this age, particularly for commercial reasons, is formally prohibited. Now I'd like you to show me your ID.'

Simone set about writing a hefty ticket while the presenter seethed and had her crew turn off their cameras. She put the young animal down on the ice. Its mother was still wriggling and whining a few metres away.

Simone bent over the pup and palpated it. 'It's going to die.'

As the presenter ordered her crew to call for the helicopter, the officer persisted. 'If you don't give me your names and addresses, I'm going to have to write a report for obstruction, which will—'

The other woman cut her off, grudgingly giving her their details. Simone handed her the ticket and walked away, in the hunters' direction.

Painchaud clapped his excited hands as she approached. 'Is that clear? Is that clear enough?'

Simone bent down over the seals, palpated their craniums. Even though the creatures were dead, the hunters were still required to crush their skulls with the hammerhead side of their hakapiks.

Ever since Brigitte Bardot had campaigned against the seal harvest, veterinarians had been weighing in on the practice, and they had deemed that this technique was the most effective and pain-free method of killing seals; everyone on the Magdalen Islands was already using it.

Officer Lord had now seen that rule number one of the harvest was respected. The second step in the process was to make sure the seal was dead by palpating its cranium. Step number three was to bleed the animal.

As McMurray, Carpentier and, surprisingly, even Marco Painchaud, quickly bled the seals, the helicopter returned, picked up the four animal rights activists and took flight. For a moment, it was whirling right over their heads.

'They'll be getting some shit-hot photos of this,' Carpentier said.

He was right. Along the horizon stretched a white line, through which the *Jean-Mathieu*'s hull had traced a delicate black triangle. A dazzling ivory fog cast the ice in compacted bluish layers around a petite scarlet pool. There was something almost poetic about the scene.

One of the activists had pulled out a camera and was shooting the whole thing from the helicopter.

The hunters started back, each dragging a prize on the hook of their hakapik. Red trails of blood streaked behind them as they leaped from one slab of ice to the next.

As they neared the spot where the presenter had inadvertently injured the seal pup, the men stopped, seeming ill at ease. They were waiting for the fisheries officer to get there. The mama seal was nudging her half-dead pup with her snout. Simone arrived at last, observed the scene. She thought about what Chevrier had told her, about the animals people left to suffer.

'Put it out of its misery,' she ordered.

McMurray cursed, freed his hook from the carcass he was dragging, raised his hakapik and struck the little one as its mother slipped into the water through a hole in the ice.

The helicopter captured it all.

The hunter returned to the group in a rage, glaring bullets at Simone, but kept his mouth shut. He knew she was right to order a suffering seal pup to be put down, but he also knew the whole world would be bombarded by the images of him killing the little creature.

'Go on, then. Go shout it from the rooftops that we kill the mothers and wipe our noses with the babies, you deceitful bitch.' The men looked on in awe as Simone's temper flared and she craned her neck towards the leader of the activists, who must have been sitting smugly in her lookout post in the sky.

The animal rights activist laughed at her from up high. But Officer Lord had already turned her back and gone on her way.

She was getting a head start on the men, blazing a trail, in spite of all the advice to the contrary. She looked up in the direction of the dinghy and saw in the distance, out on the deck of the *Jean-Mathieu,* Bernard Chevrier waving his arms wildly, a signal the others might take for a victory dance. Simone knew precisely what he was doing. He was signalling for her to wave the helicopter down again, to climb aboard, to fly away with the activists. She ignored him. That was out of the question. She'd had enough of his paternalism, not to mention McMurray's chauvinism, Lapierre's authority, Painchaud's insanity, Carpentier the poacher's shiftiness, and the activists' hypocrisy. It had sickened her to order an end to the seal pup's suffering. She had enough rage running through her to climb back aboard the *Jean-Mathieu* and tell them all to go to hell.

Behind her, Painchaud yelled to the sky: 'Yeah, bitch. She told you, didn't she?'

His maniacal laugh fell flat on the ice as the helicopter gained altitude.

The hunters were focused on putting one foot in front of the other, struggling to keep their balance as well as the heavy hauls hooked on their hakapiks. They made it back to the dinghy, left the carcasses there, then went back to the shore to fetch the other seals they had bled.

Michaël Lapierre attached the carcasses to a line to tow them through the water, back to the trawler, giving Simone a satisfied smile. Ticked off, she turned away. She knew what he was trying to communicate: that he was proud of her. She knew that look. Whenever she slapped a poacher with a hefty fine, the men at Fisheries and Oceans Canada beamed with the same sort of air that translated to: 'Our feisty female can really show you where to shove it.' Those eyes of his would do nothing for

her, though. She was the observer on board and they could all
go screw themselves: the seal hunters, the activists, even
Joaquin Moralès!

An hour later, they were finally back on board the *Jean-
Mathieu*. The fisheries officer went inside while the crew hoisted
the dinghy clear of the water, raised the gangway and dressed
the carcasses. They had the music blasting out on deck. Simone
cleaned herself up, grabbed her notebook and went to sit in the
wheelhouse, where Chevrier was steering the trawler on a
cautious course to the west.

'That's a lot of wind for a helicopter to risk flying in to come
all the way out here.'

She didn't reply.

'I can't believe the danger some women will put themselves
in just for a couple of seals. It's beyond me, anyway.'

Without giving Simone a chance to respond, Chevrier turned
up the volume of the music with a disgruntled hand.

こ&

The Tour de Gaspé skiers had to hurry to get back to the ship,
since the cold had left the captain no choice but to set sail
straightaway once the skiing was done. The Saint Lawrence was
freezing over and they had to depart Quebec City without delay;
and unfortunately they couldn't stick around for the festivities
in the Old Town that evening.

Érik, Joaquin and Nadine made a beeline for the bar.
Standing at a huge window, they were almost the only ones
watching as the moorings were cast off. The other skiers had
probably opted to stand under a hot shower instead.

'First round's on me.' Sporting a sweater with retro motifs,

Érik swaggered over to the bar; now was the time to steer the conversation towards Simone. He came back with the beers. Then he launched right into his argument, calling Nadine as his witness when Moralès reached for his bottle.

'Did you see your former colleague here's taken off his wedding ring?'

'This is my right hand, Érik. I've never worn my ring on that side.'

But Nadine played along. 'Doiron told me you got divorced.'

Lefebvre nodded as keenly as if he was the one who had gone through the whole process and signed the papers. 'And that means you're single again.' Gleefully he raised his bottle to toast this new civil status, but Nadine was not in agreement.

'No. He's not single, he's divorced.'

Érik leaned in her direction with a charming smile. 'And what's the difference?'

'I used to be married,' Moralès said.

But it would take more than that to put the matchmaker off his stride. 'Hey, I was asking the psychologist!'

Down on the wharf, acrobats and choral singers had gathered to give the ship a send-off. A few small groups of perky skiers had ventured out on deck to watch and were cheering the city their own lively farewell.

Nadine was selective with her words. 'When you're single, you fill yourself up. You take up the space.'

'What space?' Lefebvre asked.

Joaquin drank a long swig of beer. He felt heavy. Sometimes, friendship involved listening to other people's theories about your own life and biting your tongue, just waiting until they were done.

'All the space there is. You learn to be enough for yourself, to love yourself, to console yourself, to occupy your time. You furnish your house on your own.'

'Your house?'

'Your house, your time, your heart. All the space there is…'

Moralès gazed at the Quebec City wharf as the ship gently cast off its moorings. The landscape was frozen, snow blackened by de-icing salt, flags stiffened by the howling wind, short, squat icicles clinging to the edges of the roof pitches. Still, there was something magical about this historic city.

'When you're in a couple, you do the opposite. You create a place within yourself for someone else. For the person you love. And when that person leaves, they leave an emptiness.'

Érik saluted the psychologist, visibly impressed by her speech.

Emptiness. That was a word Joaquin would remember. But he knew he would find new furniture for himself. He just wished that time would go by more quickly. That the boat would pick up speed. That spring would thaw winter. That the migration would get under way. He hated the season of self-pity.

Lefebvre was enchanted. 'Incredible. So you've got a guest room in your heart now.'

Nadine stifled a laugh with her beer.

'Right, well, I still have to fill you in about Simone—'

'Have the team tracked down the friend of the kid who was beaten up, then?' Moralès had to cut Lefebvre off. He had no desire for him to touch upon Officer Lord in front of Nadine, so he'd latched on to the first subject that sprang to mind.

Dumbstruck by the abrupt interjection, Lefebvre opened his mouth, closed it, opened, closed it again.

Nadine answered the question. 'Yes. They've got him.'

Joaquin anchored his gaze on the shore. He had done

precisely what he shouldn't have. A man could not constantly fill his empty bedrooms with dramas, homicides, dead bodies.

'Is he all right?'

'Yes, but he's terrified.'

What was Lefebvre going to tell him about Simone? The last time Joaquin had seen her, he was sure he had made a complete fool of himself. She had been sitting in the open workspace at the Gaspé police station, her head bowed as she filled out an investigation report. Walking by, he had paused behind her and held his breath at the sight of the little vertebra teasing the skin at the nape of her neck. The C3, or perhaps it was the C4. Compelled by some giddy, hypnotic urge, he had stretched out a hand and touched the delicate mirage of perfection. Simone had sat bolt upright as if she'd been bitten by a snake, and the oasis had evaporated. He had stuttered over his words and left the room, bumping into the door frame as he went.

'Have your officers questioned him?'

Maybe she'd met someone in the Magdalen Islands. That was a possibility. Joaquin should have contacted her sooner, perhaps, but … but he was in the midst of getting divorced. He felt old to be courting a woman. That was the truth of it. Old, ridiculous. Divorced and filled with emptiness.

'He says Buster was always with his partner. Like all the dealers. But here it's pretty clear that he went on his own to beat the crap out of the kid. We don't know why.'

With a thrust of its engines, the ship slipped away sideways from the shore. '*So long, farewell…*' A group outside burst into song with the gleeful abandon of a choir that doesn't care if it's crooning off key.

'At last.' Lefebvre, glad of the distraction, slunk away to the bar again.

Nadine gave Joaquin a tip of the chin, as if to say, *What's up with you?* Or maybe, *So, are you on board with the case?*

Before the detective could respond, however, the psychologist's phone rang. She reached into her pocket for it. Moralès held his breath. It must be the homicide team. Maybe the kid had regained consciousness. Maybe they had found Buster. Or identified his partner. Or maybe they had figured out the motive for the beating.

Nadine frowned. 'I have to go.'

She left the room.

'Happy hour!' Érik Lefebvre passed his colleague another beer.

Joaquin put down the empty bottle his hand had been clinging to in vain, took the full one his friend was offering.

Through the window, at the end of the Quebec City wharf, he could see the great, lolloping head of Bonhomme Carnaval, its smile as static as it was silly. The winter festival mascot kicked a leg in the air and waved a grand, goofy goodbye to the cruise ship, which responded with one long blast. Moralès shivered. In the chill of the day's end, the echo of the fog horn on the river, caught between the cliffs of the old walled city on one side and of the town of Lévis on the other, reverberated in him like the tremulous, plaintive cry of a beast kept at bay.

One hundred years of solitude

'We're not in the right place.'

Érik Lefebvre made the statement with assurance, before he had even opened his eyes, as if he had a GPS unit built into his brain or he'd had a stroke of genius in the night and had combined it with a nautical ephemeris table to calculate the ship's position. Joaquin looked out of the porthole. His cabin mate was right. The boat, which should have been docked at the wharf in Sainte-Anne-des-Monts, was at a standstill in the middle of the Saint Lawrence River. The lights of a coastal community twinkled in the darkness.

'We're caught in the ice.'

The two men got dressed and went up on deck. Outside, the northerly wind packed a powerful punch, the cold biting at their skin. Through the windows of the cockpit, they caught a glimpse of concern on the crew's faces and apparent alarm among the organisers. The captain, whom they had met on their first evening aboard, was speaking into a VHF radio handset with an animated, albeit serious, air.

A pale light illuminated the transparent, frozen dawn. To starboard, they recognised the seaside industrial area of Matane, its breakwaters two rocky arms reaching out to them. In the background emerged the serene outline of the mountains.

'I didn't bring my skates.'

They headed to the cafeteria. Moralès showed no sign of a smile. Standing by the coffee machine, he was chomping at the bit. The called-off happy hour in Montreal, Nadine's last-minute arrival on board, the attack on the young dealer, the ski day cut short in Quebec City, and now the ship at a standstill had all taken a bite out of his plans to rest and relax. He was weighed down, but he wanted to feel like he was on holiday. On the run. Weightless.

'Are you going to make the best of the situation and dive into that kid's case with the delightful Nadine?'

Joaquin glared at Érik, picked up a tray, made his way to the service counter, where he was hoping to get a veggie omelette. His friend followed, and was now doing battle with some strips of bacon.

'Otherwise, what are you going to do? Want to pitch a ball at a glove with me out on deck?'

Moralès put some bread in the toaster. 'No, don't worry about me.'

'I can't fathom you, Moralès.'

'Back in the autumn, Officer Lord called me a loser heading for early retirement.'

'Ah. That's why you've been like this ever since we left. You're missing Simone!'

Joaquin went to sit at a table with his breakfast.

A jubilant Érik was one step behind. 'I've got her number in my phone, you know.'

Moralès stabbed his fork into his omelette. 'Stop it, Érik. I'm not going to investigate with Nadine and I'm not going to call Simone.'

'Neither of them?'

'Neither of them.'

'Can I know why?' Lefebvre asked, with his mouth full.

'I'm on holiday.'

'It's the right time to reach out to a woman and—'

Joaquin cut him off. 'In the last year, I've moved house, got used to my new boss, been given the run-around by a bunch of fishermen and fed a pack of lies by my wife; I've opened my door to a son in a crisis, I've lost my friend Cyrille and I've gone through a divorce.'

Lefebvre counted the points on his fingers like a baseball score.

'And now, I just want to enjoy my week off and do some skiing.'

Érik erased the score. 'Impossible. We won't be able to ski today. So what's your plan B, then?'

Thrown off course for a second, Moralès hesitated. Then caught himself. 'Reading.'

'You're going to read?'

'I'm going to read, yes.'

'Are you a reader, Joaquin Moralès?'

'I brought a novel with me.'

Lefebvre nodded like a conciliatory life coach, ate a spoonful of fruit yogurt.

'I've even got a book for you, too.'

Érik widened his eyes in surprise. That morning, he was wearing a sweater in tones of yellow and orange on which a sun was perpetually setting. 'Oh, really?'

'A poetry collection.'

'Are you serious?' Lefebvre seemed entirely awed by this charming surprise.

'It was the bookseller in New Richmond who chose it for you.'

'Mélanie? I didn't know you went to bookshops…' Lefebvre leaned against the backrest of the bench seat, thrilled by the day's new prospects. 'Bookshops and booksellers are passions of mine. Right, well, if you're not working on the investigation, do you think Nadine would be up for playing some ball?'

🦭

Before dawn, the cold and the damp penetrated every layer of clothing. Bernard Chevrier was already up, and so were McMurray and Lapierre. Simone was taking her time. She had waited for them to leave the cabin before extracting herself from her bunk.

Eight-Inch flew into the galley like a gust of wind. Lucien Carpentier was steering the ship while the skipper was finishing his breakfast. The young cokehead slurped his yogurt.

'Chevrier, you'd better find us some seals today. Is that clear?'

'Aye. There's some on Henry Island.'

'You said that about Margaree Island, and there was nothing there.'

'Well, if the helicopters come and scare them away…'

Eight-Inch carried on as if he couldn't hear. 'No way we're going back to shore empty-handed. I want to cover my costs, is that clear? Is that clear enough?'

Bernard Chevrier stood up. 'It was your old man who chartered the boat and your uncle gave him a family discount.'

'We need a good haul. A fucking good haul.'

Chevrier filled his travel mug with coffee and went up to the wheelhouse to take the helm. Trying to have a conversation with Eight-Inch was like talking underwater: the sound never reached his ears.

The northeaster had picked up and was carting its loads of ice into the strait. On the horizon, not a thing. There *was* no horizon. Only a windswept whiteness pushing the crests of the waves southwards, the swell rolling and collapsing, the slabs of pack ice, more and more of them, rising and falling. Somewhere out there, not far off, was Henry Island, nestled near the coast of Cape Breton Island, at the mouth of Saint George's Bay. Its shoreline, Chevrier hoped, would be stocked with seals. The men could fill the hold and go home. He settled into the captain's chair.

Carpentier went down to the galley. McMurray came up to the wheelhouse. Lapierre wasn't far behind, followed by Painchaud.

'There. Over there!' Eight-Inch yelled.

They all gave a start. Carpentier came running from down below. Painchaud pointed at something. Chevrier already had his binoculars in hand. The murk tore apart for a moment and the sparkling shore of Henry Island emerged, peppered with minute specks of grey.

'Six seals.'

'Did I find 'em or did I find 'em?'

Tony McMurray gave Lapierre a quick glance. 'Well done, Painchaud. But that won't be a very big haul, will it? I've heard stories about a crew that killed fifteen hundred seals on a single trip, just last year.'

'There were ten of us on board,' Bernard Chevrier chimed in.

Lapierre ignored the skipper. 'How much does a pelt fetch, already?'

'And the meat as well. Réjean Vigneault, he'll buy the lot off us for his butcher's.'

McMurray's shoulder rolled back in its socket involuntarily; his grey balaclava sat perched on top of his head. He stared at Lapierre, who could see the hunter had understood. He knew why they were there. And he was all right with that. Carpentier hadn't been kidding when he said he'd found a guy who had what it takes.

'A decent haul, I reckon that'll put your daughter through vet school and bankroll one or two all-inclusives down south for your wife, won't it, Lulu?'

Carpentier the poacher laughed out loud, making his belly shake up and down. 'For the right price, I'd cart around no end of bloody suitcases!'

Bernard Chevrier threw cold water on the excitement of the moment.

'If you think you're going sealing to get rich, get real. You'd be better off staying at home.'

Michaël Lapierre turned to Marco Painchaud. 'You really want to fill this hold to the brim, don't you, Eight-Inch?'

Painchaud was sweating buckets. His face was covered in perspiration as thick as a layer of grease. 'No way we're going back empty-handed.'

Lapierre sketched on his face a slow smile of satisfaction that spoke to McMurray, who scratched the back of his head and led Carpentier down the stairs to get the rifles ready.

Eight-Inch nodded his head of dirty hair frantically. 'If I want the trip to be lucrative, it's gonna be lucrative. all right? Is that clear? Is that clear enough?'

Lapierre gave him a tap on the shoulder and the two of them went downstairs, while Chevrier guided the *Jean-Mathieu* towards the coast.

A moment later, Officer Lord came up to the wheelhouse. 'Where are they all?'

Chevrier pointed to the seals on the shore. The crew were up front, at the prow. The skipper turned to Simone. His broad body embedded in his seat, he continued steering the *Jean-Mathieu* with a cautious hand as he spoke to her.

'Now it's just the two of us, tell me what you're doing on board, will you?'

She was observing the men. 'My job.'

He shook his head. 'No. In general, you fisheries officers only show up while we're at sea – you have a field day with your surprise inspections. You come aboard a coast-guard vessel. You accost a trawler and comb every inch of it, searching for the slightest offence – flushing out the accidental catch, measuring the hakapik handle that's half a centimetre too long. Then you slap your ticket on the table and you go on your way. So what I'm wondering is why your bosses put someone right here on board instead of having the coast-guard boat follow us.'

'Because there's a storm brewing and no one wants to dispatch a whole team out to sea for one tiny crew that refuses to wait for a window in the weather.'

'The guys said it wasn't you who was supposed to be on board.'

'They were supposed to be getting an officer from Gaspé. He was sick and had to stand down at the last minute. They sent me instead.'

Simone cursed herself for giving the skipper an answer. She didn't owe him any explanations. But talking to him relieved the pressure. The scene the previous day had wakened an anger in her. A rock-hard, heavy anger she'd been carrying for years and never let go.

'You're not happy about being here, that's as obvious as an eye in the middle of your forehead.'

'No, I'm not happy about it.'

'That supervisor of yours, Jean-Guy Thériault, I know him.'

'The order didn't come from him.'

'Aye. Who did it come from, then?'

'From the boss in Gaspé.'

A punishment from the top brass.

'And Jean-Guy didn't offer to take your place?'

'Yes, he did.'

'Why did you refuse?'

'Because he and his wife have three kids and the youngest is still in nappies, because going aboard ships is part of my job. And because I've got overachiever syndrome, so I've always got to prove to myself that I've got what it takes – that I can measure up to a bunch of men! Are you happy now?'

Chevrier decided to take it steady. No, he wasn't satisfied; if she was a proper officer, she must have proper motivations. He tried another approach to get her to open up.

'Well, Simone, I've always been of the opinion that fishing belongs to fishermen, not people who play at being police but who've never gone out in a storm, who've never torn a net and cursed the coral, grounded a propeller in the shallows or put a crack in a hull between two slabs of ice. You officers, you consult with your lab biologists to see how many codfish, crabs and seals there are over the other side of Dead Man's Island, but you've never put your hand in your pocket for a permit, changed a transmission or forced a winch. You've never dug a hook out of your forearm. No. The only risk you fisheries officers run is getting a stain on your sleeve from the ink in your pen when you're writing a ticket. And even then, the shirt on your back's paid for by your employer.'

He marked a pause before he carried on.

'But you, you're courting even more danger by coming aboard a boat full of men.'

Like getting raped or going overboard.

'A single woman observer on board: let's be honest, that's a bad idea.'

Chevrier had come to the conclusion that there must be another reason why she was on board. Maybe she wasn't just a fisheries officer. He wanted to find out for sure.

'So I'm wondering, what makes you so interested in this job of yours?'

Simone took a moment before giving him an answer. The truth was, she liked him, his memories and his gruff manners.

'How many years have you been fishing and hunting, Bernard Chevrier? Since you were eight years old?'

Time meant nothing to him right now. He was focused on the approach they were making through the ever more tightly packed ice.

'Longer than that. My old man, and his old man too, were hunters and fishers. I was raised on saltwater.'

The men shouldered their rifles.

'When you were young, you must have come across those factory ships that came to round up the fish in international waters? The ones that gobbled up all our resources?'

They fired.

'I saw a few of them.'

'And you must have seen some of your friends out there, fishing like they wanted to empty the whole sea?' She put her binoculars down and turned to him. 'You know as well as I do, Carpentier used to poach by the boatload, don't you?'

'Aye.'

'Aye? Wake up, skipper! If the fisheries officers hadn't been there to protect the resources, you would have stopped fishing a long time ago because there wouldn't be any more fish in the sea.'

Chevrier was no fool. He hadn't poached a lot himself, because often it was more trouble than it was worth, but he'd seen folk sell full hauls offshore, and it had pained him to see his sea being emptied into the holds of foreigners. She was right, but that was no reason to prove her so.

On she went, insisting, baring her teeth almost. 'And with all those catches offloaded under the table, Carpentier can't have sold his licence for much, eh? Have you asked him if he got a fair price for it? Seeing him having to skate around out there on the ice, I'd say he didn't.'

Chevrier knew he hadn't. Carpentier had made a mess of it all. He had always declared small catches but then strutted about with cash lining his pockets, which had ruffled a few feathers on the wharf at Grande-Entrée. For years, he had folk believe there wasn't much to be caught where he fished. As a result, when he was forced to sell up, five years ago, his licence was all but worthless, since he'd only ever declared small quotas in his zone. His buyer, Longuépée, had said to him: 'No one's going to pay for a zone with no lobsters in it.' He had put a paltry amount on the table, and the poacher had been forced to accept it. Carpentier wasn't just broke. With the fine he'd landed, he'd been driven to the brink of bankruptcy. He'd had to sell up quickly, at a deep discount, without a chance to up his quota.

The officer had found her confidence again. 'It's because I love our resources that I'm on board, Chevrier. And often, I wonder if you fishers and hunters appreciate them as much as I do, or if all you care about is killing everything that moves so you can line your pockets and not give a damn about leaving nothing for your children to find.'

'Aye, you're right about the fish. But the seals, there's too many of 'em!'

Lord knew that. 'I'm not here for the seal quota. I'm here to make sure it's a clean hunt.'

Chevrier stayed silent. The conversation had run out of steam, and Simone was on her way out to shadow the crew on the shore. He wasn't much of a talker, anyway. He'd found out what he wanted. The girl was really who she said she was, an officer. Just a Fisheries and Oceans Canada officer. The reality of that was head-splitting for him. He had been hoping, especially since he had seen her sneaking a peek at her phone, that she was a police officer, working undercover for the drugs squad maybe, and had her eye on Painchaud. Someone who knew how to defend herself, had backup on standby.

But no.

It had been a long time since Chevrier had been in the thick of things like this. He switched the radio on, listened to the shipping forecast. Carpentier and McMurray would do anything for money. Painchaud had a coke habit. And Lapierre looked like a guy with connections. He pored over the marine chart. There weren't many options. If he was to persuade the men to fill the hold with anything other than dope, he'd have to steer clear of the coast of Nova Scotia, head deep into the Northumberland Strait and skirt around the other side of Prince Edward Island, over towards New Brunswick.

All the way to Pictou Island.

🦭

Érik Lefebvre came back to the cabin, out of breath and in a sweat.

'So, that novel of yours?'

Moralès looked up with heavy eyes. 'What about it?'

'Is it interesting?'

'It's all right.'

'What's it about?'

'It's about a guy who…' He was searching for the words, realising this was something he'd never done, summing up a novel. 'It's the story of an explorer who founds a village, with his wife and their kids, but…'

But what? Suddenly, it seemed unclear to him.

Lefebvre tossed the book Moralès had given him earlier that day onto his bunk. 'Wow. Sounds exciting.'

'That's just the beginning.'

'So after that, does he go on to found a town?'

'No. The hero, he wants to discover things, but he gets swindled.'

Lefebvre leaned against the bathroom door frame with a mocking smile. 'What's the title?'

'*One Hundred Years of Solitude.*'

'Was it Mélanie who recommended that?'

Joaquin scratched the back of his neck, admitted it wasn't. 'Not really.'

'Right, well, Moralès, when you get divorced and you're depressed, instead of calling a woman and going out to join her in the Magdalen Islands, you're telling me you'd rather spend your holiday on a boat stuck in the ice, holed up in your bunk with *One Hundred Years of Solitude*?'

'When Sébastien washed up in the Gaspé this past autumn, he accused me of abandoning my Latin American roots.'

'So, for your Mexican soul to rise up from the ashes, your son suggested you read a Colombian novel?'

Joaquin knew he was going the wrong way about things. Far from feeling weightless, he sensed he was wallowing heavily in the depths of his being. He had to bounce back. But how?

'The guy in the book, the hero, he goes round in circles and everything crumbles around him. He goes crazy.'

Érik pulled up a chair, sat down in front of his friend. 'Perhaps you shouldn't be reading a book that turns you upside down like this. You could be having a whale of a time with the Tour de Gaspé gang, you know. They're singing their hearts out and playing all kinds of games up there...' He stopped, knowing those weren't the kinds of activities Moralès enjoyed. 'Or you could read a good crime novel. Now that's relaxing, because you're not the one leading the investigation.'

Lefebvre picked up the poetry collection he'd tossed on the bed, opened it, chose a page as he spoke.

'I've already read the book Mélanie gave you for me. It's the story of a guy who wears cowboy boots and says: *"May the heart-breaking horizon of my soul / seed skies of starry constellations / and in the light of day madly / may I love you / like one loves no more".'*

He closed the book.

'That's beautiful and all, and it tickles me that my bookseller's sending me poems about a guy who wears cowboy boots. But I'm not that guy. Sure, I can get a bit poetic when I'm in love. And I do wear cowboy boots. But I'm my own person. I'm Constable Érik Lefebvre. I crack the case, I cuff the guy who killed the husband, and then I give the widow the eye. I live a frivolous life, and not just because the world is one strong undertow and I'm trying to keep my head above water. No. It's just who I am. I live with no wife and no children. I'm a free spirit.'

Lefebvre made a sudden, bizarre movement with his head, as if he'd just punched himself in the face. Knocked for six, it took him a moment to grasp the gravity of a revelation only he had seen. Then he tossed the poetry collection back onto his bunk.

'What I'm saying is that novel of yours might well be Latin American, but Joaquin, you're not that guy. You're your own person.' Lefebvre got up, pushed the chair back under the desk, grabbed his towel and went to take a shower, closing the door to the bathroom behind him. A second later, he pushed it open again and stood there, wearing nothing but a thong. 'Right, well, you know what? Earlier on, I was in the gym, riding a stationary bike. A bike is supposed to get you somewhere, not to spin on the spot, are you with me on that? At one point, it occurred to me that I was doing this on a ship that was supposed to be moving forwards, but was stuck at a standstill. I was riding a bike on the spot, on a ship that was sailing on the spot. Can you imagine, in spite of all my effort, I wasn't getting anywhere? I wasn't moving a metre!'

Joaquin smiled at last. 'It's a good thing the earth is still turning…'

'Anyway, it made me realise that I was doing exactly the opposite of what I love. Me, my passion is pitching balls at a hundred and fifty kilometres an hour. I live in the lightning bolt of the moment. When I take it easy, I start thinking and it makes me melancholy. I'd rather be in the action.'

Apparently surprised to discover how philosophical he could also be, Lefebvre fluttered with excitement.

'I don't know how you can just sit there in your bunk, read your book and think about your divorce, how you can be on holiday without diving right in to Nadine's investigation. I know I couldn't.' He went quiet for a second, thinking. 'It would be like … inhibiting my inner nature.' And with that, he disappeared into the bathroom again.

Moralès stared for a moment at the closed door, listening to the sound of the shower and the din of his colleague singing at the top of his lungs. He went back to his reading, then paused to run through again in his mind what Lefebvre had just said, and got up. He scanned the room for something to use as a bookmark, pulled out of his wallet a little origami bird Officer Lord had left on the table of his kitchenette at the auberge that past autumn, slipped it carefully between the pages, set the book down on his bunk and hurried out of the cabin.

ᘓ

Aboard the *Jean-Mathieu*, Marco Painchaud had hauled up on deck all the pelts the men had left out in the water overnight, having dressed them and hooked them onto a line the day before. Officer Simone Lord had tagged them all with a tie through their now-empty eye sockets.

Painchaud had opened the hatch doors and gone down into the crab trawler's hold to stash their haul. Michaël Lapierre had used the winch to crane the pelts over to him, and the youngest of the crew had stacked them to starboard, fur to fur, fat to fat. Next, Lapierre had passed through the hatch the bagged cuts of the carcasses, which Painchaud had then placed in bins on the portside. The cold in the steel trawler's belly was enough to preserve it all until they were back at the wharf.

Meanwhile, Carpentier and McMurray had lowered the dinghy into the sea. Escorted by the fisheries officer, they had gone to retrieve the freshly killed animals, which they had bled on the shore then dragged back to the boat behind them.

Now out on deck, they were starting to dress them. Lapierre, however, went inside to get cleaned up and go and see Chevrier. The skipper was ready.

'Aye, I've set us on course for Pictou Island. There's always hundreds of grey seals on the shore there. I wasn't sure, because of the bad weather, but anyway, we'll be all right.'

Lapierre, the picture of calm, was watching him. 'I don't think we should be going too far into the strait. Seems the wind's too strong for that.'

The skipper insisted. 'Got to keep hunting. Going back with an empty hold after six days at sea, that'll look suspicious. We've barely got fifteen of 'em down there.'

Lapierre turned to look out on deck. Armed with knives, the men outside had skinned the seals. Carpentier and McMurray were gutting, boning and meticulously carving up the carcasses, while Painchaud hooked the pelts on to a line to lower them into the water for the night. Lapierre wiped a hand across his forehead. It was the first time since they'd been at sea that Chevrier had seen him like this.

'You all right, son?'

Lapierre looked at him. 'Everything you've told me, about the Islands and the sealing, it's … I don't know.'

'You've been in the city a long time.'

'Yeah. I'd forgotten everything that goes on back home.'

'You regret leaving, then.'

Lapierre cast his gaze offshore, observed the bluish white of the sea, the hemline of the waves, the horizon and its piles of pale grey clouds, the deck flooding with blood.

'I'll give you twenty-four hours for your little trip,' he said. 'We'll fill the hold with seals. But after that, we're going to be heading east. And I'll be the one setting the course.'

Chevrier wasn't waiting to be told twice. He steered a course to the southwest and accelerated, in spite of the increasingly hazardous opacity of the ice in the Northumberland Strait.

'Aye. Over Pictou way, there'll be plenty of seals to make you rich. Maybe you won't even feel like doing that detour of yours after that. That'd be better for everyone, the girl included.'

Immediately, Chevrier regretted bringing her up. It would be better for the crew to forget she was a girl, forget she even existed.

But Lapierre flashed him a predatory smile. 'I'll take care of the officer, all right.'

The skipper whirled around to face Lapierre. 'There's no way you're laying a finger on her. She's with me.'

'I told you I'd take care of her. Now, before I head out, you're going to give me your phone and I'm just going to…'

He pocketed the device Chevrier handed over reluctantly, and then disconnected the VHF transmitter.

'Just to make sure you keep your mouth shut.'

ᨒ

In her cabin, Nadine had turned the second bunk into a work space with photos, printouts and handwritten notes all arranged in a strict order. She opened the door when Moralès knocked, invited him in and offered a chair that seemed to have been waiting just for him. He studied the documents one by one as she brought him up to speed on what the team believed had happened.

'We know why Buster completely lost it. The day before yesterday, our guys went to the school to pick up the kid's best friend – a youth by the name of Prudhomme. He's in shock. He said his mate was bragging about making a mint. He was a mathematical genius who wanted to be an accountant for the Hells. He'd been dealing for them for the last eight months and, according to Prudhomme, he ran a tight balance sheet. That was his trademark, in fact. He wanted to prove he was better than the rest.'

Moralès was holding a sheet of colour photos that showed the young man who'd been savagely beaten.

'The thing is, he got himself into a bit of hot water…'

Moralès didn't ask if the kid was dead. It would be next to impossible to survive a beating like that, and if Doiron's unit was the one handling the case, that meant things were likely to take a turn for the worse. Today, Buster was wanted for aggravated assault. Tomorrow, he'd be wanted for murder.

'Two weeks ago, the kid bragged to his mate Prudhomme that he'd loaned a thousand dollars to his supplier. He said that was going to make him a partner of sorts with the Hells in a deal that would pay big money.'

Moralès imprinted the image of the youth in his mind, the spatters of blood on the walls of his mother's living room, the red pool that had seeped into the light-blue rug she'd had to throw in the garbage. Objects, in spite of themselves, were often the carriers of an indelible memory.

'He got himself caught up in something dodgy. But why did Buster go and lay into him?'

'We don't know. Last week, the kid told Prudhomme he'd have news about his big scoop in a couple of weeks.'

Moralès gently placed the photo of the young man in his hospital bed on the bunk in front of him. That kid was somebody's son. The detective tried to put together a scenario:

'The kid lends money to Buster to help him bankroll a drug shipment. Then he goes bragging about it at school. He says some things he should be keeping to himself. Buster gets wind of it and comes over to teach him a lesson.'

The psychologist shook her head. 'I doubt it. A thousand

dollars, that's not exactly big bucks for the Hells. They wouldn't put a young dealer in the hospital for that, especially if he's good at his job. Maybe it's got nothing to do with the dope. Prudhomme swears he doesn't know. He reckons even the kid had no idea what the money was for. If he did, he'd have been bragging about that too.'

'What's Buster going to do with a thousand bucks?'

'We don't know. Buster's not a big thinker. The day the brain cells were handed out, he was probably outside, putting a line of coke up his nose, if you see what I'm saying.'

Moralès winced. 'The goon on the hockey team, that kind of guy.'

Nadine pulled a photo out of a folder. It was a close-up of a man around thirty-five years old, with long hair and a thick moustache. A goofy smile revealed a gap between two teeth.

'Racketeering, pimping, drug dealing. Six arrests, four years behind bars, all in all. Accessory to murder, unsubstantiated – remember that shitster Charland, in Granby three years ago? Always got a prostitute on the back of his bike, never the same one. Up until now, he's always put gloves on before he picks up an iron bar to mess with a girl or a shopkeeper—'

'Or a small-time dealer.'

'Yes. But this time, he forgot. There are so many prints, all over the kid's place, he could almost plead that it was a set-up.'

'If he'd been trying to kill the kid, he wouldn't have gone about it that way.'

'I don't think that was his goal.'

'What was he trying to do, then?'

'Get him to talk about the big scoop.'

'In that case, it wouldn't have been him sponging a thousand bucks off the kid.'

'Prudhomme doesn't know.' She handed another photo to Moralès. 'Meet Buster's partner.'

'Who is he?'

'Stone. Stone Lapierre. More than nine years, they've been working together. Stone's the leader. Outwardly, he never says a word. He listens. He can even be quite endearing. He's the kind of guy to bail his buddies out when they're in trouble. He's got charisma. If he was a singer in a rock band, he'd go down a storm. A Hells supporter, like Buster. Neither of them are members, but they'd like to be. Got a similar rap sheet to his good friend. Drugs, racketeering, but without the hookers. And not as violent either. He's the type who gives the orders.'

'The coach. He's the one the kid lent the money to.'

'Maybe. I imagine he's the one who made sure Buster put the gloves on when he was about to throw a punch. Which makes me think he wasn't around when the kid got beaten up.'

'Where is he?'

Nadine shrugged. 'That's probably what Buster wanted to know when he went knocking at the kid's door.'

Joaquin put the photo back in the file. 'And what about us, what do we know?'

The cops tended to keep an eye on most members of biker gangs, but their supporters were so numerous, they could fly under the radar.

'Our officers are actively hunting for those two shitsters.'

Moralès nodded. All he could do, for now, was learn as much as possible about the two men and try to anticipate their actions. He picked up the file for one of the criminals, opened it. This kind of reading he could handle. But just before he got stuck in, he took another hard look at the photo of the young man.

'What's his name?'

Nadine smiled. 'Beaudry. Simon Beaudry. Welcome to the case, Detective Moralès.'

⚜

The slabs of ice were tearing at the prow and clawing the hull like wild animals – testing the patience of the crew and the resistance of the steel. A shrill lament echoed around the all-but-empty hold. Since the morning's haul, words had become a rarity. Eight-Inch had spent the rest of the afternoon biting his nails, sitting down, jiggling his legs frantically, getting back up and starting all over again. Carpentier took care of the cooking.

Late in the day, Lapierre prised himself off the leather bench he'd been lounging on with another hunting magazine, leafing with unruffled calm through the minutes of this excruciating expedition. At four in the afternoon, as the daylight was approaching its end, he went out on deck with a satellite phone to make a call as monosyllabic as it was swift.

McMurray, in the cockpit, took the opportunity to have a look at Chevrier's navigation plan.

'Where are you taking us, now?'

'Where the seals are.'

'Because you're the one who gets to decide?'

The skipper clenched his jaw, the way a man did whose job it was to find a fine colony of seals. The grey gold of winter.

Eight-Inch, edgy as ever, went out on deck for a piss. The trawler was making slow headway, but the spray had still covered the surface with a fine film of ice. From the wheelhouse, McMurray had half an eye on him, but kept Lapierre in his sights as well. With his legs far too straight, Painchaud began to empty his bladder. He turned his head to spit downwind. Suddenly, the boat lurched as it hit a slab of ice and McMurray saw Eight-Inch skate off down the deck with his dick hanging out. The stream splashed him all the way up to his face. Lapierre was the only one to laugh. Chevrier was staring straight ahead, and McMurray stood still as stone; he understood the cards were all on the table now. It was a brazen plan, one that would put anyone on edge. Especially a little guy like Painchaud. But the youngster was too far gone now to take a different tack. Carpentier wouldn't change his mind either, he was too broke to go home empty-handed. No. The one they needed to keep an eye on was Chevrier. He was too old for escapades like this.

When Eight-Inch came back in, Lapierre was waiting in the vestibule. He told him to go clean himself up. Meanwhile, he went and opened a bottle of wine. Having a drink would calm their nerves. McMurray went down the stairs.

Chevrier stayed at the helm until the darkness came. Night was still falling early, even though the sun was extending its hours and things were moving in the right direction. The fisheries officer brought a plate of food up to him. The atmosphere was charged; she could sense it.

'What's going on, skipper?' Simone's voice was heavy.

Chevrier doubted she made a habit of waitressing. If she'd brought him his meal, it was to soften him up and get him to talk. He would have rather Fisheries and Oceans Canada had sent a man. He wouldn't feel so responsible.

'It so happens I'm not the type to go home with a light boat.'

'I hope you're not going to do something stupid, Chevrier.'

The skipper gave a hearty laugh, but it rang false. 'I'll do nothing you might regret, my pretty officer.'

She got a bit pushier. 'Step aside so I can check your course.'

'Give me a bloody break with the course, will you? You said you liked the hunt, didn't you? Well, a hunt is what you're going to get.'

A second of silence, then she was back at it. 'You're headed for Pictou.'

'Aye.'

'It's past nightfall. When are you going to stop?'

'With the moon, it's light enough for me to keep going.'

'Through the ice?'

'Aye.'

'Listen, Chevrier—'

'No. I won't hear another word. Now shut your bloody mouth and let me get on with my job!'

'Why are you getting your back up?'

'You're the one getting it up. You're a pain in the neck, Simone Lord. Now you listen to me: you need to quit asking questions, is that clear?'

The officer moved closer to him and lowered her voice, to make sure he was the only one who heard her. 'What's your fucking problem, Chevrier?'

The skipper shot her a sideways glance. *My fucking problem is that Painchaud's betrayed his uncle. My fucking problem is that no one's here for the seals. My fucking problem is that one of the guys is not a hunter by any stretch of the imagination, but he's shit hot at firing a gun. My fucking problem is that the crew were expecting to have another officer on board, but you were the one Fisheries and Oceans Canada sent. Do you understand? My fucking problem, girl, is that you're not on anything remotely resembling a normal seal hunt, but you're too wet around the ears to notice and you're in danger of losing your hide out here!*

That was what Chevrier wanted to say, but he could hear

McMurray's heavy steps coming up the stairs, so he just shrugged his shoulders.

'My fucking problem is you.'

ぷ

At the end of the day, riding on the rising tide, the ship finally floated free and got back on course, in the wake of a coast-guard icebreaker. The holidaying skiers clapped their hands in excitement, snapped photos, raised their glasses to the captains' respective healths. That evening, most of them went out on deck to hoot and holler at the fireworks the town of Sainte-Anne des-Monts had set off to salute their passing.

In the background, the majesty of the Chic-Chocs' snowy summits was veiled by the overcast night. The skiers knew they'd missed out on a course as leg-busting as it would have been breathtaking, but the organisers of the trip had popped the champagne corks and gloom had soon given way to gaiety. Here and there, little groups had splintered away and were challenging each other to sing-offs. There was a sense of celebration in the air.

The mouth of the Saint Lawrence stretched north to an invisible shore, lost in the glacial blues. Even the lights of Sept-Îles were hidden in the mist. The ship seemed to be sailing into space.

Moralès, in spite of the bonhomie of the skiers around him, remained pensive. He had spent the afternoon studying the case file. Now, he had to wait for the field officers to get their informants to talk. This was the time for patience, the window when he wanted to be skiing, to be active.

He watched Érik courting Nadine with his natural, disarming

charm. She was laughing. Joaquin knew she could be quite the man-eater. She had a penchant for waking, sweating, among rumpled sheets that carried the scent of the whirlwind of the night that had followed a hard working day. It took her mind off things. But she had a tendency to psychoanalyse her lovers, she had once confided in him. It twisted relationships and squeezed all the wrong juices out. One thing time had taught her was that her heart would never allow her to stand before an altar or behind a pram.

He envied them, her and Érik.

He didn't have that sense of ease with strangers. That lightness. He felt weighed down. By himself, by his age, by his seriousness, perhaps; by a deep, intrusive nostalgia that had been rising in his throat since he moved out to the Gaspé Peninsula. He thought back to Bonhomme Carnaval, in Quebec City. He must look a bit like that, a ridiculous mascot of a man with a clownish smile, while beneath the costume, within himself, lurked a man of silence divorced from love. Whose bedroom lay empty.

Moralès looked out at the river as it opened up into the darkness; bell towers, luminous, were scattered along the shoreline. These were the markers of sacred places, made for eternal unions. Mascots, with their great ridiculous heads, he mused, had no place in those churches. He would have to learn to live in solitude.

The bitter wind had driven the other skiers back inside. Joaquin shivered. Érik was right. He shouldn't turn himself upside down over a book, there was no sense to it.

With a cheerful wave of her hand, Nadine went in, too. Now Moralès, Érik and the husband and wife from the Magdalen Islands were the only ones left at the deserted prow of the ship.

The loving couple came to stand beside them, cheeks ruddy from the breeze, blood warmed by booze.

'When the wind's up like this in the Islands, you don't tie your dog up outside, or else he'll be flying like a kite.'

Lefebvre laughed. Before them, the river turned into an estuary. To the east, the wilds of Anticosti Island were sheltering in the cloak of night. 'Did we tell you? There's a friend of ours spending winter in the Islands.'

'Oh, is that right?'

'She's a fisheries officer. She's out there monitoring the sealing. I think time is dragging for her.'

Joaquin pricked an ear.

'Well, you should give us her name before we go. I know everyone in the Islands. When we get home, we'll track her down and have her over for supper.'

That made Lefebvre happy. He admired the welcome that Magdalen Islanders were famous for.

'How about you, Réjean, have you been out seal hunting this year?'

'Yep. I went out for the grey seals earlier this month.'

'Do you go over land or by boat?'

'Both. Depends on when you go. The people in the Magdalen Islands, we're hunter-gatherers. We take what nature gives us. It was the First Nations who taught us that. The grey seals, they were the first fresh meat of the year for those who came before us. They have their young on the shore in December, and the hunt gets going when the pups are weaned. After that, there's the harp seals, and we'll be after them from the middle of March. For them, you've got to head out into the pack ice.'

Head hunkered in her hood, Réjeanne watched with a gentle

smile as the distance between the two shores grew and the river made a break for it into the estuary. 'Réjean's building quite the market for seal meat.' She admired her husband, that was obvious.

'It's a meat that's free from hormones, very lean and very red, because it's wild,' Réjean said.

'He also teaches sealing courses.'

'Oh, really?' Lefebvre asked.

'I have to show the guys how to preserve the carcass. If I don't, I might end up with tainted meat. And the last thing I want is to butcher my business.'

Lefebvre kept asking questions, as if he wanted to try his hand at seal hunting. 'Is it complicated?'

'They're not hard to kill. It's the same as for a pig or a cow in a slaughterhouse. You have to crush the skull with a club or a hakapik to the forehead. A hakapik's a hook, with a hammer-head kind of thing on the other side, on the end of a handle about this long.' Réjean stretched his hands, wrapped up in warm mittens, about a metre and a half apart. His ear lobes had gone red in the wind. 'The hunters kill the seals with the hammer side, check the skull is crushed, bleed the creature with a knife and use the hook to drag the carcasses to the water's edge. It's all regulated with fancy words, now we've got the animal-rights groups chasing after us, but it's the same it's always been. My old man used to say, "You smash their head in, slice 'em open and turn 'em on the cut." They've just changed the vocabulary so it sounds smart.'

Joaquin was starting to feel cold, but Lefebvre was still going strong. He seemed to be wishing he had bigger eyes to take it all in.

'I've seen photos. They bleed a lot, eh?' Lefebvre continued.

'No more than any other animal, but the blood gleams brighter on the snow than it does in my slaughterhouse.'

'And if you go by boat, do you chop them up when you get back to dry land?'

'No. We skin them on board so the meat doesn't get contaminated. We start by dressing them. It's a strange word for it because we're taking the skin off; it's more like we're undressing them. We put the pelts in seawater to soak, then to preserve them, we stack them up, fur to fur, fat to fat, down in the hold, on one side of the boat. We chill the meat in food bins overnight, then the next day we bag it up and store that in the hold too, but on the opposite side of the hull. The temperature stays around minus ten to minus twelve degrees Celsius down below. Things keep well down there.'

'And you keep all the parts?'

'Just about. We keep the ribs, the nerves, the heart, the liver, the shoulders, the fillets. And for the fat, people are looking into turning that into omega-3 gel caps. There's talk of using the guts as another kind of bait for fishing. And the paws, I candy them.'

'I didn't know seals had paws.'

'Flippers, most folk call them.'

'And what do you do with the skins?'

'We used to sell them, mainly over in Europe, but the animal-rights groups are winning the battle to boycott the market for real fur in favour of synthetic, petroleum-based rubbish. It's stirring up a whole lot of trouble.'

Réjeanne was now hopping up and down to stay warm. Beneath her hood and her hat, she wore her hair very close-cropped, which, Moralès knew, highlighted her regal air, the way she held her head high.

'The animal-rights activists worry more about the seals than they do about wars and famine. That's not normal, I often think.'

'And things will get tricky pretty quickly if there's a decline in sealing. We're harvesting barely ten percent of a population of hundreds of thousands. If we don't keep their growth in check, they'll eat all the fish and crustaceans.'

Érik Lefebvre was shivering, but seemed oblivious to it. He was trying to recall the text Simone had sent him the other day. 'Where are the boats right now, then?'

'At the moment, the trawlers are all docked at the wharf. The wind's bringing the ice down and there's a storm brewing in the Maritimes. Navigation's going to be perilous.'

Lefebvre remembered the name of the vessel Officer Lord had mentioned she was boarding. With a knowledgeable air, he dropped it into the conversation.

'Right, well, I think the *Jean-Mathieu*'s out at sea.'

Réjeanne frowned, visibly intrigued that her friend from Gaspé seemed so well informed.

Her husband, only too happy to be talking about sealing, chimed in: 'The *Jean-Mathieu*'s quite the vessel. Versatile crab trawler, aluminium cabin, steel stabilisers. Belongs to Denis Éloquin. He's the guy I go aboard with, usually. You're right, that boat is at sea, but it's not Denis at the helm. It's his nephew who's chartered it from him.'

Lefebvre nodded energetically, as if he were privy to all this.

Réjeanne leaned closer, now with an air of suspicion. 'How come you know the *Jean-Mathieu*'s gone out? Is it because you've had dealings with Denis' nephew?'

Lefebvre took a step back, rocked from one foot to the other to warm himself up. 'No. Why would I know him?'

Mr and Mrs Vigneault looked at one another indecisively.

Réjean chose to hazard an answer. 'He might have had some trouble with the police before…'

'How so?'

The Vigneaults shrugged. Even though they knew, they cared too much about Denis Éloquin to speak ill of his nephew.

'Which way was the *Jean-Mathieu* heading?'

'Probably over New Brunswick way.'

The butcher rubbed his hands. 'Well, I'm not as warm as I was. How about we head in?'

Back inside, Lefebvre signalled to Moralès that he wanted a word. The police officers said goodbye to the Magdalen Islanders, and Joaquin followed Érik all the way back to their cabin. As if he was hatching a serious plot, Lefebvre closed the door cautiously behind them. He switched on the light, then his phone.

'This morning you said to me, "I'm not going to investigate with Nadine and I'm not going to call Simone." Now you're on the case with Nadine, you have to get in touch with Simone.'

A dumbstruck Joaquin took off his coat.

'Right, well, maybe she's the very reason you decided to get a divorce?'

'No.'

'Don't mess me around, Joaquin. She came down on you like a ton of bricks at first, and two weeks later you had her eating out of your hand.'

Suddenly exasperated, and not taking care, Joaquin broke the wooden hanger he was placing his coat on.

'*En la Madre!*'

Lefebvre stepped in his direction, reached for another one and hung up his friend's coat.

'It's not even a metaphor, you made supper for her.'

'I've only just got divorced.'

'The time is ripe. You have to reinvest in your capacity for love.'

'It's a woman we're talking about, not a poker table!'

'Did you hear what the Islanders said? That boat, the *Jean-Mathieu* that's gone out to sea with that sketchy guy?'

'You're reading too much into it, Érik…'

'Simone is on board.'

Joaquin all but folded up from the shock, pulled over a chair, sat down on it heavy.

'Right, well, she's been keeping me posted, from time to time.' Lefebvre handed him his phone as proof of the fact. 'Four days ago she went aboard. I've asked her to send me updates, but I've not heard anything.'

Lefebvre leaned over the desk, picked up a pen and paper and wrote down a number.

'You and me, we're very different, Joaquin. Me, I pitch balls. But you … maybe you really do have a guest room inside you that needs someone to live in it.' Érik slid the note to him. 'I know she's not indifferent to you, so you should at least write to her.'

Joaquin looked at the numbers as if they represented an indecipherable code. Hypnotised by the puzzle, he neglected to notice Érik leaving the cabin, barely even heard the door close behind him.

The grey gold of the ice floes

The night was unfolding like a painful slow-motion race, between waves flattened by ever-denser slabs of ice and the howling northeaster hurling its cursed chop down the strait.

Simone had knocked back a glass of wine at supper. Lapierre had forced her hand a little, arguing the troops could use a boost to their morale after four days at sea. It was true, the crew had been through an especially tense few hours. Carpentier and McMurray had been harping on about the idea of heading east, while Eight-Inch seemed to be constantly on the brink of exploding.

Even though Simone never usually drank alcohol at sea, this time she had let Lapierre twist her arm. It was better to allow herself to relax than let the tension mount higher and risk the urge to slit everyone's throats with a skinning knife. But by the end of the meal, she was seriously ready to drop with fatigue. That was hardly surprising. Over the last three nights, she had slept a mere six nervous, restless hours in her bunk. In spite of her altercation with the skipper, she decided the wheelhouse was the safest place for her to lie down.

Simone woke with a start. She had the impression she hadn't closed her eyes for long, yet she felt like she'd been jolted from a deep sleep. She stayed lying down for a moment, sensing something was happening. She opened her eyes. Chevrier was standing in the cockpit, clenching his teeth. He was murmuring a mantra of 'aye, aye' to himself, trying to steady his nerves, it seemed.

Just as she was sitting up, the trawler heaved over the icy lip of a wave. Chevrier yanked the wheel hard to port. Simone had to hang on so she wouldn't fall. In the cabin beneath them, the men cursed. Objects were thrown onto the floor. The trawler heaved once more. The skipper attempted another manoeuvre, to no avail but noise. A terrible screeching of metal. Bernard Chevrier shifted the transmission into neutral, turned anxiously to the screen that showed the engine room. Simone finally managed to haul herself upright. Outside, the ice had seized the crab trawler in its grip, pitching it slightly to starboard. The current was carrying the vessel and the floes out into the strait. The officer understood that Chevrier, eyes glued to the screen, must be wondering if the hull would hold up to the pressure of the ice.

'Well, fuck me ragged.' McMurray appeared in the wheelhouse, flanked by Carpentier, and by Painchaud, who was rubbing his eyes.

Simone wove her way between them and dashed down the stairs. She turned to starboard and hurried from one side of the boat to the other.

A worried Lapierre was only a step behind her. 'What's going on?'

'We're caught in the ice.' Simone switched the light on and went down the narrow stairwell that led to the hold. He followed. The walls were creaking around them. Down below, she made for the engine room.

Lapierre seemed paralysed by fear. 'Fuck. We're going down!'

Simone reached out to touch the external wall, which was lined with frost. 'It's just the paint.'

The pressure on the steel was so high, the paint on the inside of the hull was peeling away. The colour cracked and flaked beneath Simone's fingers. She looked at Lapierre, who was frozen too, in his own way.

'It's over,' Simone said.

Lapierre didn't respond.

'We're not moving. Do you understand? The boat is at a standstill, the ice has stopped squeezing it. If the hull was breached, there'd be water coming in. One of the bilge pumps would've started up. Everything is all right. We're not sinking.'

Lapierre pulled himself together, nodded in silence, unable to speak.

'I think Chevrier put the propeller in neutral at just the right time, otherwise we'd have heard it clunking against the ice.'

'OK.'

'Are you all right?'

'I hate boats. I hate sleeping all squished in a bunk no bigger than my hand and being shaken every which way. I hate it!'

Simone avoided asking him why he'd come aboard, then. Now was not the time. 'We've got a good skipper.' She climbed back up the narrow stairs.

Up on deck, the men were in a whirlwind. Before she even saw what was happening, Simone could hear McMurray and Carpentier running around, lowering the gangway.

'Stop, Painchaud! The hook's caught in the railing.'

She made her way over to the vestibule.

'Oh, for fuck's sake! You've torn something off.'

'Calm down, the weld's just come undone. Is that clear?'

Michaël Lapierre pulled on his coat and went outside.

Bernard Chevrier called Simone over from the top of the stairwell. 'Come see.'

She quickly followed him.

'We're stuck, but have a look at this.' He tipped his chin.

Simone turned to see. Chevrier had managed to steer the trawler within a few cable lengths – less than a nautical mile – of Pictou Island. The shoreline filled the horizon, with seals as far as the eye could see. It was more than a colony, it was a windfall, an X marking the spot on the map for the treasure trove Chevrier had promised the crew. The sight took Simone's breath away.

'We've got about thirty-six hours of this northeaster. After that, the wind's going to ease, so the ice should break up in tomorrow night's high tide. But in the meantime, the hunting's going to be easy. And lucrative.'

Simone hadn't heard Chevrier moving around in the early hours of the morning, but he had had Lapierre and Carpentier haul up the previous day's pelts, which they'd been dragging behind them in the water. The carcasses, too, had been put away in the hold. The trawler was ready to bring its next haul on board.

Chevrier was visibly relieved. His sister would be furious about the paint, though. Denis would have to give the engine room a fresh coat, but he'd be happy to see his nephew come home with a good haul. Now, Chevrier had to persuade the crew to abandon the idea of that detour. Maybe there was a chance he would succeed.

Simone grabbed a muffin, pulled her coat on and went outside. The crew were all in high spirits. She made her way down the ramp, saw that one of the rods in the railing had been forced out of joint. It was sticking out at a sharp angle and would be a hazard to anyone coming aboard. She remembered the exchange she had overheard between McMurray and Painchaud. She tried to push the rod back into place, but it was impossible. The metal was too stiff.

The hunters had abandoned their rifles and were making for the shore, hakapiks in hand. Carpentier was leading the way, followed by McMurray. Suddenly, she saw the leader sink up to his waist in water. His sniggering colleague helped him out of the hole, and the poacher forged ahead as if there was nothing to it, fuelled by adrenaline and blazing the swiftest trail to the colony.

Marco Painchaud, crazy as a loon, set off at a run and passed them all, hooting and hollering.

'I'm going to be the first, I'm going to be the fir—'

That was as far as he got. He slipped and went sprawling headfirst on the sheer ice with a 'Wooooh!'

The men bent over laughing.

Painchaud's slide, and his whoops of joy, came to an abrupt end as his face connected with a seal's hefty rear end.

'I know you're excited, Eight-Inch, but you don't have to go kissing their butts.'

Painchaud didn't hear Lapierre. He had scrambled to his feet and was slip-sliding on the icy spot while four huge seals, furious at being disturbed by such an abrupt influx of human heat, turned on him with a growl.

'My hakapik. My hakapik!'

Eight-Inch had let go of his weapon in his fall and was crawling over the ice trying to reach it.

By now the hunters were on their knees with laughter. Painchaud grabbed hold of his hakapik, struggled back to his feet and raised his arms in the air as the seals charged his way.

'I'm going to be the first.'

For the first time in months, Simone Lord realised that she was laughing, and heartily. That she was all right. In spite of the tensions, she told herself, in a way she was a part of this crew.

The men got down to work on the ice. The sun shone bright

on the horizon. The officer did her job overseeing the culling. The hakapiks in McMurray's and Painchaud's hands hammered to and fro in a jerky cadence, while Carpentier and Lapierre bled the carcasses.

There was a gleeful energy to the team, which contrasted with the bleak, sinister backdrop. Eight-Inch was unrecognisable and seemed to be in his element, toiling away in good humour and mumbling the word 'cash' at the slightest opportunity. Carpentier was going on about how he would have suitcases stitched out of sealskin for his wife, and how impressed the chambermaids at the all-inclusive resort would be next month. McMurray seemed sceptical. Still, in spite of his shoulder tic, he was the quickest of them all on the job. Only Lapierre had an air of mystery and sadness about him.

Simone checked that the skulls were all properly crushed.

'Let's start taking them aboard.' It was McMurray who gave the order.

'I'll get the quad out on the ice.'

Carpentier was doubtful about Painchaud's idea. 'Not sure it's thick enough.'

Eight-Inch didn't give a damn. 'If it goes through, my uncle can claim it on his insurance,' he laughed.

Michaël Lapierre wiped his nose on his sleeve and ended up leaving a broad streak of blood on his cheek. He and Marco Painchaud made their way back to the *Jean-Mathieu*, establishing a safe route. Then they winched the quad down onto the ice and drove it cautiously to the shore. They hooked a first load of carcasses to the back of the vehicle and hauled them to the trawler while the others continued with the culling. Painchaud came right back to fetch a fresh batch of seals, while Lapierre stayed on board to start dressing the carcasses.

Chevrier gave him a hand. 'That's seventy-five we've got already. Let's start with that.'

Simone looked over to the trawler. It seemed far away. She realised it was almost noon and she was starving hungry. Since daybreak, the work had been done by the book; she could allow herself a break. She set off for the boat, following the quad's tracks. This time, it was a tougher trek across the ice. Slipping in the viscous pools of blood, she quickly found herself walking in a narrow, stagnant stream of frozen red that cracked beneath her feet.

She clambered aboard with her head in a bit of whirl. Mere hours earlier, the bleak whiteness had been dotted by only grey, lifeless bodies; now it was tarnished by crimson stains as the comings and goings of the quad steadily traced a map of scarlet, carmine, vermilion scars across the frozen strait.

Simone went inside for a bite to eat. In spite of the carnage out there she felt a sense of relief, and wondered why. It occurred to her, as she was giving her hands a thorough washing, that she had sensed an unsettling tension in the men the previous night. For a moment she almost suspected there was an agreement, a secret pact between the members of the crew, an understanding that had terrified Chevrier and driven him, perhaps, to navigate these hazardous waters all night, to run the trawler aground in the pack ice, to steer a stubborn course for Pictou Island, into another brewing storm.

She suspected Eight-Inch had stuck his nose in too much coke and run up some risky debts with someone. Who, though? Lapierre? He was the only one who didn't really hunt or fish.

She went to find her Fisheries and Oceans Canada paperwork holder and carried it up to the wheelhouse. From there, she could keep an eye on the action through the window while she wrote her report. She really did need a break. Still, something nagged at her. If Eight-Inch owed Lapierre money, that would explain why the young cokehead had pressured Chevrier to sniff out a colony of seals, and fast. If not, then what? What had given the old sea dog so much grief the night before?

Now they'd found a colony like this, it should defuse the situation. Simone pulled herself together. The fatigue must be playing tricks on her. Maybe all this was just a figment of her imagination. It was probably just loneliness and nerves that had set the soundtrack to a horror film playing in her mind. She cast a glance outside. If the weather didn't turn too harsh, they would soon be on their way home. She started calculating. Chevrier had said they would be stuck until tomorrow night. In three and a half days' time, they should be back on dry land. All being well.

She opened her folder and seized the chance, while she was alone, to switch on her phone. There were new messages waiting in her inbox.

⌀

During the night, the ship sailed past Rivière-au-Renard, where the shrimp trawlers in their winter dry dock cast giant shadows over the port. Rounding the point of the Gaspé Peninsula, Joaquin had gazed with amazement as the cliffs of Forillon Park emerged in a sliver of moonlight like the grand prow of a formidable vessel surging from the saltwater, as if ready to surge forth and defy this estuary reluctant to call itself the Atlantic.

Moralès had barely slept. He had idled around the empty, silent bar, contemplating what lay beyond the national park in Gaspé Bay, where he and his team had discovered the coral bride the previous autumn. It was Simone Lord who had dived down and brought the woman's body back to the surface. Angel Roberts, a woman Simone feared she may have condemned to her fate.

They'd had a hard time working together, he and Simone. She had welcomed him at the police station in Gaspé like a dog to a bowling green, but Érik was right. Since the night he made her supper, everything had changed between them. Moralès had talked about the past, about his grandmother, about the things we inherit without realising, the things we do without understanding, the things that define us. He had approached her as she stood leaning against a kitchen cupboard and he had reached a hand out to grab a rolling pin. She had thought he wanted to kiss her. That was obvious. Unsettled, she had flinched, and he had sensed her uncertainty. That precise moment of fragility had moved him.

The last few months had turned him upside down.

Surely Érik was right: he shouldn't let himself feel weighed down by reading that book. It was dangerous for him to immerse himself in a nostalgia that was not his own. Still, Joaquin couldn't help but feel an emptiness. That space he had created, once upon a time, with Sarah, was now a place deserted by passion. A place on which, by taking off his wedding ring, he had shut the door. Excruciating sweet nothings whispered out to sea, and then rolled back to his feet, echoes in the shorebreak.

He was thinking about Simone. With a sigh of relief, or surrender, he had to admit he'd been thinking about her all winter. Without a sound, the spirit of that woman – either because of, or thanks to, the memory of that moment of vulnerability – had come to inhabit him.

The coast drifted by, gently and without resistance, to starboard.

Joaquin had learned to love Sarah in the urgency of youth, of emigrating, of expecting a child, studying a common language for them to converse in. Now that he was embarking on his fifty-third year, and as both the unhurried pace and profound forces of the tides caught up with him, would he be able to find connection once more? To be with a woman who wasn't fresh from her teenage innocence, but who had lived a life, built character, inherited happy diversions and trying times of her own? A woman who would have a seat at his table, who would quiver as he drew near and feel the desire for intimacy?

'They've tracked down an informant and questioned him.'

The detective was startled. He hadn't heard Nadine approaching. She sank heavily into the seat across from him, spent a few seconds observing him with a furrow of her brow. Joaquin kept looking out to sea, embarrassed to have been caught by surprise in such a private moment.

'I thought you'd be sleeping,' he said.

'How long have you been here? It's morning, Joaquin…'

Nadine turned away too, waited for her colleague to get hold of himself. With a gently purring of its engines, the ship was advancing towards Percé Rock, in all its spectacle and splendour. Some skiers had risen early to marvel at its appearance in the early morning.

'Where are we at, then?' Moralès asked.

Nadine went ahead. 'The guy said Stone and Buster owed the Hells a bunch of cash. To pay off their debt, Stone decided they'd take care of landing a shipment of drugs. A big one. We figure he must have approached Beaudry for a loan, probably because he heard the kid bragging about wanting to be the banker for the Hells, and then he slipped off the radar.'

'Has he made any calls?'

'Not on his mobile.'

'No transactions with his bank cards?'

'None at all.'

'That's why he went to the kid to borrow the cash, so he could be untraceable.'

She nodded. 'Yes. The drop's supposed to happen any day now. That's what the snitch said. Prudhomme, the kid's mate, said he'd heard the same thing.'

'Why did Buster fly off the handle?'

'Because if he and Stone don't bring back the drugs in time, the Hells will come down on them like a ton of bricks.'

Through the window, Moralès caught a glimpse of Percé Rock in the pink of daybreak, the faintness of a morning moon hanging over it. 'Stone kept Buster in the dark about his plans. That's why Buster went to Beaudry's. To see if the kid was in on what his partner was up to.'

'The kid must have been shooting his mouth off about slipping money to a guy with the Hells, and word got round to him…'

Moralès pictured the Hells wannabe losing his rag. 'You said Buster was high as a kite all the time.'

'Yes. He must be freaking out about Stone and his plans.'

'So he ended up losing it.'

'And he sent the kid to hospital.'

The detective was thinking. 'Where's Buster?'

'We're still looking for him.'

'And Stone?'

'The drugs squad are on the case, but there's no sign of him anywhere.'

'If Buster's panicking, that means he doesn't know where his partner is, either. But if Stone is bringing the drugs into the country, why didn't he keep Buster in the loop? Why is he not staying in touch?'

'Because he's dead?'

Nadine might be right, but the detective had his doubts. 'Or because he can't. If he's turned off his phone, it's because he doesn't want to reveal his location. Triangulation zones are quite broad, so I think we can assume he wouldn't be too concerned if he were somewhere like Montreal or Quebec City. So he must be in a small village, a hole of a place in the middle of nowhere, maybe not far from the border. He knows, if he contacts Buster, he'll be found straightaway.'

'So he's not calling. But where is he, do you think?'

'How long has it been since he dropped off Buster's radar?'

Nadine dug around in her file, counted the days. 'Two weeks at least.'

'With a thousand bucks for a month in his pocket, he can hardly stretch to a five-star hotel. Since he doesn't seem to trust his friends, maybe he's holed up in a cheap motel. Where would you crash if you were strapped for cash?'

Nadine shrugged. 'At my mum's place.'

The detective stared at her. 'Where's he from, this Stone?'

Nadine leaned over her file again, then sat bolt upright. 'From the Magdalen Islands.'

ↄ

Simone switched off her phone.

She had left the Gaspé Peninsula behind to embark on a Magdalen Island winter, and she had carried in her baggage the near certainty that Joaquin Moralès would get in touch with her. That they would bridge this distance with the thrill of a possibility.

When you carry a little hope, the horizon is easier to traverse.

But he had given no sign of life and Simone, though she didn't dare admit it to herself, had been bitten by the infinite, silent beauty that lay offshore and had begun to suffer the effects of its poisonous fangs. In the last four months, the disappointment of waiting had turned the Islands into a prison, and the sea had taken on the bitter taste of disillusionment.

Her hands were trembling a little. Now was not the time to be venturing into her vulnerability. Not here, not now, while the men outside were slaughtering a colony of grey seals. A sip of coffee went down the wrong way, and she coughed. Tears streamed down her cheeks.

She took a deep breath to calm her heart, looked outside.

Painchaud and Carpentier were carrying the carcasses aboard the trawler. The bleeding trails of that morning had swelled to streams of a pinkish red, frozen by the biting cold into long crimson corridors over the bluish ice, every one of them leading back to the boat.

Suddenly, without understanding why, Simone regretted coming aboard the *Jean-Mathieu*. Bernard Chevrier's words were flotsam bobbing back to the surface of her mind. He had felt betrayed, it seemed, floundering in anger, enraged to the point where he might make bad decisions. It struck her that perhaps this was how she herself had been acting for a long time. She'd been ruled by resentment and defiance. *I'll show them I can do it and rub their noses in it.* Her decisions were governed by what others thought of her, and that was making her miserable.

Lapierre, McMurray and Chevrier were making short work of dressing the seals.

She could see it now. Her friend Érik Lefebvre was right when he said that Simone acted like an overachiever. That she gave herself homework to do. That she didn't know how to have fun.

In the absence of all this rage and resentment, and if she had made a decision for herself alone, what would she have done? Her gaze wandered beyond the ice, disappeared in the distance.

Diving. That was what she loved. She could have opened a diving school. She thought about the beauty of what she had seen around Percé and Bonaventure Island, about the sand eels, the shorthorn sculpins, the snow crabs, the giant lobsters, the feathery anemones, the purple coral, the supple sponges, the sea strawberries. She remembered the silence, her breath in the regulator, the beating of her heart.

She wished she could scuba the world away, be in love, weightless, floating free of the pain.

The horizon was blurring before her eyes. What Lefebvre had said too, was that she didn't know how to love.

Officer Lord drew herself tall, stuffed her phone to the bottom of her bag, donned her outer layers and went outside. Out on deck, the ferrous stench of death made her a little light-headed. She cursed her distaste, hoped it wasn't too obvious to the crew.

Bernard Chevrier, his waterproofs drowning in blood, gave her a wave. 'I hope the smell's not turning your stomach too much.'

With her neck warmer pulled up over her mouth, Simone didn't answer.

Tony McMurray's left shoulder rolled back in its socket involuntarily. 'Well, fuck me ragged. Looks like the cat's got the singer's vicious tongue!'

This time, she looked him square in the eye. 'I don't know what turns my stomach the most, dead animals or live men.'

'Well you can be a nasty little bitch, can't you?'

⚓

The day was filled with singing and strolls in the sun around the deck of the Tour de Gaspé ship. The skiers were expecting to make land by supper time and be back on the snow the next morning.

Nadine had been in touch with the investigation team in Montreal. Moralès had read the contents of her file twice over before returning to his cabin, going down to the gym, spinning the pedals on a bike and telling himself he wasn't strictly going nowhere since the boat was in motion, having a shower, going round in circles and deciding to head up to the lounge, where he found Érik, sitting alone in a shirt bearing a giant orchid pattern and waving to him.

Érik looked excited and seemed to be hiding something under the table. Here and there, the skiers who had been hoping to slide on the snow every day that week were wandering around, playing cards, joining voices to sing the choruses of popular songs, looking out at the shore, to the horizon, waiting as best they could.

'So, have you written to Simone?'

Joaquin said nothing.

Érik seemed disheartened. He took a sip of sparkling water, then launched into a tirade he had apparently learned by heart. 'Simone Lord, she's rich from her parents. Well enough off, anyway, to not have to work.'

'How do you know that?'

Interrupted, but not sidetracked as such, Érik smoothed his thin moustache. 'I had a thing with her sister, one year … She was passing through the Gaspé, and you know how I like to service and protect the tourists. Anyway, I – how should I put it? – served as a bit of a confidant as well as a guide to Suzie Lord. She told me their parents had sold some land up in the Laurentians and that had guaranteed some sort of income for her and Simone. She owns a little yoga studio, herself. You should see how flexible Suzie Lord is.'

His eyes widened to an immensity that reflected the lasting impression left by a contortion as deep, inverted and inimitable as the scorpion pose.

'Simone could have stayed at home, meditated and signed petitions about the environment. Found a husband, procreated, eaten sushi. But no. She was one of the first women to train for the coast guard. After that, she decided to become a fisheries officer and save the wildlife. And still she keeps going, in spite of the fishermen and their barbs.'

'Why?'

A focused Érik Lefebvre was now looking for something to touch, take, stack. Joaquin had seen him engage in this ritual several times before – assembling a collection of random objects for as long as it took to stabilise his thoughts.

'I've always thought Simone was a slave to a sort of over-achiever syndrome. Do you know what I mean? Women who take it upon themselves to be perfect their whole life long? But I was wrong.'

He stood up, went over to an adjacent table and retrieved an empty, dirty champagne glass, hesitated, set it on its side.

'There are some people who stand before the sea and feel compelled by it, like there's something sucking them in. You're like that too. You got divorced because you moved out to the Gaspé Peninsula. Because you found yourself looking out to the big blue and got sucked in by…' Lefebvre left his words hanging.

By the weightlessness, Moralès completed the sentence in his mind. Perhaps it was this he found so painful. Up until then, he had been sure he loved his wife, Sarah. It was with her that he had furnished a bedroom. Made a house a home. Built thirty years of his life. And what was left of that now?

Lefebvre got up again, brought back a piece of driftwood so straight and whittled you'd swear a sculptor had painstakingly worked it for hours, with tools that existed only in the ethereal workshop of the waves.

'Apparently, when people get divorced, they often think they don't know how to love. It was Nadine who said that to me yesterday. But it's not true. Of the two of us, I'm the one who's never learned to love.'

Érik looked astonished by his own observation, then dashed over to a corner of the room, as if he had already spotted, when he came in earlier, an object he could go and fetch later – predicting from the outset that it would be a part of an uncertain, yet probable, accumulation of things. Moralès couldn't see right away what the object was, because he had taken advantage of his friend's brief absence to lean across and sneak a peek at what Lefebvre was hiding on his seat. It was the poetry collection by Yves Boisvert – *Aimez-moi:* 'Love Me' – that the bookseller had sent for him.

Érik came back. He saw that Moralès had picked up the book, but didn't mention it.

'She's not an overachiever. She's a woman who's only ever met guys … who didn't know how to love. Right, well, I imagine that's what made her turn to the ocean. Because it was easier that way.'

He uncurled his fingers. It was an hourglass he had fetched.

'As for me, in spite of all the adventurous affairs that have swept me off my feet, I'm heading for forty with my hands empty. As if all I'd learned to do was tread water.'

Lefebvre was assembling the delicate objects he had accumulated with the precision of a goldsmith. Atop the dirty champagne glass, which lay immobile on its side, he balanced the piece of driftwood.

'I've always said I was waiting for the perfect woman, but we both know they're untouchable, don't we?'

Moralès stiffened. Hearts laid bare made him ill at ease.

'Érik, I think you've been spending too much time with Nadine.'

Lefebvre sighed. 'Well, she is a phenomenal psychologist.'

The slightest of angles in the wood held the piece in place. Lefebvre contemplated his montage before reaching for the hourglass.

Moralès gave him a wry smile. 'She herself is an untouchable woman.'

'I've noticed.'

Érik Lefebvre perched the hourglass delicately, time yet to pass topmost, in the middle of the piece of driftwood balanced atop the dirty champagne glass. The golden sand slipped slowly through the neck of glass.

He watched it flow and carried on as if his words were for that very object.

'Call Simone Lord, Moralès. Take what you know about love and share it. Because you're still thirsting for a little salt in your heart. And she needs some of that, too.'

Joaquin looked at the precarious installation, through which the numbered grains of fate appeared to be slipping, before stemming the flow of his friend's thoughts.

'Érik, can you ask the Vigneaults if they know anyone from the Magdalen Islands by the name of Michaël "Stone" Lapierre?'

The murder of Simone Lord

Jagged shards of voices, that was what had woken Simone. She was sure of it. She looked at her watch. It was nearly three in the morning. She had managed to sleep roughly an hour. In the cabin, all was silent. The trawler's generator was smothering the sounds from outside.

Exhausted from the long day and the biting cold, Simone had closed her eyes for a while. Out on deck, the men were still at work. At the end of the afternoon, they had decided to harvest another twenty-five seals, even if it meant working into the night. The forecast had confirmed the storm was heading their way, so they had made the most of the calm while they could.

She got up, crossed the darkness of the galley, went into the vestibule, to the bottom of the stairwell, to see where they were. The deck was flooded with harsh light. Through the porthole in the door, she saw Carpentier, crouched with his back to her, dressing a seal while, out on the ice, Painchaud and Lapierre were doing a round trip with the quad.

'Aye, we've got enough seals to fill our pockets!'

Simone flinched at Chevrier's voice, retreated two steps into the shadows. Behind her, she felt the rack of grimy coats hanging in the entryway. Something in his tone had given her goosebumps. He was yelling, on account of the noise, but there was a thread of tension in his voice too.

'Now all we have to do is tell Lapierre to call off his guy and head home to the Islands. We'll be there in two days.'

An urgency. There was an urgency in the skipper's voice. The same urgency Simone had sensed yesterday, when he was navigating too hastily through the ice, in search of the shore.

'He's not going to call anything off, for fuck's sake. I didn't come back from Mexico for three or four seal skins.'

Cautiously, Simone crept towards the door. Where were the two men? She could see only Carpentier, who had straightened up and was looking out to starboard. He stood among the animal carcasses, observing the altercation. The officer wanted to get out of the entryway, but the poacher turned her way, and she sensed he was scanning the darkness. Very, very slowly she retreated, huddling in a hollow of hanging coats. There was no way he could see her, she was almost certain; the powerful flood-lights on deck were all on, while the bulb above her head was dark. The porthole in the door must look like a mirror from the outside. Simone's hands were clammy. At last, Carpentier turned away and looked out over the starboard side of the vessel again.

'Aye, but you're not the one calling the shots, McMurray. I say, tomorrow night, we turn around and head home with our pockets full.'

Carpentier flexed a feisty jaw, as if he had a big chunk of stringy steak to chew on. He approached the two belligerents. Simone felt her way cautiously through the darkness, out of the vestibule, along the corridor beside the stairwell, to the end, where another porthole offered a glimpse of the starboard side of the deck, at the top of the steps leading down to the hold.

Blades in hand, McMurray and Chevrier argued as they butchered the meat into quarters and packed it into the big food bins. Stacks of carcasses were strewn all around them. The floor was awash with blubber.

Standing with his back turned, McMurray stiffened, gave Carpentier a look. A motionless Simone saw them exchange a nod of agreement. McMurray let go of the seal he was dressing. Overalls glistening with blood, he clambered over the slippery skins to Chevrier, who pulled his knife out of the carcass he was butchering. Simone shrank into the shadows.

'Now you listen to me, you great fat oaf. I told Lapierre we were going to do this detour, so we're going to do this damned detour, all right? I don't want any hassle with the…'

As his voice was drowned out by the approaching quad, McMurray left his words hanging.

Chevrier puffed out a proud chest. 'Aye, but Lapierre's the one who set up a rendezvous. Not you. You don't decide a damned thing around here.'

'You cheeky fu—'

Eight-Inch Painchaud burst into the frame. 'Oi! You're not getting paid to chit-chat. Is that clear? Is that clear enough?'

In the harsh glare of the floodlights, Simone saw his sly smile souring to a sinister grimace. There was nothing left of his previous adolescent glee. Now he was every bit the deranged villain, the authoritarian psychopath. The others got the message, keeping their mouths shut and knuckling down to work again.

Suddenly, the door flew open. The officer froze, unsure of her next move. If it was Carpentier, and he had reason to come down to the hold, he was heading her way; he would find her and realise she'd heard everything. If she stayed there, huddled beneath the stairs to the wheelhouse, he would know she had witnessed the scene through the window. If she went down the other stairs and got caught in the engine room, she would have no excuse for being there. Discreetly, she craned her neck into the corridor to try and see who it was, and what he was doing. It was Carpentier, as she'd suspected. He took off his boots, ducked in, towards the galley.

Simone was petrified. She had to move, and fast. She had to get out of there. She ventured a cautious step forwards, then another. Silently, she made her way to the foot of the stairs. It was too late to go back to her bunk. She tiptoed up the steps, found herself in the dimly lit wheelhouse. Hopefully no one had been up there in the short time she had been snoozing in her bunk and then slinking about, so no one would know she'd been on the move and suspect she might have heard something she shouldn't have. She could hear Carpentier back in the vestibule.

He opened the door and yelled out, 'The girl's not in her bed!'

A shiver ran through Simone. Through the window of the wheelhouse, she saw McMurray snap his head up. His overalls were slick with blood, and in the harsh light, his eyes were full of fury.

'Find her!'

Carpentier's heavy footsteps came up the stairs. Simone hurried to lie down on the leather bench and turned on her side so she had her back to the room, trying desperately to calm her breathing and pretend she was fast asleep.

The poacher was in the wheelhouse now. Simone heard him turning on his feet, looking around, like a man under stress. She heard him catch a breath. He'd found her, she knew it. Without a sound, he went back down the stairs, opened the door again.

'It's all right. She's fallen asleep upstairs.'

Simone didn't register the response, only a movement. Carpentier must be putting his boots on again. He went outside.

Officer Lord sat up with difficulty. Her body was shaking. She went to find the satellite phone. The device wasn't where it should have been. Neither was the VHF transmitter. She dug frantically in her bag, grabbed her mobile. Switched it on, prayed the battery wasn't dead. It was working, but her hopes were dashed. No signal. She switched the device off. *Think. Think, Simone Lord!* She switched her phone on again. If the device had been able to receive messages when they passed Souris, maybe it could send them too, when the trawler moved again and came within range of a telecommunications tower.

Quickly, she drafted a note:

Jean-Mathieu, departed Magdalen Islands, gone sealing in Pictou vicinity. Crew planning detour to pick up drug shipment.

She added their GPS coordinates, then hesitated. Who should she send the message to? She realised her superior might be in on the plan. He had asked her to go aboard at the last minute. Why? She gasped with horror as the unthinkable dawned on her. Her superiors were not expecting her to return to land.

Simone sat heavily down on the stool. She would write a report on the seal harvest that would allow the *Jean-Mathieu* to dock and unload its cargo of drugs, buried in the seal pelts and meat, with impunity, while the police would busy themselves investigating her disappearance at sea. She couldn't see any other possibility. Her superiors had sacrificed her. Her hands were shaking so much, she struggled to locate Moralès in her contacts and press the send button. Her message stayed where it was, with the addition of a red exclamation mark. Still no signal. Again, and again, she pressed send. In vain.

She pulled herself together. She had another resource: Bernard Chevrier. He had figured out what was going on. That was why he had tried to persuade her to jump ship, she realised. She was not alone. He was the skipper. He would protect her.

Noises, more noises, outside. The quad motored away. Shards of voices. She switched off her phone, stuffed it in her bag. Terrified, she decided to stay in the wheelhouse for the rest of the night. If the men were working shifts on deck, she'd rather avoid being in the cabin and risk being cornered by McMurray and Carpentier. She had left her coat down below. Her flick knife was in the pocket. She rummaged in her bag, retrieved a little penknife, courtesy of Fisheries and Oceans Canada, folded the blade open. She hoped she wouldn't need it. Still, she would remain on her guard. Too panicked to venture over to the rear window, she returned to the bench and lay, with a lump in her throat, and waited, in a night laden with menace, for the light to return.

During the hours that separated her from the sunrise, Simone heard the hunters coming and going. Exhausted, paralysed by fear, she stayed there, huddled on the leather bench, until dawn. Only at first light did it occur to her, with horror, that not once in the whole night had the skipper come up to the wheelhouse. Chevrier had gone out there, and failed to return.

&

Moralès stepped into his skis. Nothing. No fresh news from Montreal. The lead investigators on the case no longer needed him, it seemed. Lefebvre had returned to the cabin empty-handed the previous day.

No, the Vigneaults knew no one of that name.

Joaquin was still on holiday – he would be back on the snow today – but his heart was no longer in it. These package holidays, the stillness of the ice, the nostalgia of reading, clearly were not for him.

Simone had not replied to the email he had spent a long time writing the other night. When Érik had told him her story, Joaquin hadn't had the heart to say he had already contacted her. He had switched off his phone and left it in the cabin to avoid waiting, like a restless teenager, for a missive that might not come.

Nadine watched her old friend distance himself impatiently from their group. That was the way he had always been, devouring the hours, as if life wasn't enough for him. Suffering the things he couldn't understand, in himself and in the hearts of those around him. In the minds of the criminals he chased. He never set out only to arrest a villain, but to grasp that villain's story and motives; to bring to light what could lead a man or a woman to take the most sordid of life's paths. She saw Érik Lefebvre, who gave her a wave before moving ahead to join Joaquin. She envied her former colleague for finding such a loyal friend so quickly.

The pack were now on their way, and the two police officers were keen to get out in front and blaze the trail, calling out to warn the skiers ahead they planned to pass them on their left. Nadine let them get on with it. She wanted to ski at her own pace. She was supposed to be on holiday, but felt heavy with the weight of that teenager in a coma, those dealers who stuffed powder up youngsters' noses to pay for their gold chains so they could swagger around the streets, kidding themselves they were kingpins. She was heavy with those who died for a few kilos of cocaine. With the responsibility of catching the shitsters – that was what she called them – and sentencing them to rot between four walls, oozing with the misery they had peddled.

She was mindful of her anger, but also surprised to find that she carried her profession like a duty to humanity. She focused on the movement of her body, on her skis sliding in the tracks in the snow, on her arms thrusting the poles, on the contrast between the warmth of her breath and the winter cold penetrating her clothing. She observed the group, the skiers in front of her, and was surprised to be searching not for Moralès, but for Lefebvre.

Joaquin had skied away from the wharf in Chandler with the devil on his heels, at too swift a pace, as if he was running away from something. He could hear the friction of his skis on the snowy surface and those of someone skiing behind him without trying to pass. Probably Lefebvre. They were well ahead of the group. The two of them skied along the shore, guided by the little flags planted by the organisers to mark the way.

To their right, a perfect carpet of ice creaked in the Baie des Chaleurs. Leaving Chandler behind, all the skiers could see was the white landscape, impeccable and silent. Through their ski glasses, the luminous expanse was tinged a warm yellow, sliced by the trees and their shadows with delicate lines of a greenish shade of blue.

🦭

'Yoo-hoo, little miss singer. Time to get back to work.'

McMurray was in the wheelhouse. Standing right there, in the stairwell. Simone shuddered.

'Need a poke to get yourself going?'

'No. I'm coming.'

He stood waiting, with his hat on, for Simone and her trembling hands to get up. Why was he waking her?

'You're already dressed.'

'I dozed off up here.'

'Aw, poor little officer…'

McMurray motioned for her to go ahead of him and followed her down to the galley. The day, in the persistent stillness of the sea ice, seemed reluctant to brighten. The wind, after settling down for the night, had turned. Picking up from the west, it was an omen of foul weather.

Carpentier the poacher stirred, directing a look of anxious silence at Simone. Lapierre came in. It was obvious he had just woken up too.

'Is Chevrier up in the wheelhouse?'

The officer froze. She shook her head a hard no.

'Can someone tell me where Chevrier is?

The men around the table shrugged their shoulders and drank their coffee, and Simone felt her spine stiffen with a trickle of icy perspiration. She didn't move, tried to act like it had nothing to do with her; she barely slowed her mechanical chewing of the toast that was losing its taste in her mouth.

'You're sure he's not up there?'

Simone struggled to swallow her mouthful. She rubbed one dry lip against the other. The silence was total. The hunters were staring at her through eyes red with either fatigue or the sight of blood.

McMurray leaned close to her. 'Sure you've not hidden him in your bed?'

Lapierre gave the men a stern look before hurrying out on deck, then came right back, cursing. 'What the fuck? Is there no one who can tell me what the hell's been going on here?'

Carpentier and McMurray didn't seem surprised. Eight-Inch, all greasy hair and white nostrils, emerged from the lavatory in haste. The three others filed outside as if mechanically following orders. Simone, in spite of having worked with the police on several investigations, remained seated, stunned by the deafening bell she could hear tolling on not only her career, but her life as well.

'Siiiimooone! Come here, Simone.'

McMurray was calling her with a voice of ill intent, the sugar-coated bark of a vicious dog owner about to punish his bastard mutt for chewing his work boots.

Simone felt like her body was laden with lead. It pained her to get up, step into the vestibule, don her boots and coat the way a convict pulls on prison scrubs, and go out on deck. The ocean was like an overexposed photograph; for a moment the hostile, immaculate white of the shroud of ice blinded her. She squinted. Then the red trails appeared, drawing lines of contrast from Pictou Island to the loading ramp. The trawler was still stuck fast, though the ice was breaking up in the distance to the east. The deck had been given a semblance of a cleaning. The men had hosed it down to wash away the blood of the seals. The tools, tidied away, were waiting for the next bout of action. More than a hundred seals, already butchered and tagged, were taking a dip in the cooling tanks while their pelts were soaking overboard.

Simone stumbled to her left, to the starboard side of the deck, where some hours earlier, in the shadows, she had witnessed the altercation between McMurray and the skipper.

The four hunters stood in a circle around the macabre scene.

What the officer noticed first were Bernard Chevrier's eyes, turned on her. Eyes bulging in stupefaction and horror, veiled with a film of whitish, translucent gel. Then his face emerged, mouth half open, stretched over the top of the neck warmer, as if the man had spoken as he expired. From beneath the skewed hat sprang a lock of black hair, tangled and frosty, pointed bizarrely skyward. The body of the skipper, dressed in his apron, was lying half prone beneath one of the hydraulic winches, in a pool of frozen blood that might have been mistaken for a seal's. His left arm was bent back on itself, as if he were trying to stem the bleeding at his neck, while the right had broken his fall. The position of the body, Simone realised, told the story of the murder.

The killer had clearly severed an artery. The blood had spurted forcefully, surrounding this husband and father in vast scarlet arabesques that spread across the metal of the deck and bulwarks.

'What were you up to last night then, little miss singer?'

McMurray cackled spitefully until Carpentier the poacher cut in.

'Hey, let's not go around pointing fingers without any proof.'

'I had no reason to kill Chevrier. What about you, Carpentier?'

'Are you crazy? I've no reason to kill anyone.'

In the midst of a woolly, nauseous fog, Simone realised this was the first time she had heard Carpentier defend himself with words. Michaël Lapierre shook his head in anger. Evidently, his plans for this trip hadn't accounted for a murdered skipper.

Painchaud flailed his hands frantically, his nervous movements accentuated either by the drugs or by the fright of seeing the corpse, it wasn't clear which. He was looking at Lapierre, as if he could conjure a solution out of nowhere. But Lapierre said nothing. He was glaring daggers at Carpentier and McMurray as they targeted the officer.

'Now you, on the other hand, little miss singer…'

'I've done nothing.' She stated it in a breath, barely a whisper. Nothing that would convince anyone in a courtroom.

McMurray's left shoulder rolled back in its socket. 'Stop messing around, officer. The coast guard guys told us you were a tough nut. And Carpentier here saw you pull a knife out of your bag.'

McMurray looked to the poacher to back him up. 'And just the other day, you were ready to slit my throat.'

'Anyone might think Chevrier pushed his luck too far.'

Simone gulped. 'Let's say we call the police and—'

'Nothing's working, not since yesterday.'

'I could never have—'

'Planted your knife in his throat?'

'*My* knife?'

McMurray smirked, the men stepped to one side and Simone inched cautiously closer to the body. Taking care not to step in the blood, she crouched down and felt a chill run through her. Sure enough, it was her knife, the one she concealed in her coat or kept by her mattress, the one with a spring-loaded blade, sticking out from the base of Chevrier's neck. So that was what Carpentier had gone to fetch, that night, when he crept in without a sound while she was hiding under the stairs. And that was how he had noticed Simone wasn't in her bunk.

'Plus, I'm sure those knives aren't legal in Canada…'

Still crouching, she shuffled back cautiously, but Carpentier gave her a vicious shove of the hip. Thrown off balance for a second, she stumbled forwards a step, then another, in spite of herself, imprinting the soles of her boots in Chevrier's frozen blood and, so she wouldn't fall, catching hold of the handle of the knife.

They skied through villages. Grand-Pabos, Petit-Pabos, then they veered to the northeast, through a forest of evergreens draped in thick blankets of snow and interspersed with silent fields. Érik Lefebvre's stride was so in sync with his friend's that for minutes at a time Joaquin could hear only a single sound with not even an echo, the swishing of his skis, punctuated by his breath and the beating of his heart. At times, the sliding of his colleague's skis repeated his own, then fell back into the cadence.

After a couple of hours, the men were the first to arrive in the village of Val-d'Espoir, which sat inland from Highway 132, the coast road Joaquin would often take when driving out to the tip of the Gaspé Peninsula. The detective had never set foot in this place before.

Surrounded by fields, the village school, rectory and church as small as a chapel stood tall in the light-filled silence of noon. Some of the villagers were out in front of the church, cheering the skiers on. Others seemed to spring from out of nowhere to block the trail.

'Come inside and warm up.'

'We've made you a bite to eat.'

Joaquin and Érik slowed in disbelief, then they saw the official Tour de Gaspé logo. This must be the scheduled lunch stop. They skied to a halt.

'Where are we going, exactly?'

'Inside the church.'

Pleasantly surprised, the men set their skis and poles aside and made their way up the five steps to double doors painted red. A volunteer pulled the handle and they entered a nave, where the pews had been uprooted and reconfigured around long tables dressed with paper tablecloths. By the choir, a hot buffet had been set up, complete with a bar topped with kegs of beer. Standing beside the kegs was Sébastien Moralès, Joaquin's eldest son. He stepped forwards with open arms and a genuine smile.

Behind him, the light of the sun shone through a stained-glass window, casting a multitude of bright, fragmented colours on the floor.

Sébastien arrived at his father's side.

'What are you doing here?' Joaquin asked.

'The microbrewery's a sponsor. I volunteered to bring the beer over. When I'm done, I've got some packing to finish. I'm moving out on Saturday, remember?'

Joaquin's ski glasses had fogged up in the heat. Sébastien plucked them off with two hands, lifted them, and rested them on his father's hat, while Joaquin tried to overcome his emotion and numb fingers and clumsily remove his gloves.

'I brought us a hip flask of tequila,' Sébastien said.

Joaquin took Sébastien in his arms for a long, heartfelt hug. Moralès senior had not cried often in his life, but in that moment, in front of his eldest son, he had trouble holding back the tears.

'Dad? You all right?'

Lefebvre said hello to Sébastien and came to his friend's rescue.

'Travel toys with our emotions.'

Joaquin smiled in response. 'You too? And here I was, thinking you were just a frivolous free spirit.'

Just then, the Vigneaults, followed by Nadine Lauzon, crossed the threshold of the nave.

'Yes, but … right, well…' Érik fell silent. He was staring at the psychologist, teetering from one leg to the other, with a hesitation his friend had not seen in him.

Joaquin turned to his son. 'Where's that hip flask of yours? I think it's time we had a drink.'

'Now, then, we'll have you tagging the pelts so we can get on with our work.'

With a tip of his chin, McMurray drew Simone's eyes to a pool of mush off to the port side of the prow, where the hides were soaking.

Carpentier the poacher, his face lighting up in a vengeful smile, gave a nod of approval. 'The wind's turned, so we should be on our way tonight when the tide comes in.'

'Who decided?' Michaël Lapierre, tight-lipped until then, had been watching the scene unfold like a man watching children play in the schoolyard, and trying to make sense of their games. 'Who decided to kill Chevrier and pin it on the fisheries officer?'

The two crooks kept their mouths shut. McMurray's involuntary shoulder did its thing.

Eight-Inch was mumbling in a frenzy. 'Wh-who did that on my boat?'

The Newfoundlander turned to Simone with an air of suspicion, but Lapierre was waiting to intercept him.

'You clown, you're not fooling anyone saying this fisheries officer's a killer. Not me, and not the police.'

Digging his hands into the pockets of a coat that obviously wasn't warm enough for a morning as glacial as this, Lapierre strode over to McMurray. He was barely any taller than the hunter, whose grubby excuse for a hat refused to cover his whole head, but he was visibly more menacing. The tattoos licking at his neck, his deeper-than-usual voice, his air of assurance and authority all made for an imposing presence.

'You do realise you've just dumped a dead body on a trawler that's going to be bringing fifty kilos of cocaine ashore? Do you really think we can just waltz up to the wharf with that?'

The men didn't answer.

'The boat's going to be searched from top to bottom because of you two fuckwits.'

Simone wished she'd heard none of that, but it was too late. The fifty kilos were already a sword of Damocles over her head. The one lifeline here was that Lapierre didn't want any bodies on board. She latched on to this idea. Maybe he would keep her alive.

Lucien Carpentier swallowed his pride, but McMurray flew into a rage.

'You don't get it at all. If we'd let him be, there would've been no detour.'

'What do you know, you fucking idiot?'

'He wanted us to head straight back to Cap-aux-Meules.'

'So you decided to kill him for that?'

'I decided what I felt like deciding. Now get off my bloody back.'

Lapierre nodded slowly. 'You pitch that overboard for me, all right. We'll say he fell, and the girl won't be accused of anything.'

Painchaud imitated and amplified the movement, flailing his head up and down like a disjointed puppet. 'Yeah, is that clear? Is that clear enough?'

Without waiting for an answer, Lapierre turned on his heels

and went in, followed closely by a Painchaud proud of getting the last word.

McMurray picked up his dignity and turned to Carpentier with an involuntary roll of his shoulder. 'Let's chuck him off the front so we're not tripping over him when we need the winch.'

Simone stood there petrified, in shock, as she watched the two men. They sauntered over to the body, each grabbed a boot and dragged the skipper to the bow, the way they had with the slaughtered seals. When they got there, they bent down to lift him up.

'Wait a sec, I'm taking his watch.' The poacher grasped the dead body by the wrist. The arm refused to budge; Chevrier had clutched a hand to his throat in a vain attempt to stop the bleeding.

'It's stiff as fuck.'

'Undo the strap.'

'What do you think I'm trying to do?'

Carpentier gave a victory cheer, stuffed the timepiece in his pocket. 'My boy'll have that. He likes big watches.'

The two men lifted the body carefully, to avoid getting themselves dirty, and tipped it over the rail, headfirst. Simone heard the sound of ice cracking. McMurray leaned overboard.

'He always was a hard-headed bastard, was Chevrier.'

Carpentier laughed like an idiot, and the men wiped their hands on the legs of their overalls.

'Better finish our breakfast.'

When they turned and saw Simone, she shuddered. She shouldn't have stayed there, hypnotised by the horror, watching these men behave like vultures. McMurray stared at her, then his slimy gaze wormed its way down her body, feeling for the curves of her breasts beneath her heavy coat, the kink of her hips, the buttocks he couldn't see, lingered at the tops of her thighs, where he'd have to force his way in a bit, like Carpentier had to force the arm to get the watch off, but maybe not so much, because the other guy had said she could be quite the singer.

Simone understood and, this time, she felt the fear, the violence of it, rising within her. She opened the door, hurried into the vestibule, tried to shut it behind her.

But McMurray was already there. He pushed the door, grabbed Simone from behind, shoved her up against the parkas hanging like hides from the hooks in the entryway. 'Right! Time for you to sing that lesson of yours this morning…'

With the palm of his right hand, he thrust her head into the waterproofs. Simone struggled, suffocating, squirmed against the wall, trying to wriggle free. In vain. McMurray slid his left hand around her waist, searching for the button of her trousers. Carpentier came in, caught a glimpse of the scene and skirted around it on his way into the galley.

He looked at Painchaud, who was slurping his yogurt.

'Women, they've no bloody place on a boat.'

'Why do you say that? We're gonna make use of ours.'

In the vestibule, McMurray was clawing at Simone's crotch, tearing the button off as he went, yanking the zipper down. In the zone now, he didn't speak, holding on to her as best he could as she fought to free herself or, at least, manage to breathe.

Simone heard the poacher chuckling in the galley.

'McMurray's sure making use of her now.'

With a smirk of satisfaction, Carpentier gave his inner thigh a stroke to show what he meant. Eight-Inch and his crazy laugh rasped back and forth like a saw. McMurray tugged Simone's trousers down to her knees, ripped her underwear open. He undid his belt, whipped out his weapon and perceived, in his right ear, the click of a rifle being cocked. He froze.

'No one touches the officer.'

Simone felt McMurray's dick deflate and hang limp against her buttocks. He backed away, opened his mouth to retaliate, but Lapierre got there first.

'You stick your fucking oar in just once, you kick off with that bullshit of yours for even a minute and I swear, you'll end up with a distress flare up your arse!'

McMurray clenched his teeth without saying a word. He was still holding Simone's head deep in the rack of coats.

Now Lapierre lowered his voice and parodied Painchaud in a whisper. 'Is that clear? Is that clear enough?'

The hunter released his prey, zipped up his fly, turned away. 'See, she can't even get a guy hard, for fuck's sake.'

He sidled off into the galley. Lapierre span around, keeping the gun trained on McMurray's back. He didn't look at Simone, spoke to her softly.

'Get dressed and go tag the pelts. Right now.'

Simone was shaking from head to toe. Her face was streaked with snot and tears. She pulled together her torn underwear as best she could, tugged her trousers up. Wiped fingers across her nose. Noticed a ferrous taste in her mouth. She had no idea if it was her lip, her cheek or her hand that was bleeding. It might even be Chevrier's blood. She zipped up her parka, went up to the wheelhouse to gather her things. When she came back down, Lapierre was still standing at the bottom of the stairs, gun in hand. Again, he spoke softly to her.

'Keep well clear of the guys. Or make sure you're not far away from me. All the time. Because even if you're not looking for trouble, trouble's going to find you.'

Officer Lord didn't answer. She went outside, shut the door, turned on the winch and pulled the line of pelts clear of the water, level with the deck. She crouched down, threaded a tag between the empty eyes of the first grey seal's skin. Tears fell on the creature's hide. She kept on tagging, filling out her report, her teeth chattering compulsively as she struggled to warm up.

In that moment just passed, Simone had understood that she was going to die. Her hours were numbered. She could start counting down. But which number should she start from? She didn't know. She kept on tagging. What drove a condemned woman to execute the tasks of her job to the letter? Why not give up now, walk a few hundred metres to the east, to the edge of the ice pack, slide between two floes and wait those few seconds for the hell to end, when the icy in-breath would make her lungs explode in a sea of frost, when her heart would cease to beat, frozen forevermore in the Northumberland Strait? Why carry on, move along to the next pelt, tag it, register it, log it in the report that would offer safe conduct for the traffickers, the killers? To what end? Her docility surprised her. Simone Lord had no survival plan in mind, no Machiavellian revenge strategy to hand. She had nothing. In the face of fear, obedience seemed to her the only possible way, but it was unlikely she would escape unscathed.

So she kept on tagging the seals. Like an overachiever.

She reflected on the decisions she had made that had led her here; she thought about her sister sitting on her meditation mat, surrounded by incense sticks burning at both ends. She reminisced about Moralès and regretted not telling him everything from the outset, during the investigation that past autumn. She regretted the blunder that had landed her in this exile, this punishment in the Magdalen Islands. Also and especially, as she tied another tag to a seal pelt, she regretted not calling Joaquin that winter, not reaching out, not reading the email he had sent the day before yesterday. Her tears became one with the ice that coated the trawler.

Later, when she went inside the boat again, she would read his message. What was it that made her want to carry on with this pathetic absurdity of a workday, while it would be far simpler, more of a relief, even, to end it all now?

A letter written by a man's hand.

ت

As it sank into the sea, the sun flooded the surface with a thick film of crimson cream and left the swell to beat it into stiff peaks. Joaquin wondered if Simone was admiring the splendour of the day's end from the vessel Lefebvre had confirmed she was aboard, the *Jean-Mathieu*. The wind was notching up; the storm would be upon them tomorrow. The ship had come down the coast to meet the skiers at the wharf in Percé and was preparing to set sail for Gaspé that evening to avoid getting stuck at a standstill again, this time because of the inclement weather.

Constable Érik Lefebvre came out on deck with the Magdalen Islanders and strode over to the detective, instantly cutting to the chase.

'Moralès, listen to this.'

He motioned for his friends to speak. The woman went first.

'We've been mulling over what you asked us. That guy you mentioned – Michaël "Stone" Lapierre – he might be Eudore's Normand's Michaël. He left the Islands, must have been twenty years ago…'

'Then I saw him, the other day, at the sealing course I was teaching.'

Réjeanne came to her husband's defence. 'He's not the one who handles the registrations. It's a secretary at the school.'

'There was one student who wouldn't stop moaning. He'd argue with me about everything, kept mouthing off that his old man never hunted that way. The angry type. It happens. Anyway, at one point, our guy raised his voice and said to him, "You're getting to be like a stomach ache. How much will it cost me for you to quit whining in my ear?" I'm pretty sure it was him. Lapierre.'

Moralès was jolted out of his daydream. 'When was this?'

'Couple of weeks ago.'

His wife clarified. 'The training finished two weeks ago.'

Moralès waited while they agreed on the date, then asked, 'Was he alone?'

'No. He was doing the course with Marco Painchaud.'

Réjean gave his wife a hesitant look. She returned a gentle nod of approval. The situation seemed critical, and keeping secrets would do no one any good.

'I told you about him the other night. His name is Marco, but his mates call him Eight-Inch. Apparently in his last year of high school he sniffed a line of coke eight inches long in the toilets. He's ... pretty hooked on the stuff.' Réjean went quiet, uncomfortable to be gossiping about a friend's nephew.

His wife carried on, so her husband wouldn't be the only one to blow the whistle on the kid. 'Eight-Inch was away a long time too, but he came back last spring. His uncle is Denis Éloquin. He's a good friend of ours. Réjean often goes out sealing with him.'

Her husband nodded, picked up where she left off, to show

he was prepared to see this through. 'Denis' sister walked out on Marco when he was a young lad. Ever since, Denis has taken it upon himself to look after his nephew.'

Moralès wasn't really interested in the Painchauds, father, son, uncle and all. 'And where do you think Lapierre is, then?'

'Well that's the thing. If you ask me, he's gone off with Painchaud on his uncle's boat. It's Bernard Chevrier, Denis' brother-in-law, who's skippering, because—'

'Gone off where?'

'To where the seals are.' Réjean hesitated, looked to his wife, who delivered the rest of the information for him.

'Aboard the *Jean-Mathieu*.'

Blood, guts and skulls were all that was left on the ice; the carcasses had been winched aboard, dressed, emptied by the men. The pelts and quartered meat from the day before had been bagged, then lowered into the hold compartments through the deck hatch.

When Simone had finished the tagging, Lapierre had told her to go up to the wheelhouse. From there she had kept a distant eye on operations, foregoing her monitoring of the slaughter this time. The hunters had returned to shore and worked until nightfall. The day's last and only ray of sunlight had flashed and fizzled between the weighty clouds and the frozen sea. One spark, then it had sunk like a stone. Simone had taken the time to pull herself together, to read and reread Joaquin's email, write a reply to him. But her message had bounced back; there was no signal.

Then, as if the detective's words had breathed courage into

her, she had decided to set a plan in motion. In spite of that one blunder she had made, she was one of those overachievers, as Lefebvre would say, who saw things through to the end. She wanted to be worthy of a man who deserved her.

The pack ice was crumbling away to the east. The hunters had finished their work. They winched the quad aboard, cleaned the deck.

Simone had been snooping; the rifles were all under lock and key. She suspected Lapierre had stashed all the weapons away to avoid losing control aboard the trawler. The emergency beacon had been disabled, the satellite phone and VHF transmitter were still nowhere to be found. All she had left was a penknife, a knife with a folding blade, to muddle her way through.

The hunters came in, took off their slaughtering gear, hung it up to dry in the small vestibule. They continued into the galley, and Lapierre shut the door behind them. Simone could hear a mad racket starting up in there. A clinking and clanking of pots and pans, cutlery, bottles. The voices were thickening, the booze making the crew heavy.

Around nine that night, she tiptoed down the stairs. No matter how much banging and crashing she did, the men were making such an infernal din, they wouldn't hear a thing. She pulled on her outdoor gear and went out on deck. The sky was packed with dense, dark clouds, the west wind was up. And she was sweating. She waited a moment, adapting to the darkness, and gradually saw her visual bearings reappear.

The men had lifted the gangway up against the boat, parallel to the hull, but without bringing it completely on board, as if they were planning on going back out to hunt. They had secured it well, however, in case of emergency. Simone made her way to the winch controls. She reached a hand out. If she got caught, she could say she'd felt like stretching her legs on the ice. That would sound strange, though. No, she would say she felt sick and had gone out to puke. She set the winch in motion.

The gangway lowered, but only partway, stopping about a metre above the ice. Someone had wrapped a chain around it so it wouldn't go any lower. Too bad, Simone would have to use her arm strength to haul herself back aboard. She grabbed a length of line, ventured onto the suspended ramp and jumped down onto the ice. Cautiously, she advanced towards the bow. Suddenly, she froze. The ice was starting to break up near the hull. Chevrier's body was half floating, half reclining on a chunk. The officer still had a metre and a half to cover before she could reach him.

Simone retraced her steps, hauled herself up onto the metal ramp. And felt a sharp pain in the palm of her hand. The broken rod in the railing had gone through her glove. Blood was trickling down her fingers. That sharp, jagged metal was a menace snarling at her in the night. She gave her hand a shake, kept on climbing. Up on deck, she swung a leg over the guardrail and clambered up to the roof of the vestibule.

Inside, the music was pumping, the portholes were pulsating to the beat; the crew were partying. Officer Lord leaned over the white plastic housing strapped to the roof. Inside it was the life raft. She undid the straps, mustered all her strength and managed to tip the housing overboard. As it plunged to the frozen sea, it bounced off the guardrail with a bang.

Simone paused for a moment. Nothing suggested the men had heard the sound. She crept down again onto the ice. The impact had cracked the housing open. Fumbling her way ahead, Simone managed to push the cracked plastic shell across the ice until it touched the water. She pulled the tab, and the raft inflated in an instant. The wind filled it like a kite, she struggled to keep hold of it. She reached for her penknife to cut through and tear off the roof fabric so that it wouldn't get in her way. It flew away in the squall. She tossed the line onto the raft, leapt aboard and braced an oar against sheets of ice to paddle the short distance to the skipper's body. The harsh wind whipping around her, it was all she could do to keep the raft in one spot.

Chevrier's body lay in a crooked position. The fall had broken his shoulder. Quickly, Simone took photos with her phone, then looped the line under the body's arms and hips, the way she'd learned when she worked for the coast guard and they had to pull an unresponsive casualty out of the water. She tied it tight, threw one end of the line up to the starboard bow scupper, ran it through the roller. She did the same thing with the other end, passing it through the portside roller. Tugging on both ends, one at a time, she managed to hoist the body tight to the hull, just below the prow, and secure it under the scuppers.

The pack ice was giving way, and fast, breaking up all around her, the windblown chop heckling at her flimsy craft. She hurried to knot the line, but something made her stop. Over the whipping of the wind and the waves, she could hear a man whistling on the deck. The tune was drawing dangerously near. Her heart pounding, Simone huddled against the hull, tucked her head beneath Chevrier's dead body. Suddenly, the life raft began to deflate. She must have snagged it on something. From right above her head, almost, a stream of piss arced overboard.

'Fucking hell. The ice is breaking up.'

Hearing the splash of his urine in the water, Lucien Carpentier, the lanky poacher, understood in spite of his drunkenness that the trawler would soon be floating free.

He finished pissing and Simone heard him go back inside. Quick as she could, she braced the life raft's puny oar against chunk after chunk of ice to punt her evermore precarious craft back towards the gangway. No sooner had she sprung out onto the ice, than the raft sank beneath the surface. If the *Jean-Mathieu*, heeling a little to one side, broke free of the ice now, it would roll hard to port, then to starboard, before it found its watery balance. She only had three steps left to go. She took them at a run and gave it her all to leap up onto the gangway. But she overdid it. On landing, she lost her balance and felt a searing pain surge through her right thigh. She had impaled herself on the jagged end of the broken metal rod. The officer calmed her breathing, kicked her foot down hard to free her leg. She bent double with the pain. A geyser of thick blood spurted from the wound. She limped aboard, just as someone on the inside switched on the floodlights at the bow and the stern of the vessel.

Simone made for the door. The wheelhouse was now brightly lit and the music had been muted. She ducked inside, doffed her coat in the vestibule, dragged her leg across the galley, into the bathroom. Leaving a broad smear of blood in her wake. She shut herself in the small room, tugged off her boots, tore her trouser leg open, grabbed the first-aid kit. Her head was spinning.

'What's wrong? Simone?'

Lapierre knocked at the door, she opened up. Her skin was clammy. He came in. He hadn't drunk much, by the looks of it. As he surveyed the damage, she explained herself.

'I went outside to pee because you said to steer clear of everyone, but then Carpentier came out. I was scared, I tried to hide, but—'

He cut her off. 'Show me.'

He leaned over her thigh, opened the first-aid kit.

'We won't be able to evacuate you, Simone. You're going to have to hang tight if you don't want to bleed to death.'

She nodded. He handed her a clean towel.

'Put that in your mouth and bite down hard. I'm going to disinfect this for you.'

She did what he said. Lapierre poured disinfectant onto the wound. It stung so sharply, Simone clung tight to whatever she could: the sink, Lapierre's shoulder, sinking her nails into his tattoos. Gently, he lifted away her fingers, placed a towel over the wound in lieu of a dressing.

'Hold this.'

He stepped out, returned a second later holding a bottle. She hated whisky.

'Here, you have a swig of this while I…'

He didn't have a chance to finish his sentence as the boat pitched wildly to the port side. Lapierre was thrown against the wall, Simone just managed to hang on, caught the litre bottle he'd let go of.

'You all right?' Simone asked him.

'Yeah.'

'Hold on, it's going to tip back the other way.'

And it did. The trawler rolled hard to starboard, then swung from one side to the other before settling back into its navigation stance at last. Freed from the ice, the *Jean-Mathieu* would soon be on its way.

'Good catch,' Lapierre said to her.

Simone took a swig of whisky, while Lapierre dug around in the first-aid kit.

'Take another one. I've not often had to stitch someone up in my life, and I didn't learn how to do it at school. This is probably going to hurt like hell.'

Powder

The trawler had been crawling painfully along the strait for some hours when Simone left the cabin and dragged her leg across the galley floor.

She had refused to have Lapierre try and stitch her leg and had settled for a tight dressing instead. However, she had asked him to switch bunks with her, since his was on the bottom. He had lifted her bags down for her, as well as her pillow and bedcovers. And hung a sheet as a curtain so McMurray would be less tempted to jump on top of her. Then Simone had fallen asleep, crippled by the exhaustion and the pain.

Now she sat at the bottom of the stairs to eavesdrop on what was happening in the wheelhouse. Up there, a tense silence was monopolising the space, interspersed with bad ideas.

'That's not the only thing. How are we supposed to go ashore without landing ourselves with an inspection?' Lapierre was anxious, and angry. 'Find a solution, you clowns, because I swear I'm about to blow your heads off.'

A surly McMurray was sticking to his guns. 'She'll get the blame if the four of us stand up as witnesses and say we saw her kill Chevrier.'

'Four fucking goons or a Fisheries and Oceans Canada officer; who do you think the police are going to believe?'

The sea had been rough for the last couple of hours. Buffeted by the wind and the swell, the trawler was struggling to make headway. Carpentier was concentrating at the helm. When he spoke, his sentences were left suspended as he turned the wheel to avoid nose-diving into a trough, then his words found their flow again. 'No one has to blame the girl. All we have to say is he fell overboard. Easily done, in a storm like this.'

'Yeah. That's what we'll do. Is that clear?' Painchaud's voice was short on confidence. His linguistic twitch floundered into a vague mumble.

An aggressive McMurray took another stab. 'But that singer of ours is gonna have to say the same thing...'

The bitch had slipped between his fingers again, and he couldn't stomach the fact.

Michaël Lapierre didn't give a shit. It wasn't the officer he was worried about. He was intending to pay her off. He knew from experience what people would do, given the choice between a generous price and a threat. Plus, he'd already started softening her up. 'What's the procedure when someone falls overboard?'

It was Carpentier the poacher who explained it. 'You have to call the coast guard and conduct a search.'

'So we're going to have the coast guard on our backs?'

'Not in this weather. We'll have to go round in circles, like we're looking for him. They'll track us on the radar.'

'We won't be able to scoot off to Newfoundland then, if they're watching us.'

'We'll disconnect the beacon. I'd do that every now and then when I was out doing business. I just said it was on the blink.' That was a euphemism of convenience for Carpentier, who had always deftly avoided the term 'poaching'.

'Can we simulate a breakdown?'

'Yes. We get out of the strait, call the coast guard, say we've got a man overboard, then we circle around two or three times to make it look like we're searching. After that, we disconnect the beacon and the radio, as if we had a power outage, then we scoot off to Newfoundland. On the way back, we'll come through the same zone, plug the stuff back in and say we didn't make for land right away because we couldn't find our guy.'

The trawler climbed a wave face. Carpentier steered it sideways down the other side. Still crunching through an icy carpet, the boat ascended another roller before Michaël Lapierre agreed.

'That sounds doable.'

'Just have to make sure all the phones and GPS's are switched off, because they'll be trying to track us and scrambling rescuers. Better make sure the girl doesn't give away our location.'

Lapierre agreed with that. 'I'll see to it. When we're not far from the Islands, we'll radio for the medics to give her treatment. She's bleeding a lot.'

'A woman on board's nothing but trouble.'

'No. Because this might mean they forget all about inspecting the boat. It'll buy us time to offload the stash in peace.'

Painchaud's presence had dwindled to feeble mumblings of 'Is that clear enough?' that were neither here nor there. Lapierre didn't ask him for his opinion. Instead, he turned to McMurray, who had been following the conversation without a word.

'That woman, the fisheries officer, she's our passport. I don't want anyone laying a finger on her. We've got to be careful.'

The order met with silence. McMurray clenched his jaw. Carpentier contorted his tongue in his mouth.

'How long before we're out of the strait?'

Simone didn't wait around to hear the answer. She headed back to the galley, then continued her laborious walk to the sleeping quarters. She had to prepare herself.

It was more than twenty minutes before Michaël Lapierre came knocking on the wood frame of her bunk.

'Are you awake?'

'Hold on.'

Simone sat up, pulled the covers over her injured leg.

'All right.'

He lifted the makeshift curtain.

'You've got a fever.'

It wasn't a question. Simone's body was drenched in sweat.

Outside, the storm had worsened a notch. The boat was still battling the sea, giving her no respite. The dressing was still saturated with blood. It was a good thing Carpentier knew what he was doing at the helm.

Simone heard the door open and bang in the wind before slamming shut again.

Lapierre went to the window for a look out on deck, came back. 'Looks like Eight-Inch needs some air.'

That was why she hadn't heard him chiming in to the conversation a little earlier. Recovering from the past night's excesses, he was too ill to even laugh like mad. It wasn't hard for her to picture him. He probably couldn't hold his balance well enough to stick his head out over the railing. Simone was right: he was puking right on the deck, spewing big chunky jets, explosive bursts diluted by the spray and, thank heavens, washed overboard.

Lapierre knelt on the floor so he could stay at Simone's height without falling. His proximity made it easier for her to get a good look at the claws escaping from the collar of his shirt and reaching up both sides of his neck. The tattoos were bluish and unsightly. Not the embellishments middle-class folk pay to have inked in the window of a fashionable tattoo studio, no; rather the marks men would perch on the edge of a prison cot to etch into each other.

'We'll be as quick as we can getting you back to shore.'

'We should be getting back tonight.'

'You know very well that we won't, Officer Lord. You heard what's happening. We're going on a detour. We have a package to pick up. If you help me, I'll give you double what I'm giving the guys. A hundred grand. I'm not crazy. I saw you didn't like working with those coast guard dickheads. Can't be any better with Fisheries and Oceans; they didn't even give you any backup. Have a think about it. It's enough cash to bankroll a fair bit of time off.'

'Where are we going?'

'Don't worry about that. We'll be on our way back to the Islands tomorrow night.'

Simone's body was burning up. And she was still losing blood. The bandages were struggling to stem the bleeding.

'What's the story with the skipper?'

'It wasn't me who killed Chevrier. I would have paid him off. A dead man causes way more trouble than a well-paid one who's alive. And he was all right, I thought, Chevrier. A good guy. It was Carpentier who did him in with McMurray.'

Her mouth dry, she nodded. 'And me? What are you going to do with me?'

'Here, on this piece of paper, I've written how many hides we took down to the hold a while ago.'

He had come by earlier to fetch a bag of tags from Simone. Together with McMurray and Painchaud, he had finished stacking the pelts and the meats while Carpentier the poacher stayed at the helm.

'Now, for everything to go smoothly, you're going to give me your phone, your report, all your official stuff.'

She pointed to the work bag at her feet. 'It's in there.'

Lapierre reached for the messenger bag, unzipped it, had a look inside, pulled out a pad, leafed through it.

'You're going to help me keep the inspectors away from the wharf when we dock. OK?'

She nodded.

He added a few handwritten notes to the report she had been working on since the beginning of the week. 'Sign here.'

It pained her to do it.

The last thing Lapierre wanted was for the boat to be inspected from top to bottom. They'd lost a man at sea, so he was hoping the officer would manage to divert the attention of whoever would be investigating so that no one would inspect the cargo. Simone didn't have that kind of power, but he didn't know that. He put the pad back in the bag, rummaged through it.

'Where's your phone?'

'I don't have one.'

He gave her a hard stare to see if she was telling the truth.

She held his gaze. 'I left it at home. I never need it when I'm at sea.'

'I'm still going to check.'

Bracing himself against the upper bunk, he picked up Simone's travel bag, tipped out all her things, repacked it all any which way. Maybe she was being honest. He couldn't remember seeing her with a phone. Suddenly the trawler pitched down violently. The hull slammed into a trough, then the bow lifted to the crest of a new summit.

Thrown off balance, Lapierre rolled to one side. He got up, cursing. 'Fuck's sake.'

Lying in her soaking bunk, Simone flexed her sarcastic tongue. 'Poor you. Careful you don't hurt yourself.'

Lapierre pursed his lips, glared at her. 'Why don't you get off my back?'

She blinked her haggard eyes half open. 'Maybe because I'm caught up in this scheme of yours whether I like it or not, and it might be the death of me.'

He sighed, turned his head one way and then the other, indecisive. 'OK. Maybe I shouldn't have left the Islands, gone selling drugs and getting up to my neck in debt. But now there's a bloody knife at my throat. Tell me, officer, what would you do in my place?'

He paused, then carried on without giving her a chance to reply. 'Forget it. You'd never find yourself in my place. Do you know why?'

Simone could hear Lefebvre's refrain in her mind – *because you're an overachiever* – but she kept her mouth shut.

'Because you lot, you folk who toe the line, you don't take drugs, you stay on the right side of the tracks and you only make the right decisions.' The trawler rolled, and Lapierre lost his balance again.

Simone's head was spinning. Through the fog of the fever, she whispered a reply. 'Look at me, Lapierre. Do you really think I've been making the right decisions lately?'

A second's silence, then the drug runner leaned close to her. 'I would have rather you hadn't come aboard, Simone, but here you are. Help me out here. All right? I won't let McMurray come anywhere near you. But don't you go dying on me.'

He let the curtain fall and took his leave as another savage shivering shook through Simone Lord. She hoped the body was holding fast at the prow, that the captain wouldn't abandon the ship.

ﾐ

It had turned out to be a long slog back up the coast from Percé to Gaspé for the ship carrying the cross-country skiers. Close to shore, the short, choppy waves had some heft to them and were rocking the boat like a humble walnut shell. The captain had been forced to steer offshore, make a detour in an attempt to smooth the waters. Propping up the bar with their Magdalen Islanders' pride, Réjean and Réjeanne Vigneault were muttering that it was a bit rough out there as they sipped their beer. Meanwhile, dozens of passengers were now green around the gills and had abandoned their windowless cabins, where they felt shaken like sardines in a can, and lay prone on the floor of the lounge, the bar, the cafeteria instead.

A hellishly nauseous Nadine Lauzon had opened her cabin door to her new nurse, Érik Lefebvre, who was only too happy to bring her water, hold the bucket, mop her brow.

'Right, well, I hope this'll set me up nicely for a psychoanalysis session or two, Freudian or not. I've got a couch especially for the purpose at home.'

Seeing his colleague feeling sick, but still smiling and in good hands, Moralès himself had taken care of calling Doiron.

'The weather's too bad for us to despatch a team from Montreal out to sea. Not to the Islands, either. I'll inform the local SQ detachment. You see what you can do from the Gaspé side,' his former boss had said.

Moralès had been cursing the wind and the ship's slow progress. Fortunately, when the vessel entered Gaspé Bay, a natural refuge from the vicious northeaster, the pitching and rolling had eased. The docking manoeuvres had still taken a while, however. The captain hadn't wanted to be too rough on the passengers, the crew or the ship.

It was past midnight when Lefebvre, Lauzon and Moralès

had at last been able to disembark. They had jumped straight into the cars the men had left on the quayside before their flight to Montreal, and raced off to the coast-guard station in Rivière-au-Renard.

On his way into the sleeping village, Moralès passed by Corine's auberge, where he had stayed the previous autumn during the investigation into the death of Angel Roberts. A snowdrift had blown across the driveway, blocking access to the front door. That was where Simone had abandoned an origami creation on the table in his apartment, where they had shared a meal in the kitchen that had just closed for the off-season. The auberge was conspicuously deserted. Driving past, he saw the lifeless sign inviting travellers to enquire elsewhere.

He turned off the road, parked in the yard behind the coast-guard station. Before he got out of his car, before anyone was looking, he checked to see if Simone had messaged him. No. No answer.

The wind stormed into the car, ripping the door from his hand. He caught it just in time and swung it shut, then hurried over to the entrance, head down against the blowing white gusts.

Two of the three duty officers were sound asleep on their respective sofas when Detective Moralès, Constable Lefebvre and forensic psychologist Lauzon blustered into the coast-guard building. The officers woke with a start, scrambled to their feet, ready to stand to attention and jump into their rescue boat. The third was keeping watch, tracking the positions of vessels at sea on a computer screen. He raised an eyebrow in surprise and greeted Lefebvre like a familiar face.

'We need to locate a boat from the Magdalen Islands that's gone out sealing. The *Jean-Mathieu*.'

The coast-guard officer pointed to the screen as if he were already on the case.

'There it is. Just on its way out of the Northumberland Strait, heading northeast. I was just watching it, as it happens. The weather's foul out that way right now.' He pointed to a blue dot on the screen.

Moralès stepped closer. 'Can we contact them?'

'Only the nearest coast-guard station can. That's the crew in Souris.'

'Put me in touch with them.'

'Tell me what you want to say and I'll pass the message on.'

'No. I want to talk to them myself.'

The guy nodded, but wasn't happy to have someone interfering in his domain. He put on a headset equipped with a microphone, plugged another into a console, handed it to the detective. Then he initiated contact with the Souris station.

A clear, alert voice responded straightaway. 'Officer Couture speaking.'

'Hi Dave, it's Francis in Rivière-au-Renard. I've got a police detective, Moralès, here with me, and he's wanting to contact a trawler that's out sealing on your patch. The *Jean-Mathieu*.'

The officer went on to indicate the trawler's GPS coordinates. The voice on the other end of the line acknowledged receipt, and Moralès was given the go-ahead to speak.

'We have serious reason to believe that a female Fisheries and Oceans Canada officer is in danger aboard the *Jean-Mathieu*. We need you to contact the vessel for us.'

'OK. Ready when you are.'

Moralès looked to Nadine, signalled for her to take the headset from the coast-guard officer beside him. The officer handed it over with a cold glare.

Lefebvre intervened, in spite of himself. 'Better watch your way with women, eh, otherwise people might think you've got some unresolved issues with your mother.'

The officer shrugged his shoulders with a sneer. Nadine put the headset on.

'Officer Couture, my colleague here, forensic psychologist Nadine Lauzon, is going to dictate word for word what you have to communicate to the vessel.'

'All right…'

Nadine took things over from there. 'The crew mustn't know that we've got our eye on them. What do you say when you contact a trawler in a storm?'

'We never do that. If the guys are sticking to their fishing plan, I don't see why we'd give them any hassle. Why are you after them? What's the girl done?'

Nadine wasn't going to answer any untimely questions like that. 'Listen, you're going to initiate contact with the skipper and ask him if everything's all right on board. Tell him it's all part of your new routine.'

He agreed. 'OK. I'll make contact, then you tell me what you want me to ask them.'

The detective and the psychologist could hear Couture calling the vessel.

'*Jean-Mathieu, Jean-Mathieu, Jean-Mathieu*, this is Souris Coast Guard. Acknowledge. Over.'

A long silence followed. Once, twice Officer Couture repeated his request. Joaquin was holding his breath.

'I don't get it, the trawler's in a zone where reception is—'
Suddenly, the response crackled through.

'This is *Jean-Mathieu*. What's going on, Souris Coast Guard?'
Nadine gave her instructions to Couture. 'Tell them you want

to know if everything is all right on board. Explain that you were concerned because of the foul marine conditions.'

Couture relayed the question to the vessel.

'Thanks for your concern, Souris Coast Guard. It's been a good harvest and we're on our way home.'

'When do you expect to be back in Cap-aux-Meules? Over.'

'By the end of the day. We should be back to kiss our wives goodnight.'

'Is everyone all right? Over.'

'Yes, except for young Painchaud, who's puking his guts up.'

As the men laughed, Nadine threw Moralès a glance. She covered the microphone in her headset to whisper a word in his ear.

'We can't ask them if they've got a Hells Angel on board, just like that. And if I insist on speaking to Officer Lord, they'll smell a rat. We're going to have to wait until they make land and then turn the boat upside down.'

The detective agreed. 'Wish them well on their way.'

They heard the radio communication come to an end.

'I'm going to spend the night here. I want to know immediately if anything changes,' Moralès said.

The officers exchanged exasperated looks.

Lefebvre came over to Moralès. 'Want us to stay here with you?'

His superior officer shook his head. 'There's no point. Find a hotel for Nadine so she can get some sleep, and see if you can get us a plane so we can fly out to the Islands as soon as there's a break in the weather.'

Nadine gratefully made her way to the exit. The day on skis and the hours of seasickness had worn her out. Lefebvre, thrilled to be tasked with missions that were right up his street, hurried to demonstrate his chivalry. He held the door open for her and they disappeared in a swirl of blowing snow.

The coast-guard officers pulled themselves together, making an effort to seem alert as Moralès, indifferent to their presence, pulled up a chair beside the VHF transmitter. As the hours ticked by, the officers sank softer and heavier into the armchairs in the small lounge area and fell asleep, content to take turns keeping watch.

🦭

It was only at around six in the morning when the *Jean-Mathieu* began to take turns of a different kind on the radar screen. Strangely, the boat had doubled back on its course. Moralès picked up the phone without asking for permission from the crew around him. It was Couture himself, in Souris, who answered.

'What are they doing?'

'I don't know. It looks like a rescue manoeuvre – what you do when you've got a man overboard.'

For a moment, all was silent. Then, a voice crackled through the VHF receiver.

'Souris Coast Guard, Souris Coast Guard, Souris Coast Guard, this is *Jean-Mathieu*. Man overboard! I repeat: man overboard!'

Moralès froze. If the sealers had thrown anyone overboard, it must be the Fisheries and Oceans Canada officer. 'Ask them if they've managed to find the person.'

The question was relayed to the vessel.

'Negative. We've slowed down and we're circling around, but there's next to no visibility and manoeuvring is difficult because of the storm. We're going to keep on looking.'

The voice sounded distant. Moralès sensed it was slipping away.

'Who is it? I want to know who they've lost.'

Couture heard the question and relayed it over the radio, but the *Jean-Mathieu* wasn't responding. Couture insisted, made two more attempts. The men listened as attentively as they could, but failed to hear a reply.

'Order them to head straight for the nearest port.'

'*Jean-Mathieu*, the weather is too bad for you to return to Cap-aux-Meules. Come back to Souris. Over.'

A long silence followed the order. Couture tried again.

'I repeat: *Jean-Mathieu*, please head immediately to the port in Souris. *Jean-Mathieu*, do you acknowledge? Over.'

More silence.

'They've stopped transmitting.'

Moralès was fuming. 'We have to send out a rescue crew.'

'That's impossible. All the small search-and-rescue stations are closed from mid-November to mid-April. It'll take a helicopter from Halifax.'

'Then send a helicopter.'

A hesitancy now crept into Couture's voice, as if he could tell that the detective had an intimate interest in the affair: 'It would be difficult, considering the weather, and almost impossible to get there in time to save whoever's fallen in the sea, because the water is freezing cold. Chances are, they're dead already. But there's a bigger problem.'

'What? What is it?'

The coast-guard officer who was sitting beside Moralès with his eyes glued to the screen took the words out of his colleague's mouth.

'We've lost their satellite signal.'

જ્

Moralès sat staring at the blank screen for another hour, for better or worse. He went round in circles, spoke to Doiron on the phone and made a nuisance of himself with the coast-guard officers – raising his voice, postulating theories and giving the waste-paper basket a hefty kick. The night team were clearly relieved to hand over to the morning shift, calling 'good luck' to their colleagues over their shoulders and slamming the door shut behind them.

The daytime team leader called for silence, made a pot of hot coffee and handed a cup to Joaquin, who nodded in thanks. The newcomer understood what was so poorly concealed beneath all this agitation. He himself had lost a cousin at sea four years ago and his family were still mourning their loss.

'Leave me your mobile number, detective. If the *Jean-Mathieu* shows up again, I'll call you immediately. The whole time I'm on shift, I'll make sure one of us stays on the lookout. We'll find this boat of yours.'

Exhausted by his vigil and comforted by the newcomer's benevolence, the detective agreed and left the coast-guard station.

Moralès was drawn to Corine's auberge as if by some kind of magnetic melancholy. Corine herself would be staying down at her boyfriend's place in L'Anse-à-Beaufils until the tourist season returned, he figured. The wind had swept so forcefully through the yard, it had cleared a narrow parking spot in one corner. Moralès tucked his car into it, switched off the engine. He recalled the subcutaneous vertebra that haunted the nape of Simone Lord's neck, the one that had teased at the surface as if to spite him and then retreated before he'd had a chance to reach out and touch it. The car windows were steadily frosting up.

Moralès shivered, started the engine again, turned the heater on. He checked the time. The Fisheries and Oceans Canada office must be open by now. He backed out of the space, turned onto the road, put his foot down and headed for Gaspé town centre.

He needed a long shower, a good shave and a hearty breakfast. He needed better wipers too, because his were leaving big sheets of frost in the middle of the windscreen. Most of all, he needed to know that she was still alive.

He walked into the grey building, approached a secretary who was making the most of the quiet time on a stormy day to water the plants, introduced himself, showed his badge and asked to speak to Officer Simone Lord's boss.

'Her field supervisor is on leave at the moment. I'll check with the area manager.' The man eyed Moralès and what he was wearing, put down the watering can, picked up the phone, dialled a number.

'Lieutenant Cumming, there's a police detective here who wants to see Maxime about Officer Lord. It seems urgent.'

Two minutes later, Joël Cumming strolled into the lobby, extending a hand. 'Come with me, detective.'

In his late fifties, with short hair, square glasses and a spring in his step, Cumming led the way upstairs and invited the detective sergeant into his office. No sooner was the door closed than he said, 'I've just heard about the disappearance of the *Jean-Mathieu*.'

Moralès said nothing in reply. His face carried the stern expression of a man who wanted answers.

'It wasn't me who sent Officer Lord out to the Magdalen Islands. Yes, she stepped out of line in an investigation last autumn, when she tried to protect a fisherwoman, but she's an excellent officer and I would have preferred to keep her here.'

'So why approve her transfer?'

Standing by his desk, Lieutenant Cumming drummed his fingers on the photos of an attractive woman and laughing children that were sandwiched between the wooden surface and a sheet of protective plastic. His gaze drifted over Moralès's left shoulder to the little multicoloured ice-fishing cabins that dotted the surface of Gaspé Bay and were taking the brunt of the wind and snow.

'You know as well as I do, sometimes a superior has to give his subordinates some slack, and sometimes that means they tangle themselves up in the wrong kinds of decisions. That's the way bureaucracy works. We fall victim to the Peter principle here like everywhere else. The dumber administrators are, the more they need to prove their power by making unjust decisions. "Pettiness," we call it.'

To Moralès, that reasoning sounded like a cop-out. 'Sometimes, not stepping in and intervening can be seen as cowardly.'

Cumming looked at his counterpart again. He wondered if he could really trust this man. At this moment, he had no other option.

'It wasn't a cowardly choice, but a strategic one. I needed to know what Officer Laurin was up to.' His fingers kept drumming softly on the desk.

'Was he the one who transferred Officer Lord to the Magdalen Islands?'

Cumming nodded. 'I don't need to tell you, a lot of trafficking goes on in the estuary. Last summer, the drugs squad conducted an investigation into cocaine shipments making their way to our shores via Newfoundland. I suspect Maxime Laurin is in cahoots with the couriers.'

'What makes you think that?'

'In the last three years, he's been the one responsible for all the fishing zones the shipments have transited through. It's almost been systematic: he's been assigning himself to the observation of those zones, while he could have been sitting comfortably in the office, like most detachment supervisors do. He's of that age when one usually tires of working out at sea. The brutal weather and the bitter fishermen end up getting the better of a lot of officers.'

Moralès figured the same was probably true of the man standing in front of him. He understood, and suddenly felt a heavy wave of weariness wash over him.

'Anyway, when I began to suspect Laurin was dabbling in murky waters, I made sure I kept an eye on him. But I could never catch him – I'm not a detective. And anyway, what would it look like if I directed unfounded suspicions at one of my team members? We've had our differences of opinion, Officer Laurin and me, over the years. And it takes a cast-iron case to catch an underling red-handed without having a finger pointed at you for harassment.'

'How does Officer Lord's transfer fit in to all this?'

'When I saw that Laurin was sending Lord off to the Islands, it struck me as an excessive penalty and I almost stuck my nose in. Then I started to smell a rat.'

'And you thought Lord was in on the drug-running too?' His tone was harsh.

Cumming recoiled, as if disentangling himself from such a sleazy suggestion. 'Not at all. Lord is above all suspicion.' He shuffled behind his desk, sat down, motioned for Moralès to do the same. 'No. I thought Laurin wanted her out of the way so he'd be free to do his thing. Because Officer Lord, you know, can be quite a stickler sometimes.'

'Committed to justice, you mean.'

Cumming smiled. 'You know her better than I do. So I said nothing, but I kept my eyes open. Last week, when it came to my attention that Laurin was volunteering to go aboard a sealing trawler that was heading out in a window of bad weather – again, as an observer – I thought it seemed suspicious. That was when I decided to step in. I assigned him to another job. When he found out, he came into my office yelling there were no two ways about it, he had to go to the Magdalen Islands right away. I explained that we already had an officer there, but he argued that a boat of seal hunters was no place for a woman. I told him I wouldn't stand for sexism in my department. And I ordered him to stay put. He became very aggressive, so I proposed he take a step back from his work. He stormed out of my office and slammed the door.'

Cumming took a sip of what must have been lukewarm coffee from a mug sporting the Fisheries and Oceans Canada logo. Moralès deduced that this was the man's way of composing himself.

'I reckoned they'd be using the trawler to move a shipment. But as long as they stayed in their sealing zone and my observer reported nothing untoward, I had no reason to contact you lot. Then, this morning, I found out the coast guard had lost contact with the vessel, so I phoned the commanding officer of the drugs squad we were working with last summer.'

So Moralès hadn't been kept in the loop. Which made sense: it was Doiron's prerogative to tell who he needed to tell. But something else was irritating him.

'So let me get this right, Mr Cumming: when you see there's a potential danger on a boat, you send a woman aboard?'

'No, Detective. Don't be sexist. Times like that, I send my

best available officer. Lord being a woman changes nothing. Few officers have her kind of nerve.'

Moralès looked away. That was precisely what he was afraid of. The line between nerve and recklessness tended to be a fine one for those who had something to prove – and especially so for an overachiever.

'Man or woman, you didn't think they'd need backup?'

'I arranged for a coast-guard vessel to go out of their way and check on them.'

'And?'

Cumming looked uncomfortable. 'Maybe they weren't the best of crews…'

'*En la Madre!*'

The curse just slipped out. Moralès figured the Peter principle must be creeping through the whole building.

'And this rogue officer of yours, Laurin, where is he right now?'

'It won't surprise you to learn he's taken the week off.'

'Where do you think I can find him?'

'At home, I imagine. I'll make sure you're given his personal address.'

On his way out of the Fisheries and Oceans Canada office, the detective phoned Lefebvre at the police station.

'Moralès, I can't get a plane to fly out to the Islands for love nor money. It's gusting up to a hundred and forty kilometres an hour out there!'

'Forget about that for now. Even if I could make it out there, there's nothing to say the *Jean-Mathieu*'s going to be docking in Cap-aux-Meules. They've not deactivated the locator beacon for nothing. They're disappearing while they handle their shipment. The coast guard's supposed to let me know as soon as the trawler's back on the radar.'

Moralès cranked up the defroster and the heater to their highest settings. 'I've got the address of the fisheries officer who was supposed to go aboard instead of Simone.'

'What? She took the place of a guy? Well, I'm not surprised.'

'It was her lieutenant who insisted on it. He thinks the other officer is in cahoots with the dealers.'

'Has he got form? What's his name?'

'Maxime Laurin. Form or not, I'm going to pay him a visit.'

'*I?* You're not going there on your own.'

Moralès knew his colleague had a point. In any case, he felt too old, that morning, to be taking any unnecessary risks. Not that Lefebvre was offering to join him; he hated working in the field.

'Is Nadine there with you?'

'Yes, she's in the conference room, on the phone with your friend Doiron. Where are you?'

'In front of the Fisheries and Oceans office.'

'Come down to the station, we'll kit you out with a bullet-proof vest and get you a team.'

Moralès glanced at his watch. It was almost noon. He started the car and went on his way. The heavy flakes had stopped falling, but the snow continued to whirl in the howling wind, spinning into haphazard drifts across the road. Visibility was still terrible and he realised, cursing the winter, that he couldn't hurry the troops along, because all the officers would have to clear their driveways and dig out their cars before they came in, their speed further hindered by the snow-covered roads.

At the Gaspé police station, however, things went more smoothly than anticipated. At the front desk, Thérèse Roch, who had been abrasive with him the previous autumn, buzzed him in the door with the eagerness of a B-movie cop catching the whiff of an emergency.

While Moralès was busy, Constable Lefebvre had assumed operational command.

'If Laurin's in with the dealers, he must be biting his nails. One of our guys is checking the firearms registry. He must have at least a hunting rifle at home, but we're not taking any risks. We're considering him armed and potentially dangerous. An hour from now, there should be enough of a break in the weather for a small team of officers from the Tactical Intervention Group to make it out here. Doiron said we could hang on to them for a day or two. I don't think we should make a move until the tactical team gets here.'

Moralès cursed, but he appreciated Lefebvre's good work. And it was generous of Doiron to loan them a tactical team for that long.

It was well into the afternoon when the tactical guys landed and they set off in convoy for Officer Maxime Laurin's place. The stubborn, testing wind seemed to be easing.

The house, over in Rose Bridge, was set back from the road. When they arrived, there was no approaching the place: the driveway leading to the house was a good fifty metres long and blanketed completely with snow. At the end of the driveway, a tractor equipped with a snow blower attachment was half buried in a drift.

'Either the guy's waiting for the storm to blow over before he clears his driveway, or he's not home.'

'Or he's dead.'

Lefebvre sighed. They were in Moralès's car, and he was sitting behind Nadine. He had wanted to be brave and jump in without his superior officer having to twist his arm, but in truth he would have rather have stayed back at the station.

The voice of one of the tactical intervention guys crackled

over the radio. 'We're making a covert approach. You stay back for now.'

It was the detective who replied. 'As soon as you've secured the premises, let us know. We'll find a tractor to clear the driveway for us.'

With a nod, Constable Lefebvre reached for his phone, dialled a number, waited. 'I know someone who lives nearby who can…'

Moralès got out of the car. The four tactical officers, equipped with lightweight snowshoes, advanced on the house. He tried to follow them, but had to admit defeat when he found himself sinking up to his thighs in snow. He turned back and got back into the car as Lefebvre was ending his call.

'The tractor's on its way.'

The Tactical Intervention Group team entered the home swiftly. Barely a minute later, the three colleagues sitting in the car heard confirmation over the radio that the premises were empty and secured. Meanwhile, an old tractor that had seen far better years rumbled past them into the driveway and set about slaying this beast of a job like David tackling Goliath.

Moralès glanced at his watch impatiently. The Gaspé Peninsula had been taunting him with its slowness since his first day on the job out here.

In a white van parked beside them sat the usual duo of forensic technicians, eating doughnuts while they waited for the boss to sort out a solution.

Once the driveway was clear, both vehicles filed in. It wasn't the most discreet of approaches, but it didn't need to be.

The sergeant in charge of the tactical unit gave them a preliminary report. 'There's no one inside. Looks like the house has been vacant for a few days. The heating's been turned down, the way you do to save on the electric bill. But someone's been in to feed the cat.'

He pointed to some faint snowshoe tracks that were still visible in a sheltered corner of the deck.

'The bowl's full for a week at least and there are two litter boxes.'

Moralès, Lefebvre and Nadine went inside for a quick look around.

'In here!' The psychologist called her colleagues over to the living room.

Érik came in clutching a portly and loudly purring ginger cat to his chest. Nadine drew their attention to a photograph of a man in a waterproof jacket and a baseball hat standing proudly on a dock and showing off the large salmon he had landed.

'Chances are, he hasn't gone very far. Maybe he's got a cabin in the area.'

'I've checked his property titles. He's only got the house here.'

Detective Sergeant Moralès was thankful for Constable Lefebvre's foresight and research skills. 'Get a couple of patrol officers to canvass the neighbours. We're going back to the station.'

'Moralès, not that I mean to go sticking my nose into your personal hygiene, but you look wiped. We'll keep at it, but you should head to the hotel for a shower. And get your head down for a nap.'

But Joaquin was restless. He drove Érik and Nadine back to the station, went for a quick shower in the locker room and then made a beeline for Lefebvre's office.

'He doesn't have a cabin, but one of his neighbours said he often goes to a fishing camp owned by one of his cousins. I'm in the process of putting his family tree together, and so far I've found eighteen first cousins who live in the Gaspé. I've given their names to two officers, and they're working their way through the list to see which ones have a cabin somewhere.'

Just then, Nadine burst into the room. 'I've started going through your list and cross-referencing it with our database. And what a bunch of shitsters they are! Half of them have been done for stealing, fencing stolen goods or drug possession.'

Another officer, who Moralès remembered seeing earlier, appeared in the doorway. 'Three phone calls in, and we can't get through to anyone anymore. I reckon the first few have sounded the alarm to the others. Not one of them's picking up now.'

Lefebvre smoothed his thin moustache disapprovingly. 'You have called them, right?'

'Well, yeah.'

'I'll pull the list of properties for all the cousins, then.'

The newcomer made himself scarce and Lefebvre got back to work.

'We should probably be expecting a family welcome when we get to the cabin.'

Nadine wasn't so sure. 'Or they're the kind to run a mile as soon as the cops show up – leaving the weakest to be devoured by the lions.'

Moralès cast the deciding vote. 'We'll bring the tactical team along for the ride.'

The detective's phone rang. It was Doiron. 'Where are you guys at?'

'Still no sign of the boat, but we've put our finger on the fisheries officer who was supposed to be handling the shipment: Maxime Laurin. We went to pay him a visit, but it looks like he's gone on holiday. My best officer is on his trail as I speak. We think he's hiding out at a family cabin.'

Lefebvre looked up for a moment, whispered, 'My best officer,' with a swell of pride; 'That's me, that is' – and went back to giving the data his full focus.

'Why is he hiding? He can't have found out all of a sudden that you were after him. Is there something in the investigation that incriminates him?'

'No. Unless the drugs squad already had their eye on him…'

The thought drifted into silence. Moralès had worked with Doiron for long enough for them to both know when a question was important. The silence between them was a fast track to a breakthrough.

'Maybe he's not in hiding. What if he's waiting to receive the shipment?'

'That's hard to believe; he was supposed to be aboard the *Jean-Mathieu*. His boss pulled him off the observation job at the last minute. Chances are, the drug-runners have ended up figuring things out without him.'

Standing right in front of the detective, Nadine could hear the whole conversation. 'He's afraid.'

Moralès stared at her.

'And not of the police.'

Constable Lefebvre raised his arms in a V for victory. 'We've got an address!'

🦭

Even without the address, the Gaspé investigators would have had no trouble finding the place. As the day neared its early end and they drove inland towards Murdochville, they soon spotted a pillar of thickening black smoke rising straight ahead of them.

The driver of the Tactical Intervention Group's vehicle switched on the blues and twos, put his foot down and zoomed ahead of the convoy. At the wheel of Moralès's car, Lefebvre accelerated in rapid pursuit, while the forensic technicians hung back to let the fire trucks pass and then manoeuvred into position to block the road. Though it was probably already too late to intercept a suspicious vehicle driving away from the area around the fire, the police had still radioed the Murdochville detachment for backup.

Two of the tactical officers swiftly swept the perimeter of the burning cabin to make sure this wasn't an ambush, while the other two dashed inside, with Moralès and two firefighters hot on their heels. Lefebvre and Lauzon soon saw the men emerge, coughing and spluttering from the smoke, dragging an inanimate body behind them. Lefebvre started in their direction to lend a hand, but was stopped in his tracks by his phone. The number for the Gaspé police station flashed on the screen.

'Constable Lefebvre, it's Thérèse Roch.'

The receptionist secretly dreamed of being roped into an investigation.

'Listen, Thérèse—'

'Standing right here in front of me, I've got the owner of the cabin everyone's looking for.'

'Put him on, then.'

'I'm afraid that's not possible. This phone line is strictly reserved for incoming calls to the station.'

'Thérèse, you alone know how urgent an operation becomes when the Tactical Intervention Group get involved…'

An indecisive silence engaged the line temporarily, then Lefebvre heard a movement that suggested Ms Roch was passing the receiver to someone.

'Hello?'

'Constable Lefebvre here. Who is this?'

'Guillaume Laurin. Seems you're looking for a cousin of Maxime's who owns a cabin in the area. That's me. My cabin's in Murdochville.'

'In future, I think you'll be saying it *was* in Murdochville.'

'I don't understand.'

'The firefighters are hosing your cabin down as we speak.'

'What? Holy shit! What's going on?'

'We're looking into whether someone might have had a bone to pick with your cousin. One big enough to try to kill him over.'

'Has something happened to Maxime?'

'Listen, Mr Laurin, I need to know if anyone other than the police has contacted you to find out the address of your cabin.'

'No.'

'Since when has your cousin been hiding out here?'

'My cousin's not hiding out. He's on holiday…' The gruff voice on the line fell silent for a moment. 'This morning, I went in to feed Max's cat, then, when I came out of his driveway, there was a guy in a car waiting for me. Out by the road. He said Max was expecting him. I said he was at my cabin and told him how to get there.'

Quickly, Lefebvre got into the car, grabbed a pen and paper. 'Did this man give you a name?'

'No.'

'Right, well, Mr Laurin, I need you to give me a physical description of the individual. As detailed as possible, please.'

'Holy shit! What the hell is happening?'

Off the charts

The trawler had come to a standstill. Simone was almost sure of it. An intense fever was ravaging her. Her body was in a sweat, shaking, her teeth chattering, her torn clothes saturated. Huddled in her sleeping bag, she lowered a hand to touch the bandage covering her wound. It was slimy and smelly. But what she found the most concerning was that the *Jean-Mathieu* was going nowhere. And yet they were still at sea. She could feel the motion of the waves rocking the hull. She realised they must have reached the spot where they'd be bringing aboard the drug shipment.

She looked at her watch. It was nearly three in the morning.

She tugged her sleeping bag down, reached for the phone she had tucked into her bandage, pulled it out. It was a good thing she had put it behind her thigh; it wasn't too damp there. She switched it on and tried to get a GPS reading. After two minutes, a dot appeared at last, to the south of the Newfoundland coastline.

Suddenly, she froze. The men were coming down the stairs from the wheelhouse.

'It's gonna be some top-quality shit, too.' Eight-Inch Painchaud sounded like he'd had an electric shock.

'Yeah, we're gonna be fuckin' rich.' Carpentier's voice was teetering an octave higher than normal.

There was a swishing of waterproof clothing in the vestibule, then the sound of the door to the deck opening and closing behind them.

Simone could breathe again. She sat on the edge of the bunk, pulled aside the sheet that had served as a curtain. Her head was spinning dangerously. She stood up, toiling under the pain from her swollen leg. The sleeping quarters were empty, as was the galley, where the light had been left on. She hobbled over to the porthole.

A string of red and green flashing lights twinkled in the night – buoys marking a long shipping channel. Silhouetted in the background, she could see land. Most likely the coast of Newfoundland. Lashed to the nearest buoy, Simone saw an inflatable life raft similar to the one she had used to hoist Chevrier's body up to the *Jean-Mathieu*'s scuppers. She deduced that another vessel had come here and tied up the raft, together with what it contained. Outside the channel, the water couldn't be very deep, she figured, which was probably why the trawler wasn't going any closer.

Simone limped across the galley. Instead of carrying on to the vestibule, she turned to her left, made her way beneath the stairs to the window, from where she had witnessed the altercation between Chevrier and McMurray, two nights earlier. To her right, the stairwell to the engine room descended into darkness. A nauseating stench of oil, rust, blood and raw flesh emanated from the hold, now that the seal carcasses were stashed down there.

She looked outside.

On the deck, the men were busy, freeing the dinghy strapped to the starboard guardrail before hooking it to the winch. So that was how they were planning to retrieve the shipment. They would use the smaller craft to fetch the life raft moored to the channel buoy, then they would winch the haul aboard.

Simone heard McMurray's heavy footsteps coming down the

stairs. The hunter pulled on a waterproof jacket and went outside to stand by the winch controls. Painchaud and Carpentier climbed aboard the dinghy. Rattling in the wind, the small craft was quickly hoisted over the edge of the railing, before it was lowered to the sea and disappeared from sight.

Through the fog of her fever, Simone was struck by horror: the men were sure to see Chevrier's dead body suspended from the prow – if not on their way out, then certainly on their return. She stood there, petrified, struggling for breath. It was over. They were going to kill her.

She heard a hysterical cry, followed by the maniacal laugh of Eight-Inch Painchaud, which seemed to crack like a whip and ricochet in the night.

'Fuck the woooooorld!'

Were those the last words Simone would ever hear? Her useless phone rested in her cold palm. If only she could alert Joaquin Moralès.

Stubbornly, she tried again, by text and by email, to send him all the information she had gathered: her secret recording of Lapierre's proposition to her about the detour for the drug shipment and his revelation about Carpentier and McMurray killing Chevrier, her own notes on the sequence of events, the photos, the GPS location of the pickup she had saved. Every last message bounced back, accompanied by a red exclamation mark – signalling her failure, her powerlessness. Perhaps the end to her story.

Where could she go? Where could she hide?

She turned her gaze to the stairs. It would be far too cold in the hold. But Chevrier had said that he and his father had once survived a night at sea by huddling under the seal pelts. On one side down there were the food bins, where the bagged meat sat waiting to be sliced, cooked, served to tourists in the next fair-weather season. But on the other side, there were the seal pelts, stacked fur to fur, fat to fat. The sea ice's grey gold.

Simone shivered, this time in fear. Tears filled her eyes. She was trapped. She thought about the words Joaquin had written to her.

There are some men who are made to pitch balls from the mound in every direction. Men who have an eye on every target, all at once.

One last time, she looked outside. The men had not yet seen the body, because they were motoring away from the side of the trawler.

I am not one of those men.

She took a GPS reading, tried to send it to Moralès along with one word: cocaine. Once she went down to the hold, the phone wouldn't be able to transmit anything. From that point on, there would be no chance of it picking up a signal and sending the messages even when the vessel came within range of a telecommunications tower.

I come from a family where the men wear a ring. Where we all sit at the same table, for life. Where we build a place to love one another.

Simone turned away from the window, from the sea, from the dark horizon of the dying storm. Down one step she went, then another. Under her left hand, she felt the rubbery material of some summer-weight waterproofs hanging from one of the many hooks on the wall beside the stairs. One more step, then she stopped. She slipped the phone into the pocket of a jacket, and began to sob softly.

I took off the ring and now, inside me, there's an empty space.

The stench filled her nostrils. Heart pounding at her temples, she was fighting the panic, the pain, the fever, the delirium. She struggled down to the foot of the stairs. Now she could no longer hear the wind howling at the trawler's rigging. She could no longer hear the whirring of the winch motor. She could no longer see the light that flooded the deck with too much white and cast its dazzling shards to the top of the stairwell.

My eyes are looking out to sea. I know that you are there.

One last step, and Simone was immersed entirely in the chilling silence of the darkness. She reached a hand to the wall, felt the flaking, frosted paint beneath her palm. Clouds of breath fogged her face. She reached for a handle. The door opened with a murmur. Then she stepped into the hold compartment at the stern, where, to her right, the seal pelts and their empty eyes were stacked. Waiting for her.

When you come back to the Islands, do you think I might join you and invite you to take a seat at my table?

She took one more step, and the door closed behind her with a whisper.

🦭

Painchaud couldn't control himself, let alone the dinghy, so he had let Carpentier take the helm. The swell was running steep, but grew calmer as they approached the buoy, probably because the channel had been carved through the shallows, beyond the breakers. Kneeling in the front of the small craft, he stretched his arms out towards the life raft, despite it still being out of reach. He was clenching and extending his fingers in a frenzy, as if he could lure the raft closer by the power of telekinesis.

'Come to me, my pretty, pretty powder…'

Carpentier could have sworn the guy was whispering sweet nothings, but couldn't hear a word in the onslaught of the wind and the waves.

Not that the poacher cared. Since he had realised that, as well as the bounty from the miracle haul of seals, he'd be pocketing a tidy stack of cash from this little detour, he had been constantly calculating and recalculating how much he'd be able to put on the kitchen table. Ida wanted a holiday in the sun? They would have a holiday in the sun. Ida wanted a big party for their wedding anniversary? They would throw a big party. Ida wanted to treat herself to some fancy clothes for both of those occasions? She would get her fancy clothes. There would be fishing in the summertime to help balance the red on the mortgages. That would be enough to shut the bankers up. With a bit of luck, he might get to do two or three more trips like this with young Painchaud and his pal Lapierre. He didn't see why the two of them would go looking for someone else instead. After all, he was the one, together with McMurray, who'd got rid of Chevrier for them. He was the one who'd had the idea of faking the rescue manoeuvre to trick the coast guard, and he was the one who'd deactivated the satellite system. He deserved a bit more than what Lapierre was offering.

This time he wouldn't insist, but next time, he'd up his price. If the guys disagreed, he could even threaten to blow the whistle on them. One way or another, he figured, he had them by the balls. Carpentier wasn't the type to take advantage. He knew the boat was Painchaud's and the contact was Lapierre's, but he was taking risks too, and that kind of arrangement should be lucrative in the long run. He knew what he was talking about. He had always been generous with his deckhands when he used to do business offshore. At some point, crews that go on runs like this develop a connection of sorts. A connection that pays well for everyone. This was the end of his money troubles, Carpentier the poacher was sure of it. He was proud of himself for going to scope out Painchaud the other night in the bar. He'd talked his way on to the right crew.

He slowed the dinghy's speed and steered them alongside the raft. 'Grab the mooring line and tie us up.'

Painchaud was agitated, his movements jerky. He took the line Carpentier handed to him and tied it clumsily to the raft. Then, in one impatient and uncontrolled movement, he stood, gathered some momentum to launch himself out of the dinghy.

'Fucking hell. What do you think you're doing?' Carpentier tried to stop him.

But it was too late: Painchaud was already soaring through the air. Fortunately, at just the right time, a gust of wind blew into the door of the raft, opening it wide for him. Eight-Inch landed aboard the flimsy craft and went flying headfirst into a tightly wrapped block of cocaine. Dazed, but running high on adrenaline, he sat up for a second before throwing himself upon the slab of coke, wrapping his arms around it and showering it with kisses.

'You're all mine, my pretty. Fuck the rest of 'em, you're all mine.' He gave the wrapping a lick of his great lolloping tongue. 'Now that's one helluva stack of cash. I'm gonna pay Lapierre back, and then some. It's the real deal, man. The purest shit there is. Gonna be one helluva trip.'

Carpentier, leaning almost horizontal against the edge of the dinghy, waved at him.

'Let's bring her aboard, then you can slip a ring on her finger, OK?'

Eight-Inch erupted in a fit of crazy laughter. 'I'm staying right here.'

Carpentier didn't think that was very smart, but then again, it wasn't exactly practical for two men to shift a fifty-kilo block from one flimsy craft to another at sea, especially in this kind of swell.

'Whatever you say. Cut her loose and I'll tow you.'

Buzzing, Marco Painchaud pulled out his penknife and sawed through the mooring line securing the raft to the channel buoy. Lucien Carpentier engaged the throttle, and the dinghy set off laboriously on its return journey to the trawler. Concerned about his cargo, he cast many a backward glance to Painchaud drooling over his betrothed. The load the dinghy was towing was a respectable distance behind the outboard motor; the mooring line didn't seem tempted to snag in the propeller. The raft was carrying enough ballast to remain stable in the swell.

At last, they drew alongside the *Jean-Mathieu* without either of them having the presence of mind to look up in the direction of the prow. They hooked the big block of cocaine onto the winch and McMurray hoisted it aboard, together with Eight-Inch, still clinging to his precious package like a leech. For a moment, Carpentier was worried the men might abandon him right there, at sea. But he soon saw the lines and hooks being lowered his way again. McMurray hauled him up, unhooked the straps and shut down the winch while Carpentier lashed the dinghy tight to the railing. Painchaud slashed the raft to shreds and tossed it overboard.

'Fuck the wooooorld! Is that clear? Is that clear enough?'

'It's fifty kilos, it's not that much...'

Suddenly, they heard someone rapping on the wheelhouse window. Lapierre signalled for Carpentier to come in and take the helm. He obeyed the order. A few minutes later, the trawler was back on its way.

Lapierre came out on deck as Painchaud danced gleefully around the package, brandishing his open penknife.

'Don't go taking a stab just anywhere, Eight-Inch, 'cause any that flies off in the wind I'll be docking off your pay.'

As Painchaud reluctantly folded away his blade, Lapierre pulled out his own knife and pierced a corner of the wrapping with a smooth, professional flourish. Then, thinking about what was yet to come, he stopped and turned to McMurray.

'You've done a seal harvest before. With the officer's report, can we be sure we won't get searched?'

'I don't reckon they'll be searching us. Not unless she snitches.'

Lapierre was still worried they were skating on thin ice. 'They were supposed to send a guy on board, but they lumbered us with the girl instead. Maybe someone suspects something. We'd best not put the stuff in the meat bins, in case we get rumbled.'

'OK. But where are we going to put it?'

Lapierre could see Painchaud was shivering with cold. All fired up to go fetch his precious cargo, the little cretin had neglected to dress warmly.

'The coast guard already inspected the survival suits and distress flares. If you ask me, no one's going to go back there and check.'

The two others agreed. That made sense. Lapierre got back to work with his knife.

'We've got fifty packets of the stuff to stash. Go!'

'We've got an address!'

Moralès hurriedly grabbed a pen and paper.

Shortly before midnight, the paramedics had driven Maxime Laurin to hospital, where he was pronounced dead. Not that he had been alive when the officers pulled him out of the burning cabin. Since then, it had been a night of pandemonium, in Montreal as well as in Gaspé.

It had become clear to the detectives that when Buster had given the Beaudry kid a beating, he had managed to extract an important piece of information from him. Stone had let slip to the youngster, when he had come to him to borrow the money, that he was going to be bringing the drugs in by boat. Once Beaudry had passed this nugget on to Buster, the latter started asking around about what had been coming in through the nautical channels, and he had latched on to the name of a Fisheries and Oceans Canada officer, Maxime Laurin, who was rumoured to have cleared the way for the couriers to move the shipments. Buster had jumped straight in his car and come to pay Laurin a visit, hoping to find out where Stone's delivery was going to be landing.

Moralès and his team had arrived not long after Buster had made his getaway from Guillaume Laurin's chalet. More than likely, he was still floating around nearby. If the drug haul was going to wash up somewhere on the peninsula, he would lead the detectives straight to it. But if it was transiting through the Magdalen Islands, the guy would have to board a flight from Gaspé or make his way to Souris, on Prince Edward Island, to catch the next ferry sailing in two days' time, when a break in the weather was forecast. Either way, Buster must be lying low someplace not far away, waiting for his partner. And the cargo.

He hadn't used his phone or bank cards, which suggested he was hiding out somewhere in which he'd be a welcome visitor. Overnight, a police operation had been set in motion to track him down. Two dozen officers had been dragged out of bed, every informant and Hells supporter who owed the cops a favour hauled in for questioning.

It was the address of Buster's lair that Doiron passed to Moralès that morning.

The Tactical Intervention Group team was now on the road for the third time in the last thirty-six hours. While the bags under the tactical officers' eyes betrayed their fatigue, none of them were complaining. To put the cuffs on guys like these was the very reason they had joined the team.

In the car, Nadine had a suggestion for Moralès about how to approach the criminal. 'Stand back and let the tactical team mess with him. In every mugshot we have of Buster, his hair's like a model's. I wouldn't be surprised if he plucks his eyebrows in secret. For him, it's all about his appearance. So let the others get heavy with him, but you make sure you're there to step in and protect his vanity. That'll soften him up and make him amenable to questioning.'

Moralès shook his head. He had a lot of time for Nadine, but he couldn't care less about Buster's eyebrows. He didn't give a damn about the drugs either. All he wanted was to find Simone alive.

The cabin had been built in the woods, at the end of a driveway that had recently been cleared. The police vehicles turned off their headlights as they approached. A single car, the plate confirming it was registered to Buster, was parked out front. A wisp of smoke rose from the chimney.

The Tactical Intervention Group officers silently sprang into action the instant they arrived, broke the door down, barged into the building. Moralès was right on their heels. They promptly found Buster and yanked him out of bed wearing nothing but a pair of Pullin boxers with a motorcycle pattern on them. Hanging to dry on the backs of chairs were clothes he had washed with a laundry detergent that smelled strongly of lavender. One of the tactical officers jokingly wafted a hand in front of his nose, while two others sat Buster down on a kitchen chair and restrained him.

'Fucking pigs! You'd rather it smelled of doughnuts, wouldn't you?'

'Anyone would think you didn't like the smell of smoke, eh Buster?'

Moralès stood in front of the killer, glaring at him. Long hair cascading over his shoulders, the drug dealer pretended not to grasp the allusion to Laurin's cabin. He had shaved his moustache and had his teeth fixed since his last mugshot was taken.

'Well, it did take me a while to stoke the embers in the wood stove. I've not been here in a while, you know.'

The premises now secured, Nadine came in discreetly. Buster had his back to her. Moralès saw her, but didn't look her way.

'Where's the boat supposed to be docking?' the detective asked.

Buster fluttered his eyelids, like a diva caught by surprise. 'What boat?'

'Your mate Lapierre's.'

'Who are you talking about?'

Moralès lunged for the villain, about to punch him in the face, but Lefebvre stepped in to stop him. 'Don't do it.'

Buster laughed. 'Oh, are we playing good cop, bad cop? You're wasting your time. I'm not scared of taking a beating from the fuzz. It'll even give me something to brag about when I'm next inside. Go on, hit me as hard as you like, mister macho Latino! I swear, you'll have my lawyer after your hide before you know it.'

Moralès had enough experience to know the guy meant what he said, and to understand he wouldn't get anything out of him right now. The guy had everything to lose. The right thing to do was leave the forensics team to gather prints and put together a case file so solid and damning that Buster would end up spilling the beans in order to bargain over how much time he'd spend behind bars. But that would take hours and, in the meantime, the boat Simone had gone aboard would slip through their fingers again.

'Take him in to the station. But just the way he is. Not one of you's going to let him put another stitch on, all right?' The detective was adamant.

Nadine's face turned to stone. She grabbed the guy's clothes and walked out. Moralès took a deep breath. He felt bad for not taking her advice, but he couldn't keep a handle on himself. He knew the psychologist would be far better than him at finding the flaw that would make the guy crack in the interview room, but urgency was tormenting him. Anger, as well.

And love too, perhaps.

⚓

The *Jean-Mathieu* had been motoring along for a while when the men finished stashing the fifty kilos of cocaine. Eight-Inch was like a child worn out from opening too many Christmas presents, rubbing his eyes, which were even redder than usual, if that was even possible. He was completely out of it, jabbering convulsive versions of 'Is that clear?' into the void.

'You and McMurray should go get some sleep. I'll see out the night with Carpentier. Let's change shifts at sunrise.'

Without a word, Painchaud obeyed Lapierre and headed for

the stairs. He must have been awake for more than seventy-two hours.

'McMurray! Take the officer a bowl of soup while you're down there. And don't you be messing with her.'

The hunter, somewhat calmer since they'd picked up the cocaine, nodded. 'OK.' He disappeared down below.

Suddenly, Lapierre heard a commotion out on deck. He went over to the window. High as a kite, Painchaud was pissing up against the portside guardrail, screaming 'Is that clear enough?!'

'Anyone would think he'd just won the Stanley Cup.' The dealer gave a woeful smile.

Carpentier the poacher, sensing this was the time to explore a mutually beneficial business agreement with Lapierre, set about striking up a friendly conversation. 'Pretty lucrative haul we're bringing back with us, eh?'

Lapierre collapsed on the leather bench seat without responding. He didn't feel like shooting the breeze. He could predict what was coming. The guy wanted more money. He knew the game. Lapierre was going to have to threaten him, and he didn't feel like playing that tune, not tonight. He was exhausted, and haunted by doubt.

'Gonna fetch top dollar, I reckon,' Carpentier continued.

When he left Montreal, he hadn't told Buster a thing. But Stone knew his partner. He was a rabid dog who could easily run amok in his absence. He was worried, too, about the investigation into Chevrier's disappearance, which was surely coming.

'Now, I've done a lot of business at sea.'

Plus, something still seemed iffy about the other fisheries officer not coming aboard and sending the girl instead. Every which way Lapierre turned he could smell a rat, and this boat wasn't even unloaded yet. But he had no choice but to deliver the gear – not if he didn't want to end up in the river, wrapped up in a sleeping bag weighted down with bricks.

'You must have noticed, I'm sure. It's a good job I'm here, you know, because without me—'

Lucien Carpentier's insipid droning was interrupted by a quickening of footsteps down below. Lapierre could hear someone racing through the galley, up the stairs. Then McMurray appeared with an anxious expression on his face.

'The singer's disappeared!'

'How so, disappeared?'

The Newfoundlander's left shoulder rolled back mechanically.

'I did what you said. I went to take her some soup. I knocked on the bedpost, and she didn't respond. I thought she was dead. I leaned over to see, and her bunk was empty. I've checked the toilet and the shower. No sign of her.'

He pointed to the screen showing the video feeds from the engine room.

'Looks like she's not there, either.'

Lapierre sprang to his feet, sidestepped McMurray and hurried down the stairs and to the sleeping quarters. Eight-Inch was there with piss all over his hands, taking off his jeans. Lapierre flicked a switch; the light was an assault on Painchaud.

'Fuck's sake, don't tell me it's time for my shift already.'

Lapierre ignored him. He shook the curtain, felt around Simone's sleeping bag, rummaged through her luggage, as if she might somehow be hiding in her backpack. He looked to McMurray, who had been one step behind him and was just standing there like a fence post, clueless.

'Get out there. Check the deck, check everywhere outside.'

The hefty hunter nodded, still sporting his grubby grey

balaclava on the top of his head, and vanished into the vestibule. Meanwhile, Lapierre went across the galley, turned to his left, switched on the hold lights, tore down the stairs, searched the engine room. Then he went for a quick look in the compartments where the products of the hunt were stored. He shivered. No, it was way too cold in the hold for the officer to be hiding there.

He went back up the stairs and found himself nose to nose with Eight-Inch, who was boiling over in a fury. 'That fucking fisheries officer! I knew we couldn't trust her for a second. We should have killed her right off the bat.'

'Shut up, will you? I need to think.'

Lapierre turned and was about to head into the galley when the door to the deck swung wide open, and in barrelled McMurray, effing and blinding his way through the vestibule.

'She's gone.'

'How so, gone? She can't just vanish. We're in the middle of the sea.'

'She's taken the life raft.'

'What life raft?'

'There was a life raft on the roof.'

Eight-Inch couldn't stand still. He was hopping with nervous aggression, banging and crashing at the walls.

'She must've slipped away while we were stashing the gear. And we didn't see a thing in the dark.'

That was possible, Lapierre realised.

'In this howling wind, we might not have heard a thing either.'

Lapierre was thinking. 'Where could she have gone?'

'We weren't that far from the coast of Newfoundland. Maybe she's managed to paddle to a buoy. The coast guard will find her there, if she moors up to it tight enough. And you took her phone off her, right?'

'I went through her bags. She didn't have one.'

'Yes, she did. I heard it beeping when we passed by Souris, on the way out to Margaree Island.'

'Fucking hell…'

'That bitch has landed us in one hell of a big bucket of shite, hasn't she?'

The silence reached out and grabbed the crew by the throat. Lucien Carpentier, who had turned on the automatic pilot, came down the stairs. He had a good read on the situation and figured the time had finally come for him to prove he deserved a bit of a bonus.

'I know what we can do.'

Lapierre looked at him, intrigued.

'I'm willing to help, but for that you're going to give us our rifles back. And give me a bigger cut.'

Stone sized him up contemptuously. 'OK.'

The poacher smiled. 'Oh, and one more thing. If we do end up finding the girl, you're going to let my pal McMurray here teach her the lesson she deserves.'

The wind had dropped as if it had taken a bullet to the forehead. The snow lay lifeless on the hard ground like a dead animal. The mercury was falling like a stone. Moralès said goodbye to his colleagues and left the station.

He had spent hours grilling Buster to find out where the *Jean-Mathieu* was going to pick up the drugs, and where it was going to make land. This time, he had followed every word of Nadine

Lauzon's advice, who had been observing the interview from another room.

With clothes on, Étienne 'Buster' Dubé had swaggered into the interview room and was slouching, head cocked to one side, in the smug pose favoured by many a TV-show criminal.

The psychologist and the detective had seen him on the screen.

'We know his game. He's going to keep his trap shut because he thinks that's going to earn him VIP treatment behind bars. He's sure the drugs are going to get here, the debt's going to be paid, and he's going to be the villain who resisted interrogation. He's going to walk tall, slick his hair back and swan around the prison yard. If he gives us the delivery address, though, his life expectancy's going to be as fragile as tissue paper.'

Moralès had listened to Nadine. When it came to the criminal mind, she had always known the best places to hit a tough nut to get him to crack.

'But that's if, and only if, Michaël "Stone" Lapierre repays their debt to the Hells. If his partner takes off with the drugs, Buster is screwed. You see? If Stone doesn't come back, Buster won't last three days inside. They'll destroy him, and no undertaker in town's going to be able to rebuild that face of his. And that's not a future our pretty little friend here will find appealing.'

She was right.

'And you be sure to remind him, he owes money to the worst shitsters in all of Quebec. A big fat wad of cash. Tell him it's in his interest to talk to us, because as soon as we find that boat, he's going to be no use to us at all and it'll be too late to make a deal. Because we'll already have our hands on Stone, the drugs, the boat and everything. All Buster here's going to have left is his brave face and his fancy Pullin undies, and they'll not do him any favours in the changing room when he goes for a shower…'

So that was the angle Detective Sergeant Moralès had pursued. The more time went on, the more the effects of withdrawal had set in, but this wasn't Étienne 'Buster' Dubé's first time in an interview room. Sweating, shaking and green around the gills he may have been, but still he managed to keep that arrogant, little, nothing-to-say face of his straight.

When the detective had paused for a break, he had found Lefebvre by the psychologist's side.

'You're good, Moralès. I'm in awe. But I've been thinking. Maybe he's just not scared. He probably thinks we have nothing concrete on him.'

Lefebvre had kept on bringing coffee after coffee, in blissful admiration of Nadine Lauzon's fiery spirit.

'Tell him the fire at Laurin's cabin never had time to take hold and you've recovered the fisheries officer's body. Say the marks on the body suggest he was savagely beaten and they've carted it off for an autopsy. Oh, and we've got his prints, his hair, his spit, his DNA, fresh as a sea breeze all over the place. Tell him we found his prints at the Beaudry place and it's just a matter of hours before the parents pull the plug on the kid's life support. Make sure he knows that all the parents in the world – journalists, newspaper readers, jury members, you name it, even crooks behind bars – dream of just one thing: giving a good hiding to shitsters like him who beat teenage kids to death.'

This time, Étienne 'Buster' Dubé had opened his mouth. 'I'm not saying anything. I know what I'm supposed to do. Wait till my lawyer gets here.'

Then the blindingly obvious occurred to Moralès. 'You're not saying anything because you don't know anything. You're such a rotten dirtbag, if you did know something, you'd have been shooting your mouth off about it. Because you've got a loose tongue, haven't you? That's why Stone didn't let you in on the secret, isn't it? Because he knew you'd go blabbing about it somewhere, and then he'd really be in trouble.'

A quiver of humiliation twitched at the crook of Buster's lips, on the right side. It wasn't much, but it was enough for Nadine Lauzon to see that Detective Sergeant Moralès had hit the mark. The guy was giving them the run-around not because he had something to hide, but because he had nothing to tell. He had found out nothing from the fisheries officer Maxime Laurin because he had known nothing either.

They would have to keep looking for the *Jean-Mathieu* elsewhere.

Now, the detective got into his car, in the parking area of the Gaspé police station, turned the heater on.

For more than forty hours he had been awake, trying to locate a woman, a boat, and now here he was, at the end of a trail that led nowhere. A dead end. At this point, his only hope was that the trawler's locator beacon would come back online.

He made his way to the exit. Where to, now? He turned right, put his foot down. The roads were empty. The sky was yellow with impassible clouds. He drove for a long time, crossed paths with only a delivery truck.

He kept going, to Douglastown, turned into a driveway kept more or less clear of snow by a neighbour's tractor. All the windows were blind, filled with the darkest gaze of emptiness. He had been here once before, the previous autumn. Back then, he'd asked Lefebvre for Simone's address. Once that case was closed, he had put his bags in the car but, before hitting the road home, he had stopped in at her place.

It had not been late, but the curtain of twilight had already fallen. He had stopped the car in the driveway, across from the kitchen window. For a while he had sat there, watching, as the fisheries officer, looking weighed down either by sadness or simply exhaustion, made supper. He had brought a bottle of wine with him and spent a long time wondering how best to introduce himself. He wasn't in the habit of doing this kind of thing. To roll up to a woman's house, knock at her door, with a bottle in hand, at meal time, it took some courage. With or without a bottle. At any time, for that matter. Moralès didn't have that courage. Boldness was an attribute a man acquired when young, single, when he had the confidence. And he had none of that. That evening, on the ring finger of his left hand, he had still been wearing the band with which he had promised loyalty and righteousness, in joy and in doubt. He had told himself he had to get a divorce. Then he had seen Simone bring two plates out and set the table for two. And he had fled the scene.

Snow was piled up on the steps, on the porch, in front of the door. Joaquin wanted to go inside, see where Simone lived, go through her fridge, linger in her living room, inhale the scent of the sheets on her bed. He wanted to enter the house the way one steps across the threshold of a sacred place, marvel at its hidden treasures, touch the relics that told of Simone's presence.

It was as if, in the space of this last week, he had started to love her more and more, to inch closer to her, or at least to what he believed her to be, to love the idea of loving her, even. Perhaps this was what faith was. Perhaps it was this kind of love, built on hope and the fantasied image of another, that inspired men to build churches.

Joaquin reached for his phone, dialled Sébastien's number. A cheerful voice answered after three rings.

'Dad?'

'Yes.'

'You OK?'

'I don't know.'

Two seconds of silence, and Sébastien was worried. 'What's going on?'

Joaquin bit his tongue. He had never been good at these kinds of conversations.

'Is it because of a case?'

'Yes.'

Sébastien was no better. He wanted to tell his father he understood, but he wasn't sure he really did understand. Sorrow was a solitary abyss. Joaquin, too, was at a loss to name it. How could he explain that he had the arms to embrace a lover, but that there was nothing there but empty space? That yes, he was divorced, but within himself there was a bedroom made up, a table set with a white cloth, a place for making tacos and, most of all, for sharing them? That he knew he could love again, with humility and devotion, with strength and desire; and that, it so happened, there was a woman he would like to – wanted to – embrace. Simone. She wore her mystery in the tease of a vertebra Joaquin would never tire of touching with his eyes and his lips. But now she was missing in action, and Joaquin feared the sound of her silence would echo endlessly within himself. How could he explain to his son that he felt the urge to love, that he was loving again, and that now, once more, the saltwater horizon was sweeping away from him the woman to whom he was opening his arms?

'Where are you?'

'In Gaspé.'

'How long's it been since you slept?'

'I don't know.'

'Wait a sec…'

A minute went by.

'There's the Adams Motel, in town, not far away.'

'I know where it is.'

'Go on, then. I'll give them a call to let them know you're on your way.'

Joaquin gave a silent nod of his head, a shadow of a sign his son could not see, but one he might sense, like everything else perhaps, before hanging up the phone.

Bodies of frost

It took half a second for Joaquin to wake up. To realise his phone was buzzing. Text messages and emails were streaming in one after the other, provoking an influx of vibrations and pings to which there seemed to be no end. He reached out to the bedside table, felt around for and grabbed the device, rubbed his eyes, didn't dare believe them, sat bolt upright, switched on the light. Simone was sending messages to him. Some of them were coming in twice, three times even. What looked like a detailed chronology, audio recordings, GPS locations … where could she be sending them from?

Moralès tried to call her. No answer. He sent her a quick text message: *Where are you?* No reply to that, either. Nothing to suggest she had received it.

He phoned Lefebvre as he got dressed. His colleague answered with a cheery albeit groggy hello, as if he kept smiling even when he was asleep.

'Simone's been sending me messages. I'm going into the station. I need you to find me someone who can track where her phone is transmitting from.'

'OK. I'll see you there.'

'Give Nadine a nudge and bring your stuff. As soon as we've located the call, we're on our way.'

'She's … who told you Nadine was here?'

Moralès hung up, called Doiron, then headed into the station.

Ten minutes later a chivalrous Lefebvre opened the door for

Nadine, who had a twinkle in her eye and a tousle in her hair. She extended a hand, and Moralès passed her the printouts of the emails he had received from Officer Lord that were relevant to the investigation.

'It's Chevrier, the skipper, who's dead. There's a recording of one of the guys, probably Lapierre, saying McMurray and Carpentier stabbed him. We've got photos too.'

'OK. Let me see.'

'Nadine?'

His tentative, almost timid tone surprised her. It was out of character for Detective Sergeant Moralès to be having feelings at work. Anger and rage, perhaps. Impatience, too. When the time came to take down a villain, his courage tended to veer the way of recklessness. He had often taken heat for it, but the psychologist was no fool. As none of these accusations had amounted to anything, it was because the SQ sometimes needed a hothead or two. At times she had wondered if it might be a cultural thing, this daring in the face of danger, if in his younger years in Mexico Moralès had lived through experiences that had made him immune to fear, or if it was something all his own, this manly strength he didn't even know he had.

'Simone sent me a personal email. Er ... if everything has to come out, for the case file, I'd like it if that one could remain confidential.'

Lost for words at the tenderness, the hesitance in her superior's soft voice, Nadine nodded. 'Of course.'

Lefebvre blew in to the conference room like a gust of wind. He was fiddling with a hair elastic and the fancy fountain pen Moralès had often seen in Lauzon's hand.

'We've determined where the messages were sent from. The signals were picked up by a telecommunications tower on

Grande-Entrée Island, at the very northernmost point of the Magdalen Islands.'

'Does the SQ in the Islands know?'

'I've got an officer contacting our colleagues out there. Right, well, we've got a plane to catch.'

The investigation team jumped into Lefebvre's car and raced off to the Gaspé airport, where the four Tactical Intervention Group officers were meeting them. On the road, they read through the new information Simone had sent.

'She hoisted the body up to the prow. Right, well, what did I tell you, Moralès? Simone's not one to do things by halves.'

'Have either of you seen my fountain pen?'

Moralès kept quiet. He had last messaged Simone an hour ago. Still no reply. If the men aboard the *Jean-Mathieu* had discovered the body suspended up front, they might well have thrown the officer overboard.

On the plane, Nadine spent the time compiling the information and planning the intervention. She had everyone's attention.

'These shitsters are armed with big-bore hunting rifles and they know how to shoot. I've been trying to find a weak link, someone we can negotiate with, but I'm not really sure who to go for. Stone: not likely. He owes the Hells so much money he's got nothing left to lose. Plus, his drop point in Newfoundland is now a no-go. But he doesn't know that yet.'

Lefebvre unbuckled his seatbelt, got up, rummaged around to find something to bring back to his seat, plucked a flight-safety card from its pocket, returned and sat down again. Nadine cast a questioning glance his way, but carried on.

'Painchaud must be snorting so much stuff his nostrils are full to bleeding. Trying to negotiate anything with him is going to be like shooting the breeze with a kamikaze on speed. But he is a guy who likes to think he's right. That's his thing. If Moralès challenges him to dock the boat like an Olympic sailing champion, he'll do it just to prove how good he is, then he'll go showing off his handcuffs like a medal. He's got the mental age of a goldfish.'

Lefebvre looked like he was about to get up again.

'Is everything all right, Érik?'

Joaquin was surprised to see him blush like a lovestruck teenager. He came to the rescue. 'He gathers things and piles them up to help himself concentrate.'

Nadine rummaged in her bag. 'Why didn't you say so before?' She handed Lefebvre a makeup kit. He grabbed it, buckled his seatbelt and set about riffling through the contents like a child given a bag of sweets. Nadine carried on.

'Lucien Carpentier sold his whole fishing operation because he got caught poaching. You should see how thick his record is. The Fisheries and Oceans Canada officers spent half a season tracking him because they wanted to make sure it'd really hurt when they collared him. He didn't give a crap about quotas or zones, and he siphoned off everything he could to the Asians. The fisheries people even had a nickname for him. They called him the Customs Man.'

Lefebvre was busy lining up the most feminine of cosmetics – brushes, foundation, pencils, lipsticks, little tubes of antiwrinkle cream and all – with the gentlest of touches. Moralès knew he wasn't missing a word of the forensic psychologist's summary.

'And then there's Tony McMurray.'

Nadine hesitated. The detective understood; she wanted to let him know there was something she wished she could spare him from. He waited.

'He's been arrested a number of times, but ended up walking away. McMurray was working aboard the Customs Man's boat the year he was done for poaching. They're pretty close, by the looks of it. Lucien Carpentier was even his principal defence witness in one of the cases.'

Again, she fell silent.

'What was he arrested for?'

'Rape.'

Érik's hands stopped moving. Joaquin averted his eyes as Nadine continued.

'He raped a girl in the Islands. She recognised him, because apparently he's got some sort of weird tic with his shoulder. She hauled McMurray into the courtroom, but Carpentier testified in his favour. When they found that out, the guys on Grande-Entrée kidnapped McMurray, carried him out to sea and made him walk the plank. But his mate Carpentier got wind of it and came and fished him out. Two shitsters just made to cuddle up together in the clink, I tell you.'

Moralès had nothing to add, but if that guy had laid a finger on Simone, the only way he'd be going into a prison cell was in a wheelchair.

'Put your beauty kit away, Constable Lefebvre, the pilot's preparing for landing.'

In the splendour of the morning sun, the rosary of the Magdalen Islands looked like a giant baited hook the sea was trying to bite onto. The wind had died down and the plane made a smooth landing.

When they touched down on Havre-aux-Maisons Island, Lieutenant Égide Leblanc was waiting on the tarmac with cars for them and the tactical team. Tall and slim with a keen intelligence in his eyes, he wasted no time in getting behind the wheel.

'I've just been speaking with the coast guard. The *Jean-Mathieu*'s locator beacon has started emitting a signal again. The trawler's nowhere near Grande-Entrée, but much further south, as if it's been heading up from the Northumberland Strait.'

Moralès watched the island landscape roll by, the colourful houses, seemingly scattered at random by the wind and anchored to the hillocks. So this was where Simone had spent the last few months. He wondered where she had been staying.

Joaquin focused his attention. 'They went on a detour, near the coast of Newfoundland. I've got a whole series of GPS points, recorded and sent to me by the fisheries officer on board.'

Leblanc went on. 'Those dealers of yours probably want us to think they've spent the last forty-eight hours circling around the mouth of the strait, trying to find their man overboard.'

'But that's not where they were. They must have come and dumped the drugs near your shores for them to pick up later.'

Leblanc was thinking along the same lines. 'Or for someone else to bring in. We need to know if a boat went out to meet them, but it's always hard to get fishermen to talk.'

Detective Sergeant Moralès turned to Constable Lefebvre in the backseat. 'Réjean Vigneault, he said he knew everyone in the Islands, didn't he?'

Lefebvre nodded.

'Do you have his phone number?'

'Yes.'

'Give him a call and ask him if a boat went out to sea this morning. From Grande-Entrée. A boat that wasn't supposed to be going out, but did anyway. Tell him the police suspect his friend Éloquin's boat, the *Jean-Mathieu*, is being used for drug smuggling, and his brother-in-law, the skipper, might be in trouble. But don't tell him Chevrier's dead, not straightaway. We don't want to spook him.'

'OK. I'll call when we get to the station.' Lefebvre was relieved. He hated going out in the field.

'You'll have to call him from the ship.'

The lieutenant turned left, onto the road that led down to the wharf in Cap-aux-Meules.

'That's the coast-guard icebreaker, right there, and you've got the tactical team with you. You're going to accost the *Jean-Mathieu*. There's no way I'm having those guys wreak havoc on the Islands. You're going to bring them in offshore. Plus, there's a cell on board the *Guardian*.'

He handed a card to Constable Lefebvre, who accepted it reluctantly and got out of the car onto the wharf.

'I'll get a team together and head up to Grande-Entrée to see what's going on there. Call me as soon as you hear anything from Vigneault.'

The coast-guard vessel was moored right there, waiting for them. Nadine was hesitant, too. She never got involved with arrests. She was used to building cases, preparing interventions, observing interviews, but always stayed in the background. Always the gentleman, Lefebvre took her bag and she followed him aboard the *Guardian* without a word. Moralès was already in the wheelhouse, where a coast-guard officer by the name of Ouellet was stationed to greet them. The Tactical Intervention Group officers boarded in turn. The mooring lines were cast off. The vessel made a swift exit from the harbour.

As the officers put on bulletproof vests, Pascal Ouellet cleared his throat. 'We went aboard the *Jean-Mathieu* last week … and we saw right away what a sketchy bunch of characters the crew were.'

Detective Sergeant Moralès checked to make sure his handgun was loaded. 'Did you see Officer Lord? She's on board too.'

Some smart arse came swaggering his way. 'The singer? Oh, we definitely saw her. Eh, Pascal? You tell 'em why we called her that back at—'

Steve Filiol didn't have the chance to finish his sentence before Moralès drove a hard right hook into his stomach. As the man folded under the impact, the detective brought a knee up to meet his face. He left him to choke on his words and turned to Ouellet.

'If anything whatsoever has happened to Officer Lord, I'm going to file an official complaint with the Canadian Coast Guard and make sure they kick you out the door.'

'On what grounds?'

'Dereliction of duty to render assistance at sea. You'll be stuck on the end of the wharf, dangling your rods for catfish before you know it. And this guy, he tripped and broke his nose. *Claro?*'

Ouellet nodded, and Filiol left the wheelhouse with a faceful of blood. Nadine was gobsmacked and didn't know how to react. Moralès immediately lost interest in the two creeps.

The weather was splendid, but Joaquin was blind to it. His heart was sinking with the fear that something serious, something terrible, had happened to Simone Lord. As they advanced out to sea, the logistical sparks of the operation began to fly: where the vessels would be positioned, how the assault team would structure their mission, what the commandeering strategy would be. Moralès couldn't stand still. He motioned to Nadine.

'Do you feel comfortable giving the detention orders to the *Jean-Mathieu?*'

Her eyes grew wide. 'That's not my job...'

'No, it should be mine.'

One of the tactical team officers handed Moralès a rifle equipped with an approach scope, and Nadine understood that her superior wouldn't be the one overseeing the commandeering manoeuvre. Because he wanted to be in the thick of the action. So that he could try and save this woman who had sent him a personal message.

She turned to Ouellet. 'Right, you're going to show me how the VHF and the loudspeaker work on this vessel of yours.'

The guy grudgingly did what he was asked.

Lefebvre came over to Moralès. 'I managed to reach Réjean on the phone. Seems there was a pleasure craft, the *Stiff Sea Breeze*, that left the harbour this morning. It was the dad of one of his butchers who saw it heading out. Belongs to one of Carpentier's old deckhands, someone he used to poach with, apparently. I've given Leblanc a call. He and his team are going to intercept the guy. Don't you worry, we're gonna get 'em.'

Érik gave him a reassuring smile, but Joaquin could sense his concern for Simone too.

The sun had set the gulf asparkle. The bluish ice floes had some space to breathe and there was a hint of warmth to the air, as if, after the glacial week, spring might be daring to make an appearance.

One of the tactical officers pointed to a growing dot on the horizon. Moralès reached for the binoculars. At last, the sturdy crab trawler was in sight, antennas sprouting from the white of the wheelhouse atop the black of the hull. The name of the vessel stood out proudly in pale letters at the bow. VHF transmitter in hand, Nadine Lauzon was waiting for the signal from her superior. As soon as the trawler seemed close enough, he gave her the go-ahead.

'*Jean-Mathieu, Jean-Mathieu, Jean-Mathieu*, this is the Canadian Coast Guard vessel *Guardian*. Acknowledge. Over.'

Ouellet gave her a sign to let her know she had initiated the exchange correctly. She did not have to repeat the call.

'*Guardian*, this is *Jean-Mathieu*. Go ahead. Over.'

'*Jean-Mathieu*, I want to speak to the person in charge of your vessel, Marco Painchaud. Over.'

Moralès could see that Nadine knew what she was doing. She was trying to butter the young guy up by calling him the responsible one in front of the others. And it worked. Mere seconds later, a haphazard voice crackled over the airwaves.

'Hey, I'm here!'

'Mr Painchaud, this is Nadine Lauzon of the Sûreté du Québec.'

She paused to give him time for that information to sink in. A maniacal laugh roared through the speaker.

'Did ya hear that, Lapierre? They're bringin' on pretty little singers everywhere these days.'

'Let go of the button, Eight-Inch, they can hear everything.'

Sergeant Ouellet looked at the floor. Moralès was a whisker away from losing his rag.

'We understand that you lost someone at sea.'

'Yeah, Chevrier went out for a piss and never came back. We spent two days looking for the guy, but if you ask me, he didn't know how to swim.'

The young cokehead released the button on the handset this time.

'Mr Painchaud, there is a mandatory procedure to follow

in this type of situation. You should see the coast-guard vessel that's coming your way, straight ahead. Please immobilise your vessel. We will be coming aboard the *Jean-Mathieu*. Over.'

The order went unanswered.

'Did you hear me, Mr Painchaud? Over.'

The trawler continued its approach. The police officers raised their binoculars in its direction.

Painchaud's voice came back over the VHF, all a fluster. 'We didn't do anything. The guy went under the ice. We didn't see any of it.'

'Did you hear my instructions, Mr Painchaud? Over.'

But Painchaud didn't acknowledge. And he had not released the button on his handset. '…either! It's not our fault if she's disappeared.'

She? Nadine didn't dare look at Joaquin.

'Who's disappeared, Mr Painchaud? Officer Lord?'

'Yeah. The singer. She's only gone and pinched our life raft, and fucked off somewhere with it. She's gonna pay for it for sure, 'cause my uncle Denis, he's not gonna be happy.'

'Put your vessel in neutral immediately, Mr Painchaud.'

'No way. This is my boat and I'm gonna dock it myself. Is that clear? Is that clear enough?'

There followed a succession of loud bangs, as if Marco Painchaud were bashing the transmitter against the dashboard and had neglected to turn it off first.

A tense silence marked an abrupt end to the exchange. As if bad news were about to be announced. This time, Lefebvre could not conceal his concern. Even Ouellet had a lump in his throat.

Moralès glared at him menacingly. 'If anything has happened to Officer Lord, I'll have you hauled in for questioning, and you'll be explaining to me why those men know the disgraceful pet name you've given to a female fisheries officer. And I will be assessing whether your attitude may have contributed to putting that woman in danger.'

Moralès went out on deck, headed to the bow of the ship. One of the guys from the tactical team beckoned him closer.

'Have a look at this.'

Moralès took the binoculars the officer was handing him. He saw the shimmering ocean, flat and calm, spotted the *Jean-Mathieu* still coming their way. Lashed right up front was a corpse ravaged by water and salt. This was Bernard Chevrier, the skipper Simone Lord had hoisted up to the scuppers so that his body would be delivered for justice and his family. The line that must have been holding his legs fast to the port side of the hull had given way. The man now hung vertically, swaying from one side to the other of the trawler's fore tip, a grim, bewitched figurehead waltzing atop the waves.

The detective addressed the Tactical Intervention Group team: 'There's a body dangling from the bow. Everyone on board is under arrest, do you hear me?'

The four tactical officers nodded.

'What are they playing at? They're not slowing down.'

The sound of Nadine Lauzon's authority came booming from the *Guardian*'s loudspeaker: '*Jean-Mathieu*, this is an order to immobilise your vessel immediately.'

Inside the crab trawler, there was obviously some unrest. Perhaps some sort of struggle. It was unclear what was happening.

'Watch out. They're armed.'

As that information resonated, Moralès saw a man step out on deck, on the starboard side. The man strode to the bow and crouched behind the guardrail with a bizarre movement of his shoulder. It looked like he was wearing a grey balaclava on the crown of his head. Moralès saw the man load a rifle and take aim at the *Guardian*.

'Take cover!'

Moralès ducked. A second later, a bullet ricocheted off the ship. He sprang up, got the man in his sights, fired. Barely a second passed. The hunter's head snapped skywards, as if in surprise, and he crumpled to the deck. Immediately, the *Jean-Mathieu* slowed to a standstill and the three remaining men on board showed themselves nervously, their hands in the air.

The *Guardian* was soon alongside the *Jean-Mathieu*. As the coast-guard officers tied the vessels together, the tactical team jumped aboard, sidestepping the body.

Moralès did not look at McMurray. One day, he might reproach himself for not saying a prayer, for not being sorry, for not having a heavy heart, for not carrying deaths like this on his conscience. He might well have to seek therapy, pursue rehabilitation, hear someone talk about post-traumatic shock, about his lack of empathy. For now, he had no desire to dwell on these shitsters, to quote Nadine. Desperately, he looked around for Simone. 'Search the boat.'

They went inside. Two of the tactical officers, followed by Lefebvre, went up to the wheelhouse, while the two others raced below deck.

Marco Painchaud was yelling in a rage. 'She was nothing but a bitch. And he was the one who told us.' He tipped his chin at Ouellet, who had stayed out of the line of fire, inside the *Guardian*. Lefebvre was observing, assimilating everything.

'Where is she?'

Lucien Carpentier mumbled an awkward reply. 'She fucked off on a life raft.'

Michaël Lapierre was saying nothing. His lawyer had taught him enough times to keep his trap shut that he had learned his lesson. But as he walked past Lefebvre, he couldn't help but mutter a snide remark. 'You're not going to find anything.'

The constable smiled. 'When you disembark, you might want to have a look up front at the present our friend Simone has left. Oh, and the police on the Islands are up north right now picking up that stash of coke you ditched just off Grande-Entrée.'

That changed the expression on Lapierre's face. As he stepped aboard the *Guardian* in handcuffs, he leaned forwards for a look at the prow of the *Jean-Mathieu*. He saw the feet of a lifeless body dangling in midair. He hesitated, looked down at the sea. He could jump, he figured. But it was too late. Lefebvre already had him by the arm and was frogmarching him inside.

'Right then, you shitster, off you go to see your mates in the clink.'

As Lefebvre stood there beaming, proud to have used Nadine's term of choice, Lapierre regretted losing his bottle. He should have jumped while he had the chance. Because in prison, he knew it'd be no time at all before he ended up as someone's blow-up doll. He swallowed his sorrows as he went down into the *Guardian*'s hold.

Meanwhile, Moralès was sniffing around the trawler's galley. The room was in a disgusting state. Lines of white powder lingered on the table. The floor was sticky with spilled yogurt. The whole place was littered with food remnants, dirty dishes, hunting overalls and greasy utensils. A streak of dried blood

not quite wiped away traversed the galley floor. The detective
followed the trail. It let to the bathroom. He had a quick look
inside, then turned to the sleeping quarters. There he found a
bunk draped in a sheet hanging limp like a curtain of lament.
He moved in for a closer look. A woman's jacket. A crumpled
origami creation. Simone's belongings. A sleeping bag that
looked like one big bloodstain. And the smell of something
unpleasant. The stench of an infected wound. Joaquin recoiled
two steps, a man fearing he might fall into the void.

Suddenly, he heard one of the tactical officers call out to
him.

'We've got her. We've found the woman!'

'Where is she?'

'Down below, in the hold.'

Moralès raced to the stairwell.

The officer called out to him again. 'Just a heads-up, it reeks
down there.'

The detective needed no warning. The damp in the air, the
smells of oil and fuel, and the whiff of meat caught in his
nostrils as he set foot on the stairs to the bowels of the boat.
On this gentlest of seas, the engine maintained its indifferent
slow tempo.

The hold was not a well-lit place. Moralès found himself
shivering. The cold down there was biting.

'We're back here.'

He ducked through a hatch door and started down a narrow
corridor with a series of doors cut into the concrete walls. To
the portside were food bins overflowing with bags of seal meat
kept fresh by the ambient temperature. The openings on the
other side had been covered with corrugated metal panels,
stacked one on top of the other to prevent access.

In their search, the officers had hurriedly opened each of the compartments part way. They had tossed the metal panels aside, and these were now impeding Moralès's progress. The floor was slippery with animal fat. Joaquin's breathing was shallow, his throat constricted. To starboard, he could see the seal pelts stacked the way Réjean Vigneault had explained, fur on fur, fat on fat. The smell was atrocious. A heavy wave of nausea came over him.

'She's here.'

In the second-to-last compartment, two men were hard at work. On their knees, hindered by their bulletproof vests and all their gear, they were struggling to shift the heavy grey pelts, stained scarlet and brown with blood, which kept slipping out of their hands. They were throwing them to one side, on top of the discarded corrugated metal panels. Joaquin stood powerless, watching this wall go up between him and Simone. His heart was in his mouth.

'Is she alive?'

The man at the opening of the compartment got up. His face was pale. 'She's lying down among the furs.'

He crouched down again to help a colleague Moralès couldn't see. The officers hurried on, dislodging the pelts any which way and casting them aside in the cramped corridor, where they formed an accumulation of darker and darker layers. In spite of himself, Joaquin noticed that the empty eye sockets of the seals had been pierced with thin loops of plastic and tags, attached by Officer Lord. He stared at her clear, meticulous, impeccable writing. She was not an overachiever, as Lefebvre had suggested, but a woman of passion the sea had swept away. Moralès felt a painful urge to reach out and touch her, this woman, to find salt in his heart by her grace.

Suddenly, the men stopped what they were doing. The one nearest the detective inhaled deeply, the way someone saved from drowning gorges on air. He backed away, still on his knees, and leaned without meaning to against the lopsided pile of fatty furs, making it collapse. With a swish and a whisper, the seal skins and their empty eyes subsided and the furs slid like dead animals to Joaquin Moralès's feet.

EPILOGUE
Land of no respite

The younger of the Langevin brothers solemnly saluted the choir, took the urn and turned to the nave. As the funeral director retreated mournfully down the broad aisle, the congregation rose with a creaking of pews that echoed through the church.

Simon Beaudry's parents had resigned themselves to unplugging their son's life support a week earlier. The kid was seventeen years old and had dreamed of becoming an accountant.

The undertaker walked slowly between the pews. The organ accompanied him, but the choir was silent. Suzie Lord was the first to step out into the aisle, followed by cousins, relatives and friends, all in mourning, all in black.

One evening, last autumn, at the end of the investigation, I made some fish tacos.

More than a few fishermen had come, in spite of their dissensions, to pay their last respects to the fisheries officer, who had also guarded the coast for some fifteen years and had saved the lives of many of them. Moralès recognised some of the faces.

I prepared everything exactly the same way you did in front of me, a few days earlier. I even set my table for two.

Nadine Lauzon had not been able to stay for the service. She had returned to Montreal with her heart turned inside out. When Joaquin had driven her to the airport, he had given her a sad, hollow smile, a rigid, empty shell of an expression, like the one Bonhomme Carnaval had sported in Quebec City, it had seemed to her.

But I dined alone.

Érik Lefebvre, hands juggling bookmarks, prayer booklets and packs of tissues, gently nudged Joaquin, who was still sitting motionless, staring at, but not seeing, a stained-glass window depicting the Virgin of the Waters. Simone Lord's reply to the detective's invitation kept riding around in his mind on an infernal carousel of regrets.

When I'm diving, I contemplate the world another way.

Moralès stood up from his pew, merged into the crowd, walked slowly towards the door. Beside him, Érik, in his matte black coat, wiped his eyes. His son Sébastien, who had now moved into a place of his own, had come from Percé. They were going to have a bite to eat together before Joaquin drove back down the coast to Caplan.

I am overcome by wonder and I hear the beating of my heart in the ocean.

Just as he was making his way outside, the sound of the great bell rang out above his head. All seven tolls of the knell caught in his throat. He stepped over the threshold of the Gaspé church to find himself dazzled by a glaring midday sun, a premature omen of spring.

I have never learned to love. Not at the speed of a baseball pitch, nor for the duration of a wedding ring.

Before he had left home, Joaquin had extracted the origami creation from between the pages of the García Márquez novel. He had taken the paper bird and spread its wings, then placed it by the window in his guest room, facing out to sea.

It must be nice to feel in love, weightless, without solitude, without fury.

At the foot of the hill, the bay of ice was a harbour for the harp seals; in little more than a week, it would be calving time. Yet Moralès would not be fooled by such tranquil splendour. The Gaspé was a devious place. A land of no respite. He narrowed his eyes, donned his dark glasses.

I would like that very much, Joaquin, to have a seat at your table.

Simone

Acknowledgements

Thank you to my first readers, Annie Landreville and Dominique Corneillier.

Thank you, Sergeant Michaël Lecours, Lynne Bibeau and Lieutenant Françoise Ouellet.

Thank you, captain of the Saint Lawrence, Jean-Phylip Picard.

Thank you to the Magdalen Islanders who helped me with my research:

To Michel Arseneault, my dear friend in Belle-Anse, for your generous hospitality and for feeding me grey seal filet mignon.

To Joël Cumming and his family for the chowder and the logistical help; to Ghislain Cumming for the helicopter hunting stories.

To Denis Longuépée and the seal hunters' association for explaining the issues around the seal harvest in plain language.

To Fisheries and Oceans Canada officers Stéphanie Poirier and Jean-Guy Thériault (retired, but quite the storyteller).

To Denis Éloquin, owner of the real *Jean-Mathieu*, and his wife Nancy, for the glass of wine, the photos, the replies to my emails.

To the crew members: Lucien Doyle (hunter), Yoannis Menge (photographer), O'Neil Poirier (my friend who makes me laugh so much) and Réjean Vigneault (owner of the Boucherie Côte à Côte whose wife really is named Réjeanne) for the images, the stories, the explanations, the crash course in butchering.

Thank you to Égide Leblanc, for whom the seals sing, and to his wife, Rachel Drouin, who works the leather.

Thank you to Pierre Luc, of course, whose love allows me to live in weightlessness from the world.

Thank you to the whole team at Orenda Books, and thank you, readers, for making me feel like writing this Moralès series.